MOTH TO A FLAME

Recent Titles by Janet Tanner from Severn House

MOTH TO A FLAME

Janet Tanner

This title first published 2008 in Great Britain and the USA by
SEVERN HOUSE PUBLISHERS LTD of
9–15 High Street, Sutton, Surrey, England, SM1 1DF.
Originally published 1981 in Great Britain only,
in paperback format only under the title
Flowers in the Valley and pseudonym of *Jade Shannon.*

British Library Cataloguing in Publication Data

Tanner, Janet
  Moth to a flame
  1. Love stories
  I. Title
  823.9'14[F]

  ISBN-13: 978-0-7278-6713-1   (cased)

All Severn House titles are printed on acid-free paper.

Printed and bound in Great Britain by
MPG Books Ltd., Bodmin, Cornwall.

FOREWORD

Some years ago, in another incarnation, I wrote historical romances under another name and they were only published in paperback in Great Britain under the name of Jade Shannon.

They were somewhat different to the books I have written in recent years, but I enjoyed them immensely, losing myself totally in a world of feisty heroines and heroes who might almost have been villains but for the highly principled character concealed beneath a tough exterior. Irresistible (to me at any rate) real men, who could be tamed for the love of a good woman, with a soft centre they hid from the world from choice – or necessity. Misunderstandings abound, and there is mystery and danger in wild and unforgiving settings.

Moth to a Flame, originally entitled *Flowers in the Valley*, was the first of these books. I am thrilled that it is to be reprinted in hardcover for the first time, and appearing in the USA for the first time in any version, and I hope that you will enjoy reading it as much as I enjoyed writing it.

CHAPTER ONE

September 1856

Heavy seas broke over the decks of the *Maid of Morne* as she ran before the wind, boards creaked and the rigging moaned like a soul in torment. On deck, Captain Abel Barnes – Bully Barnes to his crew – watched the sail with a shrewd eye. A lifetime at sea had taught him exactly how long the sails and spars would stand the strain, and he relied on no one but himself to choose the moment to reduce canvas. He did not snug down at nightfall as had been the habit of so many masters. He sailed on, taking full advantage of the winds to make a fast passage. That was what the ship owners expected – what they were determined to have. If he drove her safely and well, the *Maid of Morne* would make Australia in less than three months and everyone would be happy.

And certainly that night there was merriment below and to spare, though the hundred and eighty steerage passengers in the 'tween decks had little to cheer for. Packed like sardines into the long, low cabin, fighting for the cookers to prepare their food and sleeping in the narrow cots that lined the walls, they had learned the meaning of discomfort in the weeks they had been at sea if they had not known it before. But they were emigrants every one, all out to make a new life in a new country where farmers were prospering and where gold had been found in the rich earth. They were too full of dreams to be put off by such little things as seasickness, hunger and lack of privacy. Their spirits were high and they kept them that way by making their own entertainment. A man with a harmonica sat atop one of the long wooden tables and the emigrants tapped their feet in time with his music and rattled their spoons; but when he had finished they turned with one accord to look for the girl who had enchanted them night after night with her singing.

'Regan – where's Regan Gardner?' someone asked and soon others took up the cry. 'Regan – Regan Gardner . . .'

In the farthest corner of the cuddy a girl who was sitting on the wooden bench straightened up, turning towards the chant with a slightly haunted look in her vivid green eyes. For all the noise and gaiety, Regan had been far away, dreaming as she so often did of other things and other places where the boards did not rock beneath her feet and her nostrils were not full of the reek of food from the galley and the stench of close-packed, unwashed bodies.

'What ails you, daughter? Smile for the people, can't you? They'll be our first audiences in the new country, don't forget.' The dark-haired, slightly-built man plucked anxiously at her sleeve as he spoke and obediently Regan lifted the corners of her mouth, though the smile did not quite reach her eyes.

He was right, of course, her father. If they were to form a theatrical company in Melbourne to entertain settlers, sheep masters and gold miners, it could do no harm for their fame to go before them. But there were times when Regan wished she had not been born the daughter of an actor, and blessed with the voice of an angel. There were times when she would have liked to be able to remain in peaceful anonymity to dream her dreams. And if restlessness stirred within her, it was not a restlessness for the applause of an audience, but for something else, something, she knew not what, that was always, puzzlingly, just out of reach . . .

'Regan, they're calling for you, girl!' Thomas Gardner urged her. Catching at her arm he pulled her to her feet and, with a small sigh, Regan gave herself up to the inevitable. She knew it was the dearest wish of his heart that she should succeed where he had failed and make a name for herself in the world that he loved – the theatre. As soon as she had been able to walk he had found parts for her in the plays he and his company had taken from village to village, and when her voice developed clear and true he had encouraged her to use it, scraping away on his fiddle to accompany her but never managing to mar the enchantment of her singing.

'If only your mother could hear you now!' he would say, his eyes bright with tears in his narrow face. But her mother was dead, and had been since Regan was seven years old. Now, it was all she could do to conjure up a hazy picture of a woman with red-gold hair as bright as her own and eyes as piercingly green. Sometimes a scent or a half-forgotten tune would remind her and she would almost feel, for a moment, the softness and warmth she had once loved. But then it would be gone, leaving only the sadness of loss and Regan was able to understand more clearly the emptiness that drove Thomas to seek success for her through her singing and oblivion for himself on the gaming tables. He had loved Nan, her mother, with all his heart and when she had died no one, not even his adored Regan, could fill the gap.

The mass of bodies in the cuddy parted to let Regan through, someone gave her their hand and helped her up onto the broad wooden table, steadying her against the roll of the ship. Beside her, Thomas scraped a note or two on his fiddle and an expectant hush fell over the crowded cabin as Regan's voice rose sweet and clear:

Oh there was a woman and she was a widow
Fair are the flowers in the valley
With a daughter as fair as a fresh sunny
meadow
The Red, the Green and the Yellow.
The Harp, the Lute, the Pipe, the Flute, the Cymbal
Sweet goes the treble Violin
The Maid so rare and the flowers so fair
Together they grew in the valley.

There came a Knight all clothed in red,
Fair are the flowers in the valley
'I would thou wert my bride,' he said
The Red, the Green and the Yellow.
The Harp, the Lute, the Pipe, the Flute, the Cymbal

Sweet goes the treble Violin
'I would', she sighed, 'ne'er wins a bride!'
Fair are the flowers in the valley.

There came a Knight all clothed in Green
Fair are the flowers in the valley
'This maid so sweet might be my queen,'
The Red, the Green and the Yellow.
The Harp, the Lute, the Pipe, the Flute, the Cymbal
Sweet goes the treble Violin
'Might be,' sighed she 'will ne'er win me!'
Fair are the flowers in the valley.

As she sang, the emigrants held their breath, entranced by the haunting sweetness. Even the children were quiet, their sobs muted as they watched her round-eyed from the comfort of their mothers' breasts. But Regan's audience was not confined to the steerage passengers. Unnoticed by them, two men had descended the companionway and stood on the stairs, listening. The one was clearly an officer of the *Maid of Morne*, but the other was marked out by his black frock coat, striped silk waistcoat and pleated shirt as a passenger of the cabin class – and a well-heeled one at that. He was slim-hipped but tall – sufficiently so to have to duck his head on the companionway – with muscles that rippled beneath the exquisite cloth and shoulders so broad and firm that they hardly needed emphasizing by the cut of his coat. But it was his darkness that was startling to all who met him – his skin bronzed by hot summers to a rich depth that not even the months he had spent at sea had been able to muddy, his hair thick, springy and almost coal black, and his eyes like pieces of jet.

And at this moment those narrowed eyes were on Regan.

Noticing his interest, the second officer, Charles Maclane, laughed deep in his throat. 'She makes a pretty picture, Zach, especially for a man forced to live like a monk these last weeks.'

Zach Casey's lip curled, almost the only outward sign of the deep agreement he was feeling. The women amongst the cabin class passengers were an unattractive bunch, but their menfolk were guarding them as if they were priceless jewels. There had been no clandestine visits to a lady's cabin to ease male needs on this voyage, and the lack of privacy in the crowded 'tween decks made it difficult for a man to find a girl willing to accommodate him, though no doubt there would be plenty who would be ready enough to go with a gentleman if the opportunity presented itself. Added to this, for the crew at any rate, there was always the threat of Bully Barnes' fury if such an episode came to his notice. He was a hard, puritanical master and if he discovered an officer dallying with an emigrant lass he would mete out harsh punishment together, as like as not, with orders to attend morning and evening prayer daily and read nothing but the Holy Bible – 'for the good of your eternal soul'.

Tonight, however, with Bully Barnes safely engaged on deck, Charles Maclane had been persuaded by Zach Casey to risk a foray to the 'tween decks, and now the two men stood unnoticed in their vantage point feasting their hungry eyes on the charms of Regan.

''Twould be worth a week of Bully's Bible reading to have her in my bed tonight!' Charles Maclane declared.

Zach Casey did not reply. As a paying passenger he had nothing to fear from Bully Barnes and he, too, was excited by the swell of Regan's creamy breasts above the low-cut neck of her bodice, her shoulders, smooth and bare, and the tiny waist a man could circle with his hands. But for all that she stood there to sing, her charms the property of the roving eyes of every man in the cuddy, there was a remoteness about her and a dignity that offered something of a challenge. Zach Casey was all man and he was used to having his way with women. But, instinctively, he knew that this girl would not come readily to his bed, or any other's, and the knowledge excited him.

As the song ended, the girl smiled around at the cheering emigrants so that her eyes seemed to dance like emeralds in her heart-shaped face. But although they stamped their feet and shouted for more, she only shook her head, holding out her hand for someone to help her down from the table. They did so, and as she lifted her full skirts carefully with her free hand so as not to trip over them, Zach caught a glimpse of well-shaped ankles and small, slippered feet.

The crowd parted and as the girl crossed the cabin to pass the foot of the steps almost immediately below him, he was unable to tear his eyes away from her.

Close to, she was lovelier than ever, her skin so smooth and perfect it more than compensated for the fact that her white net dress was far from new. An evening dress discarded by some lady of fashion, Zach decided. But even when it had been first made, it was doubtful if it had graced the wearer more than, in the autumn of its life, it graced this girl.

As if sensing his eyes on her, she looked up and for a moment he held her gaze with his own. Then, with a toss of her head, she turned away. But as she did so desire got the better of Charles Maclane's discretion and he stepped down to her level, catching at her arm.

'Don't run away! Wait and talk with two poor gentlemen!'

Her chin came up and she looked pointedly at his hand on her arm.

'I am sorry, sir, I do not think I know you.'

There was a faint burr of some English dialect in her voice that had not been apparent in her singing, but Zach smiled to himself at her sharp rebuff of the clumsy approach. So he had been right! he thought triumphantly. Actress she might be, but this girl was no easy plaything to be won too soon by a look of riches about a man.

'My friend meant no offence,' he said swiftly, stepping down himself to her level. 'He merely wanted to ask you how it is that steerage passengers have such entertainment as this, while we in the first class have only the doubtful talents of our own selves to keep us amused.'

She lifted her eyes to his; dimples played in her cheeks.

'These talents, such as they are, are the talents of the steerage passengers you seem to look down upon,' she replied tartly. 'Because we cannot afford to travel as you do does not mean we do not have virtues of our own!'

'Indeed not!' Zach's eyes travelled the length of her shapely body and, beneath his gaze, colour flooded her cheeks. With a swish of her skirts she turned away. A thin-faced man Zach had not noticed before pushed his way through the crowd and he recognized him as the fiddler who had accompanied her singing.

'We are players by profession, sir, and if you wish we could come to your saloon and entertain the first class passengers as we entertain here,' he suggested eagerly.

Zach and Charles Maclane exchanged glances and the man hurried on: 'I should perhaps introduce myself. I am Thomas Gardner, and this is my daughter, Regan.'

Zach's eyes returned to the girl. 'Regan! An unusual name.'

'But one I hope you may some day come to recognize,' the older man smiled. 'I intend to form a theatrical company in the new country and, if I am not much mistaken, a little culture and amusement will be more than welcomed there.'

Zach's dark eyes flashed. 'Indeed? You think, perhaps, that the natives are all savages?' he asked in amusement.

The older man stared for a moment, perplexed, and Zach laughed aloud.

'If you do, you may not be so far from the truth. But there are those of us who live well, despite the virgin nature of the land.'

'You have already been there?' Thomas asked with interest.

Zach's hands found his hips and for a moment his stance seemed to portray the casual arrogance of the new country. 'I have never lived anywhere else,' he said simply. 'I was born an Australian.'

'Then why . . ?' Thomas broke off abruptly. He had no wish to offend this fine gentleman by too many questions, but it was all he could do to contain his curiosity. At the outset, Thomas had been heartily seasick – it was beyond him why anyone should make such a long voyage not once, but twice.

'I have been to England on business,' Zach said briefly. 'But I assure you, even on a clipper as speedy as the *Maid of Morne* it sometimes seems to me as if I have been far too long on the high seas.' His eyes returned to Regan and the challenge in them was barely disguised. 'That is why your offer to entertain us is more than welcome,' he finished.

'Then you mean to accept my offer? Oh, you will be pleased with us, I know,' Thomas babbled eagerly. 'Regan is a most accomplished performer.'

'I have not a doubt of it,' Zach said with irony and his meaning was not lost on Regan. Hurriedly she turned away from the dark challenge of his eyes, her cheeks burning dully.

'My friend Mr Maclane is an officer of this ship and he will make all the necessary arrangements,' Zach continued smoothly as if he was quite unaware of her discomfiture. 'Will you not, Charles?'

'Oh yes, yes of course,' Charles Maclane muttered hastily, but already his eyes were greedily raking the cabin for another wench whom he could invite to share his bed. This red-haired, green-eyed beauty with her haughty manner was not the only girl in the steerage, even if she acted as though she thought she was. And a father at her elbow was a complication he would rather be without. Let Zach have the pleasure of taming her – and may it be worth the trouble. He, Charles, would find a bedmate more eager to please him – and the hell with Bully Barnes.

'We shall expect you to entertain us the morrow, then,' Zach said. His eyes sought and met Regan's for one long, meaningful moment before he turned and walked back up the steps and out of her sight.

In her narrow bunk at the side of the cuddy, Regan lay wide awake and staring into the murmuring dark.

It was never quiet here, she thought. Always there was the sound of the waves and the wind, the creaking timbers and the sighing sails. And even when they became a part of the background there were the sounds that came from a hundred and eighty people crowded together – the coughs and snuffles, the cry of a child, the laboured breathing of a pair of lovers as they tried to take their pleasure under cover of the darkness without disturbing their neighbours.

Listening to them, Regan found her thoughts returning to the tall, dark gentleman from the cabin class who had commanded their presence in the saloon as if he owned the ship. Why she should think of him now she did not know, except that there had been something in the way he had looked at her that had spoken unmistakably of desire – a desire as fierce and burning as the one driving the unseen lovers who panted in the darkness. He wanted a woman, she supposed, any woman, and because he knew she was an actress he considered her fair game. But he would soon learn he was mistaken. He was not the first to make the incorrect assumption that she would fall eagerly into his bed and he would likely not be the last. The fact that he was more subtle in his advances than his ship's officer friend would make no difference. He would get the same short shrift – as had all the others before him.

Perhaps it was because of the way of life she had been raised to that she had built up such a wall around her virginity, Regan thought. It would have been easy – too easy – to become a lady of pleasure, although she knew it would break her father's heart. A lesser man, poor and struggling as they so often were, might have encouraged her to trade on her good looks and prompt fine gentlemen to part with at least a little of their wealth, but not Thomas. He loved her too much, and was too ambitious for her to allow her to take a penny piece from anyone if it had not been earned by her voice or by her dramatic talents. And Regan had taken her lead from him. She was eighteen years old now, and as chaste as the day she had been born. Not even Richard had been allowed to do more than kiss her – nor would he until the day they were wed . . .

Richard – Richard Gammon, her fiancé. Regan closed her eyes, trying to picture his fair-skinned face with its dreaming blue eyes and sensitive mouth, but the vision was uncomfortably hazy – almost as blurred as that of her mother, dead these eleven years. But that was ridiculous! thought Regan. It was little more than a year since she had seen Richard – though sometimes it seemed like a lifetime since he had sailed away to seek a fortune for them both in the new country on the other side of the world.

Under cover of the darkness she pursed her lips, trying to relive the sweetness of his kisses and the tender love they had shared.

Just when it had begun she did not know, for as long as she could remember, Richard had been there. His mother had been an actress too, travelling with the same company, and Regan's earliest memories were of turning out a costume trunk with Richard and dressing up in exotic garments they found there. Later they had gone to school together, protecting one another from the curiosity and jibes of the local children who looked on them as no better than gypsies. With Richard she had run through the summer-sweet meadows, paddled barefoot in the sparkling streams and explored places they had never seen before and would never see again. And long before they had shared that first uncertain, trembling kiss Regan had known they were meant for each other.

We would be married by now if it were not for the gold, she thought, and in spite of herself she smiled as she remembered his eagerness when he had told her about it.

'Just think of it – gold lying in the ground for the taking!' he had murmured, his blue eyes shining with excitement. 'Oh Regan, you have always looked like a princess. When I have made my fortune, you will be able to live like one!'

'Take me with you Richard!' she had begged, but he held her away, shaking his head gently.

'It's no life for a woman in the diggings, they say. But we'll not be parted for long, I promise you. Let me go on ahead, and when I find gold, I will send for you.'

And so he sailed away and she was left to worry and wonder if she would ever see him again. When he had been there to set her alight with his dreams and his enthusiasm it had been one thing, now, left alone, the doubts and fears came crowding in. Suppose his ship was lost in a storm? Suppose he was attacked by natives or by convicts – for Australia, was, after all, a penal colony where murderers and thieves had been transported for more than half a century.

And when his letters began to come they did little to comfort her, for although Richard painted a romantic picture of the goldfields the miners sounded a fearful lot, crazy for gold and taking the law into their own hands when things did not suit them. Richard, she knew, was not like that. He was gentle – a dreamer. How could he survive amongst such men?

Months passed, long and lonely, and Regan began to wonder if Richard would ever send for her. He still wrote often enough, telling her of his hope and the excitement he felt when he knelt on the ground and saw the shining gold dust run through his fingers; and he told her too of his loneliness in the long evenings when a day's digging was done and there was nothing but a visit to a grog shanty to ease the boredom. But never did his letters contain the summons for which she waited.

It was Thomas who finally seized the bull by the horns and suggested they should wait no longer. Things were not going well with his company since Richard had left and Thomas knew it could not survive if Regan went too. But supposing they were to start afresh in a new country! There was precious little entertainment there, Richard had said – and if gold had been found, there was most likely a fortune to be made by providing diversions for the newly rich. The only problem that he could see was how they would live while they were making their fortune in the new country. Never in his life had Thomas been wealthy enough to set aside a nest-egg for a situation such as this.

But then fate stepped in to take a hand. All his life, Thomas had been a gambling man who could not resist the turn of the cards or the roll of the dice. With the cheerful optimism that marked out his kind he had always been convinced that this time, at least, Lady Luck must be on his side, and more often than not the conviction had proved his downfall. For once, however, his optimism had been rewarded. A gaming session with two rich and inebriated strangers at a country inn left Thomas with a pouch of sovereigns – and it was enough for him. Two passages were arranged on the *Maid of Morne* and Regan had time to write just once to Richard, asking him to meet them in Melbourne when they berthed, before they set sail towards the new land where Thomas was so sure fame and fortune awaited them.

In the darkness, Regan smiled to herself. His endless enthusiasm was matched only by Richard's, she thought. In many ways they were so alike. Why, it had been all she could do to persuade him not to spend the sovereigns all at once on first class cabins for the voyage, instead of saving them to provide for their needs when they reached Australia. But she had succeeded, and now he slept with the pouch containing the sovereigns and a ruby ring which had once belonged to her mother – the only thing of value that they owned – beneath his rough pillow. He was in constant fear that it might be stolen by one of the other passengers while he slumbered. Even now she could hear him tossing and turning in the bunk above her as he did every night and she was sure his anxiety was part of the reason.

'Wealth – it brings with it nothing but trouble,' he had told her often enough when she wondered where the pennies for their next crust would come from. 'All the wealth I shall ever need is to be found in God's good earth.'

Well, now they were sailing towards a country where the wealth in the earth was just that. And where Regan would find that other treasure her father always told her was beyond price – love.

Yet suddenly the restlessness was alive once more in her, stirring her in a way she could not explain. Was it imagination – or did she really not miss Richard as much as she once had – as much as she should? What was it she wanted, and knew instinctively she had not yet found?

Determined to sleep, Regan closed her eyes and to shut out the sounds of the cabin she began to sing softly to herself. For some reason when she had sung for the enjoyment of the passengers earlier, she had left off the last verse of the song. Why, she did not know. But now the words came unbidden to her lips.

There came a Knight in yellow was he,
Fair are the flowers in the valley

'My bride, my queen, thou must with me!'
The Red, the Green and the Yellow.
The Harp, the Lute, the Pipe, the Flute, the Cymbal,
Sweet goes the treble Violin.
With blushes red, 'I come,' she said;
'Farewell to the flowers of the valley.'

CHAPTER TWO

Next day Thomas could talk of nothing but the invitation for Regan to entertain the passengers of the cabin class and when the time approached he took her to one side, looking her over with all the pride of a father.

'We must impress them favourably. We may not be granted such a golden opportunity again,' he told her for the hundredth time.

Regan laughed. 'Listening to you, Father, one would think our lives depended on it!'

'So they might!' His mobile face was serious. 'The sovereigns will not last forever.'

'And you wanted to fritter them away on a first class passage,' Regan reminded him.

'For your sake, daughter. You deserve better than this place.' He reached out and twisted one of her curls so that it fell tantalizingly along her jawbone. 'Still, you are as beautiful as ever, even though I say it myself. And that does you credit. It is not easy to remain so in this black hell-hole.'

Regan smiled but said nothing. She dared not confess how her body cried out for the luxury of a tub of warm water, nor confide her longing for privacy to change her undergarments. If she did, her father would squander the precious sovereigns even now on a cabin for her and they would be left to face the new country penniless. So she had done the best she could in the circumstances, gaining a little privacy by hanging her cloak from the corner of her bunk and hiding behind it while she put on a clean chemisette and stockings, and peering at herself in a cracked piece of mirror to pinch colour into her pale cheeks and tidy the tangle of red-gold curls.

'You grow more like your mother every day,' Thomas murmured wistfully and then, as if the sentiment had reminded him, he fumbled in his pockets for the sovereign bag, loosed its cord and drew out the ring that had once belonged to Nan. 'Wear this tonight for luck, my Regan,' he begged her.

A gasp of surprise escaped Regan's lips.

'But I thought you said . . .'

'That you should not wear it lest it encouraged some ruffian to attack you for it. That's true. But tonight you will not be rubbing shoulders with scoundrels, adventurers and the poor who do not know where they will find their next crust. Tonight you will be with gentlefolk, and the ring makes you one of them.'

As he spoke he had turned so that his back was towards the passengers in the cuddy and the ring was shielded from their sight. But even with no light falling upon it the huge ruby glowed with a depth and richness all its own and Regan reached out to touch it reverently.

'Mother . . .' she whispered.

'It was her most prized possession,' Thomas said simply. 'I bought it for her when our fortune was running high and I would never sell it however low we sank. She needed that one luxury, Regan.'

Regan nodded. Although she had heard the story many times before it never failed to move her and without warning she felt tears pricking behind her eyes. She raised a hand to wipe them away and Thomas took it, drawing it into the shelter of his cloak and slipping the ring onto her finger. 'Who knows, little one? Tonight may mark a change in our fortunes. Now, no tears. They will make you blotchy and plain and that is not like you.'

For a moment Regan stared down at the ruby glowing on her finger as it had once glowed on her mother's. Then she caught and held her father's arm. It meant so much to him that she should do well tonight! For his sake she must forget that she no longer enjoyed singing for the pleasure of others. Then, if his theatrical venture became a success, perhaps she would be able to slip away quietly with Richard to a home they would build with the profits of his gold mining, and others would be only too pleased to take her place with the famous Thomas Gardner Company.

'I will do my best, Father,' she promised.

'Of course you will.' He patted her hand. 'Now come, my dear. It is time for us to go. Our audience will be waiting!'

He led her between the emigrants who stared after them with curiosity and sullen resentment of their good fortune, and up the stairs leading out of the cuddy.

As they emerged onto the deck the stiff breeze, heavy with salt spray, caught Regan's breath and tore at her skirts and she shivered, drawing her shawl more tightly around her. Neither father nor daughter was certain which way to go and as they hesitated a man who had been standing in the shelter of the wheelhouse to talk and smoke broke cover and hurried towards them.

'My friends, you have stolen the advantage of me. I had intended to escort you to the saloon. But it seems I have delayed too long.'

As she recognized Charles Maclane, Regan stiffened, remembering his advances of the previous evening. But to her relief, after a quick, appraising glance when he confirmed that she was every bit as desirable as he remembered her, Charles directed his attention towards Thomas. Last night he had satisfied himself with a passably pretty emigrant lass who had accepted what he could offer with a pleasure that matched his own, and if he was not mistaken, he would find her in his bed once more tonight. With his man's hunger assuaged somewhat he could view Regan with a little more detachment – though he had to admit he would still like to taste her charms if the opportunity arose.

Now, he touched Thomas's arm and pointed towards the stern of the ship. 'Come quickly – you will catch your death of cold out here,' he advised. 'This wind is for making a fast passage, but there the pleasure ends, I fear. Follow me.'

He led the way to the covered section beneath the

poop, then stepped aside for Regan to go ahead of him, and she almost gasped in surprise as she found herself in a large, pleasantly furnished saloon.

No expense had been spared, it seemed. In contrast to the scrubbed benches and tables in the 'tween decks, the woodwork here was polished mahogany and teak, and the settees were upholstered in rich velvets. The ceiling was higher, too, so that the place had an airy feel about it after the stale mugginess below and the passengers looked relaxed and as if they might even be enjoying their voyage.

Almost involuntarily, Regan found herself searching their number for the tall dark man who had accompanied Charles Maclane to the 'tween decks the previous evening. She had expected him to be here to greet them – since it was he who was responsible for their being here, it seemed the barest courtesy.

As if reading her mind, the second officer touched her elbow and pointed to the farthest corner of the saloon.

'Zach is engaged in his favourite pastime, I fear, where it's as easy to lose track of time as it is to lose money.'

For some reason, Regan's cheeks flamed. She did not want anyone, least of all this plausible officer, to think she had come here for the benefit of the arrogant Australian whose narrow look had assumed so much. But her eyes automatically followed Charles Maclane's direction and as they came to rest on the corner table she drew up short, embarrassment forgotten, as she recognized the nature of the 'pastime' he had referred to.

'They're playing dice!' she said sharply.

Charles Maclane nodded.

'One of the few diversions possible aboard a clipper,' he explained. 'I have seen fortunes won and lost at that table, and with a bottle of rum to sustain them, they often play until morning. But such a game would be a novel amusement only to you, Miss Gardner, if I am not much mistaken.'

Regan smiled faintly, all too aware of her father standing close behind her. She dared not look at him – she did not want to see the light that would have come into his eyes when he heard the sound of the dice rolling on the table top. Gambling was a sickness with Thomas – a fever that made him forget all else. Sometimes, as in the inn game from which he had brought home the precious sovereigns, he won. More often he lost. But losing never seemed to deter him, never made him more cautious. As a child, she had more than once heard her mother weeping and remonstrating with him, when he had returned having lost every penny he had earned, but always his answer was the same: 'I couldn't lose – I had the winning hand!' he would say, sounding more hurt and puzzled than remorseful. And: 'It'll be different tomorrow. I'll win a fortune for you, my love. It's time Lady Luck smiled on me.'

Of late years, things had been better. Thomas had had neither the wherewithal to gamble, nor the opportunity. But now she could imagine all too clearly the eagerness that would be itching in his fingers and her mind flew to the precious sovereigns that were all they had to make a fresh start in a harsh new country and fear made her mouth turn dry. Without them, they would be destitute. But Thomas would not see it like that. Given the opportunity to gamble, he would see only the fortune he could make if the luck ran his way.

Abruptly she turned away from the table and the men who sat there rolling the dice.

'Perhaps we should begin our concert, Father. If Mr Maclane will show us where to go . . .'

'Why certainly!' Charles Maclane had clearly been accepted by officers and passengers alike as the man best able to organize saloon entertainment, and as he led them to the space which had been cleared to form a makeshift stage, an expectant hush fell on the assembled company.

Thomas, the lure of the gaming table forgotten for the moment, tuned his fiddle, and soon Regan's voice rose sweet and clear, charming them all as she had charmed the emigrants in the steerage. Only the few women amongst them looked askance at her bare shoulders above her white net gown. The men merely enjoyed it. Once, between songs, Regan fancied she heard the click of dice at the corner table and fear of what might happen if they were still gambling when the entertainment was done added sharpness to her dislike of the arrogant Australian.

Why, it's plain he does nothing but drink, gamble and look at women in a way no gentleman should, she thought crossly.

As her last sweet notes died away, applause rose rapturously from the occupants of the saloon and a smiling Charles Maclane appeared at Regan's elbow.

'Miss Gardner – a pleasure indeed! Last night I thought you sang sweetly, but tonight you excelled. Now, Zach Casey wishes you and your father to join him at his table . . .'

Regan stiffened. It was just as she had feared – temptation would be put too easily in her father's way here among the monied passengers. They could afford to lose in an evening, as like as not, the same amount of money that would keep her and Thomas alive for a year. And who did this conceited Australian think he was, in any case, to summon them to his presence like a king issuing a royal command?

'I assume you act as his messenger, Mr Maclane,' she said sweetly. 'In that case, perhaps you would convey my regrets to Mr Casey and tell him if he wishes to see me, he will have to ask me himself.'

'And that I will gladly do!' Regan swung round in surprise to see Zach Casey himself standing beside her. 'You were magnificent, Miss Gardner, and I thank you for entertaining us so well,' he went on. 'Now, let me play host to you and your father, I beg you.'

His tone was beyond reproach, but his black eyes raked her with the same insolent appraisal as the previous evening and Regan felt the warm colour flooding her cheeks.

'I fear you mock me,' she returned tartly. 'I find it difficult to believe you needed entertaining at all.'

'Regan!' Thomas admonished, but to the surprise of them both, Zach Casey only threw back his head and laughed.

'You need not be jealous of the table, my dear. I am sure your singing can exert the same power over a man and make him a far more willing captive. Now, will you join me?'

Regan experienced a moment's panic. Somehow she must keep her father from this man's table, she knew, for once there he would too easily be persuaded to gamble with the little they had. Hastily she searched her mind for an excuse.

'I thank you, sir, but it is late and I am tired . . .' she began, but he was not to be discouraged so easily.

'Not so late that you cannot spare me a few minutes, surely,' he pressed her.

'Zach – I hope you do not intend to keep the lovely Regan all to yourself!' an English voice cut in, and with a rush of relief Regan turned to see a handsome young man moving through to join them. In stature he was as broad as Zach, though he was several inches shorter, and his fair hair and light eyes made him the complete antithesis of the Australian. 'Permit me to introduce myself,' he said with a smile. 'My name is Dickon Trenoweth. Like you, I am voyaging to the other side of the world for the first time, to join my brother in his business ventures.'

Glad of the diversion, Regan turned her attentions to him. 'Really, Mr Trenoweth? And what business ventures are those?'

Dickon's smile broadened. It was a strange smile, Regan thought in passing, humourless somehow and not quite reaching those light eyes of his. Fleetingly, she was reminded of a smiling theatrical mask that disguised who knew what.

'My brother's holdings are many and varied,' he said now. 'Jud has been in Australia since I was a young child and now he owns half a township, I believe, as well as his land. Is that not so, Zach?'

A flicker of impatience crossed Zach's dark features and Dickon went on: 'By the strangest coincidence his land and Zach's adjoin. We have met halfway across the world, yet we are to be neighbours.'

Zach laughed shortly. 'It's true Jud Trenoweth's farm adjoins my father's land, Ballymena. But he has yet to learn the vastness of the country. "Neighbour" in Australia has a very different meaning to the one he is accustomed to.'

There was a faint edge to his voice and Regan was

unable to prevent a small twist of pleasure.

So you think Mr Trenoweth is an intruder! she thought. He, at least, can get under your skin!

'It seems, daughter, that we are not the pioneers we thought ourselves,' Thomas put in. There was a jagged eagerness in his manner that dismayed Regan and she knew the nearness of the gaming table had had its effect on him.

'Gentlemen, I beg you to excuse us,' she said swiftly. 'It is time my father and I returned to our own quarters.'

'But you will sing to us again another evening?' Dickon pressed her.

'I'm not sure . . .' she floundered, searching for an excuse, and before she could stop him, Thomas had leapt upon the invitation.

'But of course we should be only too delighted! Tomorrow you may think is too soon but . . .'

'This moment could not be too soon!' Dickon contradicted him. 'And it will be my pleasure, if you will permit me, to escort you back to your own quarters.'

With a sweeping bow he gestured to them to go before him and as they left the saloon Regan was aware of Zach's eyes following them.

They were like two magnetic poles, he and Dickon, she thought – complete opposites. The one proud, arrogant and dark, laughing sometimes, too loudly, but rarely seeming to smile, the other fair, smooth as satin and smiling, if such a thing were possible, too much! That they did not like one another was evident – their rivalry was plain for all to see. And I do not like either of them! thought Regan. If they are a sample of cabin class passengers, then I am glad we are travelling steerage, for all the discomforts!

When Dickon Trenoweth had bade them goodnight and they were alone, Thomas turned to Regan, chiding her gently.

'Why were you not more charming to our patrons?' he asked, his mobile face puzzled. 'They could do so much to help us with our venture in the new country. And surely it is better to spend our evenings in that well-furnished saloon than in this black hell-hole.'

Regan frowned. 'At least in this black hell-hole, as you call it, you cannot gamble away our sovereigns,' she told him bluntly. 'The people here have nothing to gamble with. But you saw the dice game going on up there just as I did – and given half a chance you would join it, wouldn't you?'

'Oh daughter, your opinion of me is small!' Thomas shook his head, regarding her with a childlike innocence that might have deceived her had she not seen it so often before. 'Have you no faith in me at all?'

'The trouble comes because you have too much faith in yourself!' Regan said tartly. 'You always believe that this time fortune will smile on you. But we have so little to lose, Father!'

'And so much to gain!' he murmured, his eyes beginning to shine.

Her heart sank. He would never change. She tightened her grasp on his arm.

'Promise me you will not gamble with them, Father, even if they ask you,' she urged him. 'If you refuse, then I shall not come to the saloon again, and good fiddler though you may be, I don't think they will want you to entertain them alone.'

His face clouded. She knew she had hurt him. But it was too important to them both for her to weaken now.

'Promise, Father!' she insisted.

He sighed, admitting defeat.

'How did I come to sire such a bullying woman?' he grumbled gently. 'Yes, Regan, I promise.'

In the evenings that followed Regan and Thomas visited the saloon several times, but each night when their programme was done Regan insisted on returning immediately to their own quarters.

It would be foolish, she thought, to place temptation in her father's way by remaining within reach of the gambling that attracted him so and besides, as she had remarked after their first visit, she was not over-fond of the attitudes of the cabin class passengers. She was, after all, in spite of her good looks, an emigrant actress and they treated her as such. Some patronized her; some, like Dickon Trenoweth, tried to talk her into their beds. Zach, when he found his invitations to join him at his table were persistently refused, ignored her, continuing with his game of dice throughout her singing so that she thought him rude as well as arrogant. But although Regan would have given up the visits gladly and had done with it, Thomas was insistent they should continue, and Regan had the sneaking suspicion that his enthusiasm was not only because of the reputation they were gaining, but also his attachment to the tots of rum that found their way into his hand – and the nearness of the damned dice.

And one evening her suspicion was proved correct. When their singing was done, she was drawn into conversation with Dickon Trenoweth and when she managed to make her escape from him and looked around for her father, she saw to her dismay that he had wandered over to the table where Zach sat with Charles Maclane and his other cronies.

Hastily she crossed the saloon. As she went, the men watched her hungrily and the women averted their eyes from her bare shoulders, but for once Regan hardly noticed. She was too intent on reaching Thomas before any harm was done. Already he was bending over the table, talking with Zach and gesticulating eagerly. Another moment and he might be seated with the others, emptying the contents of his pouch onto the table.

'Father!' she said sharply. 'It's time we were leaving.'

He looked up, and the excited light in his eyes alarmed her still more.

'But Regan, I am doing no harm!' he pleaded.

'Father, you promised me!' she insisted. 'You must excuse him, gentlemen. We must return to our own quarters.'

Thomas shrugged helplessly. 'My daughter does not approve of me chancing my money, I fear.'

'But women are there to do as we tell them, my friend, not the other way about.' Zach's eyes raked Regan with studied insolence as he spoke and anger flared in her like a fire. Who did he think he was, this conceited Australian? If he was typical of the men she would encounter in the new country she could have wished she had remained in

England! With an effort she bit back the sharp retort that
rose to her lips, though her eyes left him in no doubt of her
dislike for him.

'Father, I beg you,' she said, taking his arm.

As Zach rose to bid them goodnight, his gallantry was
somehow as mocking as his rudeness had been.

'Perhaps it is as well you do not stay with us, old friend,'
he said gravely to Thomas. 'The game will likely last all
night and the stakes will be high. Perhaps some other time
you will join us.'

'Perhaps,' Thomas agreed sadly.

Without another word Regan led him from the saloon.
She was shaking, both from the encounter with Zach and
the narrow escape she had had from losing her father to
the gaming table, and when they reached the emigrants'
cuddy, she turned to him with determination.

'I don't think we should go there again, Father,' she
told him. 'Why the rich gentlemen should wish to draw
you into their game I don't know, but it seems to me that
they do, and with stakes such as they can afford, you could
lose the little we have almost before you know it.'

To her surprise he sighed resignedly. 'Perhaps you are
right,' he agreed. 'Now I think I shall retire. The sight of
fortunes being lost and won has wearied me. So you see
you have nothing to fear.'

'Oh, Father!' Tenderness flooded her and she reached
up to kiss his rubbery cheek, anxious suddenly to express
her love for him. 'I'm sorry if I upset you, but it's only for
our good.'

'Yes.' He smiled at her and twisted a red-gold curl
between his fingers. 'But you must remember, too, that
my motives are just as pure. I, too, only want what is best
for us, Regan.'

'I know,' she murmured, and when she had undressed
and lay down in her bunk a warm contentment seemed to
separate her from the whispering cuddy. Perhaps at last
he had realized the folly of his ways, she thought. Perhaps
if they could find the success he dreamed of he would be
satisfied enough to leave his old habits behind forever.
That indeed would be something worth working for.

*   *   *

Regan awoke suddenly. Her heart was pounding against her ribs and there was a trembling in her limbs. Her first, terrified thought was that the ship had foundered. But the murmuring dark was unbroken, the waves still roared with the same rhythmic pattern and the boards creaked comfortingly around her. Yet something was wrong, for all that. She knew it instinctively and she lay for a moment wide-eyed and shivering before carefully raising herself and swinging her legs over the edge of the bunk.

Beneath her feet the floor rocked and she grabbed at the edge of her father's bunk above to steady herself. Then she stopped, the breath catching in her throat as the first hazy suspicion assailed her. It was just as if . . . but no, that couldn't be . . .

Swiftly she turned, running her hands across the bunk, and a small sob escaped her lips. It was empty! He was not there! But where . . .?

The very second the question crossed her mind, she knew the answer. The pointers were all there, too clear to be ignored. Her father's ready acquiescence to her plea not to go to the saloon again, his eagerness for them both to retire instead of dreaming and planning as they sometimes did, into the early hours, the brightness of his eyes despite his disappointment, the slight unsteadiness of his hands. She had put that down to the rum he had consumed, now she knew differently. And as if he were right beside her now, she seemed to hear Zach Casey's mocking tones:

'The game will likely last all night.'

How long was it since he had left the cuddy, Regan wondered _ hours, or minutes? She had no way of knowing. With shaking hands she reached for her dress and struggled into it. If he had only just gone, and in so doing disturbed her, she might still be able to avert disaster. But somehow, sickeningly, she was sure he had been gone longer than that. There was an air of quiet in the cuddy, as if no one had stirred for a very long time.

Her dress fastened, Regan reached for a shawl, thrust her feet into her slippers and hurried to the companion-way. As she emerged on deck the wind, icy-cold and blowing as hard as ever, bit into her, and spray soaked her dress and hair before she had gone more than a few yards. But she scarcely noticed. All she was aware of was the light that was shining out into the pitch blackness from the cabin beneath the poop _ the cabin where, if she was not much mistaken, the gaming was still in progress.

Pulling her shawl across her face to shield her from the driving wind, she ran along the companionway and into the saloon. Then, with the door banging to and fro behind her she stopped, uncertain.

The saloon was almost empty now. Most of the passengers had left for their cabins. But at the corner table a group of men stood watching two players who sat over the rolling dice. Facing her was the darkly hateful Zach Casey. And the other side of the table, his back towards her, sat Thomas. For the moment they were too engrossed in their game to notice her, but when she went down the steps Zach Casey looked up and his eyebrows lifted sardonically as he saw her. Then his voice rose, carrying clearly to her above the roar of the waves outside.

'Your daughter has come to watch the play, my friend. Perhaps now your luck will change!'

Thomas turned and as he did so Regan's heart fell like a stone. There was no mistaking that look. She had seen it too often before – the face of defeat. Slowly her eyes took in the table – the bottle of rum, half-empty, and the glasses, the dice and the dice-cup, the pile of gleaming sovereigns at Zach Casey's elbow. And her father's pouch, flat and empty, bearing witness that her worst fears had been realized.

'Oh Father how could you!' she cried. 'You have lost everything!'

'It was just a run of bad luck, Regan!' Had it not been for the despair in his eyes, making him old, it might have been the face of a disobedient child that looked up at her. 'It was going my way, daughter. I was making us a fortune – and I still could if I had but something left to wager.'

'Will you never learn?' she asked softly and then as the hopelessness and despair welled up in her she whirled round on Zach. 'You're no better than a thief!' she cried. 'To take the little we have when you have so much!

You've plotted and planned this, haven't you? You've seen the way my father looked when he saw a game. And you've encouraged him to lose everything we have because you could afford to wait for luck to turn your way. I despise you, do you know that? Despise you!'

For a moment there was silence as the men around the table stared at Regan in amazement.

'Miss Gardner . . .' Zach began, but she cut him dead, turning to her father and laying a hand on his arm.

'Come, Father!' she urged him. But suddenly his eye fell on the ruby ring glowing on her finger and he caught at her hand, hope bursting in his face like sunrise after a dark night.

'Regan – wait! We have not lost all!'

Her eyes followed his glance and her heart seemed to stop beating. Her mother's ring! Usually after their visit to the saloon she took it off and gave it back to him for safe keeping. But tonight she had been preoccupied when she retired and she had forgotten she was still wearing it. So he had not lost it with the sovereigns, but now . . .

'Oh no, Father!' she whispered. 'No – not Mama's ring!'

He caught at her hand. 'Give it to me, daughter. I can still win back all I have lost – and more. You see, Mr Casey? It's a ruby. And it is no imitation, I promise you.'

Zach appeared to hesitate. For a long moment he sat there, his eyes going from the ring to Regan's face and back again. He was mocking them, she thought, enjoying every second of their discomfiture. Then, with a lazy movement, he pushed a great pile of sovereigns into the centre of the table.

'I'll take you on,' he said slowly. 'One last roll of the dice – your ring against all the money I have in front of me. There's three times what you lost to me here, and I wager it all. Will you accept, my friend?'

Thomas glanced pleadingly at Regan. 'Daughter – we have no choice! The ring – I must have it . . .'

Regan stood motionless. She felt as if her heart had turned to stone within her. Then slowly, very slowly, she eased the precious ring from her finger. To risk it broke her heart. But what choice did she have now? For a moment she held it in the palm of her hand, too choked by tears to speak. Then with an abrupt movement she put it down on the table.

'Damn you both,' she said softly.

Zach Casey's eyes met hers briefly and in them she saw what looked like a glint of triumph. Then he reached eagerly for the rum bottle, refilling their glasses.

'Let us drink to the game before us,' he said softly. 'And may the best man win!'

The tension around the corner table was so thick it seemed to hang like tobacco smoke in the air. All eyes were turned now to Zach and his opponent. Never, it seemed, had two men been more sharply contrasted. Never had more hung on the roll of a dice.

Someone offered Regan a seat but she shook her head. She did not know how she could bear to watch, but neither could she leave now and she stood beside the table, her fists clenched so tightly in the folds of her skirt that her nails cut deep crescents into her palms.

'We wager all on this one game, do we not?' Zach asked. There was amusement in his voice and Regan hated him more than ever. He was enjoying their discomfort, she was sure. And if he won again he would take his dues without hesitation. He pushed the die-cup towards Thomas, his lips curling. 'Let the game begin!'

Regan glanced at Thomas. Perspiration stood out on his face like a thin mist and he suddenly looked years older. Yet still there was that strange light in his eyes – even now, on the edge of ruin. With a shaking hand he shook the cup; the dice rolled out onto the baize table top. A gasp went around the assembled company – a good throw! Eagerly he separated the matching pairs and the dice rolled again. Regan held her breath, hardly daring to look until she saw the tentative smile begin to curl the corners of her father's mouth.

'I'll leave it there, I fancy.' His voice was slurred. Tension had heightened the effects of the rum and he sat back watching like a cat through narrowed eyes as Zach's strong brown hands closed over the cup. For a moment he waited and the company held their breath. Then, with a mocking glance at Regan, he shook the dice onto the table. One by one it seemed they turned, clicking slowly over. One by one, like pieces of a jigsaw falling into place. The watchers gasped in amazement. But for one dice they would be an unbeatable combination, the five sixes. Zach did not look up now. His eyes saw only the dice. The one that spoiled his throw was returned to the cup and rattled and Regan found herself praying as she had never prayed before. And she was answered. A two! There was a dead silence now in the saloon. Not a soul spoke or even, it seemed, breathed. Again Zach raised the cup, but unlike Thomas, his hand was quite steady. Once, twice, he shook it and the dice rolled over and over until it came to rest. Would it be? Could it be?

It was! A six! Their breath came out in a concerted gasp and Thomas seemed to slump in his chair. It wasn't possi- ble – he'd played a winning hand and this devil had beaten him! Now, in helpless torment, he glanced at Regan.

She was standing quite still, her face white but expres- sionless. Then, with a determined movement of her slen- der shoulders, she reached out to help Thomas to his feet. 'Come, Father,' she said softly.

The men around the table parted to let them through. But before they had gone more than a step, Zach's deep voice arrested them.

'Wait!'

They stopped, though Regan could not bear to turn to look at him and he pushed his way through to them. In one hand he held Thomas's pouch, in the other the ruby ring and a handful of sovereigns.

'Wait. I'll not take your last penny and see you starve.' He opened the pouch, dropped the sovereigns and the ring inside, and pushed it towards Thomas. 'Here, take it.'

They stared at him, Regan in disbelief, while Thomas's eyes filled with tears of gratitude and he stretched out a shaking hand.

'Oh, how can I ever thank you . . .'

Zach dropped the pouch into his hand, but made no attempt to move from their path. 'You misunderstand me, my friend. You cannot play me at dice and not pay for your wager. I still intend to take some dues – but I will exchange your stake for something you can afford to give.'

Seeing their puzzled expressions, he threw back his head and laughed. 'You still don't know what I mean, do you? Then let me put it more clearly. I will not take your sovereigns and leave you destitute. I will take a richer prize – your daughter!'

A gasp ran around the assembled company – a gasp of delight and disbelief, and before Regan could move, speak or even think, his fingers had fastened around her wrist, drawing her towards him in a grip of iron.

'You shall pay your father's debts for him,' he murmured. 'And the exchange will be my gain. You are worth more, sweet Regan, than a sackful of sovereigns.'

Then his arm tightened around her waist like a band of tempered steel, drawing her so close against him that the breath was squeezed from her lungs in a tortured sob and his lips covered hers, searching, demanding, possessing.

CHAPTER THREE

To Regan it seemed the kiss would go on forever. Breathlessly she struggled, but it was useless. His vice-like arm held her pinioned against him so intimately that she was left in no doubt as to the hard reality of his maleness, while his free hand gripped the back of her neck to support her under the fierce pressure of his searing lips and probing tongue.

Dimly she was aware of the gasps that came from the other men, but if Zach, too, heard them he did not let them deter him. Rather he held her tighter still, as if to stake his claim once and for all. The cabin swam around her, blood sang in her ears so that she thought she would faint and still he held her, his mouth crushing hers, his arm making her captive and his hard thigh pressing her to him so that every curve moulded to the answering swell of his body.

Panic rose in her in a bubbling tide, but she was caught as securely as a bird in a snare and it was only when she thought her lungs must burst that he released her, so abruptly that her shaking legs almost failed her and she steadied herself with one hand against the table edge while the other covered her stinging lips.

For a moment she was too shocked to speak. Never had she been kissed like that before. Never had Richard violated her so, forcing his tongue into her mouth in that way – no, not even when they were alone. But this cruel-faced stranger had insulted her before all his friends and now stood looking as pleased with himself as if he had just bagged the fattest bird in a pheasant shoot.

The thought incensed her still more and lent her the impetus to find her tongue.

'Is this for their entertainment, too?' she flared. 'Are they well pleased with your little show – you blackguard!'

Thomas, who was standing like a man stunned, recovered himself at the sound of her voice. Staggering a little, he pushed forward and faced Zach angrily.

'You swine!' he cried, his voice slightly slurred from rum. 'How dare you treat my daughter like a common whore?'

Zach smiled slowly and let his eyes run insolently over Regan, lingering a moment too long on the creamy flesh above the neckline of her gown. Then: 'If you do not want her treated like a whore, then you should not allow her to dress like one!' he advised calmly.

Regan gasped, her hands involuntarily covering her breasts. But Zach seemed unaware of her now.

'Do not use the word "whore" too readily, old friend,' he told Thomas. 'Your daughter will not be the first to sell herself for security, many a wife has done the same. And her life with me will not be unpleasant, I assure you. I can offer her many more comforts than you ever could. In this harsh new land it has taken many years to amass them.'

Regan stared and the feeling of faintness began to overcome her again. His voice was blurred, she thought, like a shout through water, and his words made no sense at all. What did he mean – selling herself for security? She wouldn't – she couldn't! And why should he speak of her life with him? He was nothing to do with her – nothing at all!

As if in a dream, she heard Thomas echo her thoughts.

'What the devil do you mean? Are you mad, Casey?'

Zach threw back his head and laughed. 'On the contrary, my friend, I have never felt more sane in my life,' he stated. 'I have made a deal with you. You leave this room a far richer man than you entered it, but I still count myself the winner. In a country where men outnumber the ladies twenty to one, your daughter is a prize indeed.'

Regan's eyes widened in horror and colour began to mount in Thomas's ashen cheeks.

'You mean – to *take* her?' he spluttered.

Zach laughed again. 'You thought to pay your debts with one kiss, old friend? Oh, your daughter is beautiful, I grant you, but I am too much of a businessman to part with a fortune for so little. No, I want more than that for my money, I'm afraid.'

In spite of the turmoil within her, Regan was determined not to allow this monster to see how afraid she was.

'You think I'd let a pig like you take me?' she cried. 'I'd die first!'

Momentarily Zach's eyes narrowed, then he shrugged nonchalantly.

'You prefer to starve and your father with you? Well, the choice is yours, my dear. But I think you'll wish you had accepted my offer before you have been long in the new country. It is no place for the weak or the old. Your father will not last long, I fear, and you – you will eventually have to sell yourself over and over again to the crazy animals in the goldfields who have not seen a woman in months and who will pay but a fraction of what I have offered. Do you know how they will use you, these rum-soaked morons who have turned to one another in their desperation? How long do you think your looks will last beneath their lust? You will come to me begging . . .'

'Enough! You go too far!' Thomas's voice had filled many a theatre, and now, though slurred a little from the rum he had imbibed, it reached every corner of the saloon. 'You have beaten me at dice, it is true. But that doesn't give you the right to insult my daughter. I challenge you, sir, to fight for her honour!'

Zach half-turned, thinking he couldn't have heard aright. Thomas was a slightly built man and a good fifteen years his senior. And he was drunk. The high flush of colour in his pallid face bore witness to that. Zach could, he knew, brush him aside with one flick of his strong brown wrist. But he had humiliated the older man enough for one night. He had what he wanted – there was no point in going on with this.

'Go to bed, old friend,' he advised. 'We will talk again tomorrow.'

But Thomas's blood was up and his sense of the dramatic aroused.

'Will no man lend me a weapon?' he demanded of the silent onlookers.

Dickon Trenoweth disengaged himself from the group. As always he was smiling. 'A duel!' he suggested. 'What more equal terms could there be? I can contribute a firearm for one of the adversaries!'

Casually he opened his cutaway, and to Regan's horror she saw he wore a revolver in a jewelled holster beneath it.

'No!' she cried, but Thomas eagerly snatched the proffered weapon and thrust it towards Zach.

'Take it – or show yourself a coward! I will find another!'

Zach's lips tightened a fraction and a dangerous look crossed his dark features. Then with a twist of his shoulders he turned away.

'I could not fight an old man like you, especially in your drunken condition,' he sneered. 'It wouldn't be gentlemanly or fair. No, pay your debt, my friend, and think yourself lucky to escape so light!'

'You blackguard . . .' Thomas was beside himself now, brushing past Regan as she ran forward to stop him and following Zach across the saloon. 'Cowardly wretch! Stay and fight!'

Zach had reached the stairs and begun to mount them

when suddenly the ship rolled violently. He grabbed at the rail to save himself, but Thomas, already unsteady from drink, was marooned in the centre of the saloon. He lurched forward and fell heavily to the floor and as he did so a sharp report rang out. For a second in time they all stared stupidly at his crumpled figure, then Regan screamed and ran to him, going down on her knees at his side.

'Father – Father are you hurt?'

In pained surprise he looked up at her, his mouth working silently, and she slipped her arms beneath him, trying to raise him. Then her eyes went round with horror and she drew back sharply, staring down at her hands. They were red with blood.

'My God!' Zach muttered. He was down the steps in a moment, crossing the saloon with huge strides and putting Regan aside as he, too, bent over the huddled body. Swiftly he peeled off his coat to make a pillow for Thomas's head and, as he turned him over to rest against it, Regan's gasp echoed around the cabin.

There was a scarlet patch on Thomas's white waistcoat – a patch that was darkening and spreading. Panic touched Regan with icy fingers and, her senses swimming, she turned on Zach.

'It was loaded!' she cried. 'Oh, you beast! What have you done to him?'

Zach's eyes darkened. 'Be quiet, little fool!' he ordered her. 'Hysterics won't help now. Have you a petticoat? Take it off and give it to me!'

'But . . .'

'Come on – hurry! We must staunch the bleeding.'

With trembling hands she raised her skirts and ripped off one of her petticoats. Then she watched in horror as Zach tore open Thomas's waistcoat and stiff shirt front to expose a gaping wound just beneath the ribs.

'Have you another petticoat?' he demanded without even looking up at her. 'Tear it up to make bandages unless you want him to bleed to death.'

A sob caught in her throat and tears of shock filled her eyes. Dear God, could this really be happening? she asked herself wildly.

'Now, Regan!' Zach ordered her harshly and automatically she stepped out of the second petticoat. It was the best she had ever owned – she would likely never own another one so fine. But without a second thought she ripped at it until the fabric gave. What did a petticoat matter now? What did anything matter?

Somehow her fingers went on tearing at the thin fabric, but around her the faces of the onlookers had blurred into a clouded tapestry. Charles Maclane was there now, helping Zach to stem the flow of blood from the gaping wound, though where he had come from she did not know. And there was Dickon Trenoweth, his everlasting smile frozen for once, coming close to her, putting his arms around her, trying even now to take advantage of her, she thought in disgust.

'Go away – leave me alone!' she tried to say, but to her surprise no sound came. Instead there was nausea rising in her throat and the saloon seemed to be swimming around her. She raised a hand to her throat, fighting against the faintness that threatened to engulf her. But it was no use. Her knees seemed to buckle beneath her, the darkness closed in, and Regan slipped quietly and almost unnoticed to the floor.

As she surfaced through the layers of consciousness, Regan wondered in confusion where she was and what was wrong. She was lying on a bunk, but a softer bunk than the one she slept on in the cuddy, and there was nothing above her to shut off the stale, heavy air from her face . . .

With a start she opened her eyes and in the same second memory came flooding back. They had been in the saloon and her father had been shot! Please God it was a nightmare! But she knew it was not.

'Father . . .' she whispered helplessly.

Someone was bending over her, raising her head to put a bottle to her lips. Momentarily she thought it was Zach, but when she turned her eyes in his direction she saw it was Charles Maclane.

'Drink this,' he said. 'Only a sip, though. It's strong stuff unless you're used to it.'

Obediently she opened her lips, then spluttered as the golden liquid seared her throat.

'It's brandy. It'll do you good. You're lucky I carry a flask for emergencies – the rum they drink would burn your insides out.'

As if this was not doing the self-same thing! she thought wryly. But for all that it made her cough the brandy seemed to clear her head and she sat up, looking around the cabin in which she found herself.

'Where am I? And where's Father?' she asked, her voice beginning to rise again as a new terror filled her. 'He's not . . .' She broke off, unable to put her fear into words.

'He's not dead,' Charles Maclane assured her. 'But he's very seriously wounded, Regan. You have to be brave.'

Brave! The cold had begun again, creeping through her veins and not even the brandy could stop it. With an effort she swung her trembling legs over the edge of the bunk.

'I must go to him!'

Charles Maclane placed a restraining hand on her shoulder. 'No, Regan. Zach is attending to your father and it's better that you stay here, out of the way.'

She screwed up her face in surprise. 'Is he a doctor then?'

'No, but unfortunately our ship's doctor is a little too fond of the bottle for his own good – and the rest of us besides. Earlier this evening he was carried to his cabin in a state from which it will take him some little while to recover. I have seen him dead to the world for a day and more after a night of excess such as this. But if anyone can save your father, it is Zach. These pioneers are hard and independent, you know. They have had to learn how to be. There are no doctors in the bush and if a leg is broken, they must set it, or if a baby comes too soon and there is no one to call upon to deliver it, then they bring it into the world themselves. And if a man is shot . . .'

Unbidden, a sob came to her lips. 'But what can he do?'

'For now he will stop the bleeding as best he can. Then the bullet must be removed, if that is possible. If not . . .'

'Yes?' she whispered.

'If not, then I think he will die,' Charles said evenly.

Regan covered her mouth with her hands, staring at him aghast. Then a commotion outside the door claimed her attention and two men entered the cabin carrying her father. With every step they took he groaned, a breathless gasp that became a shriek of agony as they lay him, as carefully as they could, on the bunk opposite to her own.

Pushing Charles Maclane aside, she ran to her father. Beads of perspiration stood out on his face and his eyes were glazed, but he recognized her at once, reaching out to take her hand in a vice-like grip.

'Oh Regan, my Regan! What is to become of you?' he moaned.

Regan blinked back the tears. 'I'll be all right, Father. You mustn't worry about me. Just think of yourself.'

Thomas's face contorted in agony. 'This is the end of me, love.'

'No!' she whispered sharply, bending over to smooth the hair away from his damp forehead. 'Don't talk so! I won't have it, Father!'

''Twas for you, Regan,' he murmured. 'I only did it for you!'

'I know!' She caught her lip between her teeth, fighting to control the tears. Thomas's eyelids drooped and closed and his fingers released their iron grip on her hand. 'Father!' she sobbed.

'The pain is too much for him.'

Regan swung around at the sound of Zach's voice. He was standing behind her, towering over her, and as he reached out to touch her arm she shrank away.

'You swine! This is all your doing!' she spat at him.

An unreadable expression flickered across his dark features, then his lips tightened in the way that was becoming uncomfortably familiar to Regan.

'I'll do what I can for him,' he said in a voice devoid of expression. 'And you may consider this cabin as your own for the remainder of the voyage.'

Regan's eyes widened. 'This is your cabin?'

He inclined his head. 'It was. It is now yours and your father's for as long as you want it. Fortunately, I had expected company on this voyage and booked a double berth.'

'Fortunately!' she screamed at him. 'What is fortunate about you being alone? If you had had company, maybe you would have had better things to do than gamble all night with those who can ill-afford to lose, then this would never have happened.'

A muscle tightened in his cheek and to Regan it seemed that his eyes were as dark and hard as pieces of jet.

'I did not force your father to play dice with me,' he said softly, 'though I knew from the first time I saw him that he was a gambler. Not even his dramatic ability could conceal that. No, he came creeping back here at the dead of night, begging to be dealt in on our game. And he would not have thanked me for pointing out that he could ill-afford the stakes for which we play.'

For a moment Regan held his eyes defiantly. She had no answer for him, but that did not mean she hated him the less. On the contrary, she hated him more for drawing attention to the weakness of the father she loved, and who now lay unconscious while her torn-up petticoats turned scarlet with his life's blood . . .

'Excuse me – may I intrude?' They turned to see Dickon Trenoweth framed in the cabin doorway. Even now he was smiling his sickly, humourless smile and Regan felt an insane urge to strike out at him too.

'By all means. Since yours was the weapon that felled him, feel free to come and gloat, so as to complete your evening's entertainment.'

He reddened, then held out a soft leather pouch which she immediately recognized as her father's.

'I found this on the saloon floor. He must have dropped it when he fell and it lay beneath him,' he explained.

At the sight of the pouch, Regan felt the faintness rise again, a wave of cold that began in the pit of her stomach and ran in shivering ripples through her body, her legs and even her arms. This pouch – these sovereigns and her mother's ring – were the cause of her father lying here now and she could not bear to touch them. Pressing her clenched fist to her lips she turned away. Zach took the pouch from Dickon's outstretched hand and tucked it into the pocket in Thomas's coat tails that spread beside him on the bunk.

'You will need these if you recover, my friend,' he said softly. 'I fear it will be a long while before you work again.'

Then he touched Regan's arm. 'Tomorrow when it is daylight I will do what I can for him. The doctor, damn him, is unlikely to have a steady enough hand to do what must be done even if he is conscious. And now you must get what rest you can. I shall be close by on the other side of the door if you should need me.'

Regan nodded, too weak suddenly to lash him again with her tongue. And besides, with the doctor lying dead drunk and useless, it seemed he was her father's only hope. For the moment, it seemed advisable to humour him, rogue and blackguard though he might be.

When the cabin was empty save for her and Thomas she sank to her knees beside him, taking his hand in hers and looking down at the ashen face she loved so well.

'Don't worry, Father, he will pay for this,' she whispered, and her tears, falling onto their linked hands, set a seal on the vow.

Next day the weather was squally so that the *Maid of Morne* rolled despite the reduced sail and Zach had difficulty in probing Thomas's wound.

'The bullet is there, wedged in deep, and I dare not try to reach it while the ship rocks so,' Zach told Regan.

'But if it is not removed he'll die – and the rascally doctor is still too drunk to help – or so Mr Maclane says,' Regan replied. They spoke in low whispers so that the older man, who lay in Zach's bunk, should not hear. He was conscious and unconscious by turns, surfacing through the mists of pain to moan and writhe, until his threshings became too much for him and he drifted off once more into merciful oblivion.

'It must be removed, mustn't it?' she insisted. 'Oh, if you are the man you say you are, do what has to be done please, for God's sake!'

'Have some sense, Miss Gardner!' Zach said harshly. 'What chance do you think he will have if the ship rolls at a critical moment and I remove half his insides along with the shot? The sea would make my hands as unsteady as those of our doctor friend. No, we have no choice but to wait and pray that the weather eases.'

'And if it does not – what then?'

'If it does not you will have to place yourself in the good Lord's hands,' he said roughly.

With difficulty, Regan bit back the sharp retort that rose unbidden to her lips. For the moment she must be civil to this hateful man – she had no choice. But oh, when the moment came she would tell him exactly what her own opinion of him was, and she would not mince her words!

The hours dragged by, hours when the ship still scudded in the teeth of the gale and Regan dared not leave her father's side for more than a few minutes. Although he was only conscious for part of the time, he seemed to know if she left the cabin and when she returned he was calling for her, feebly, so that her heart turned over and she ran to him, holding his hand in hers as if he were the child and she the parent.

'It's all right, Father, I won't leave you,' she assured him, and he drifted off again, satisfied.

Towards evening, however, his condition worsened. He tossed and turned in a fever, forehead burning, eyes wide and bright in his flushed face. He was soaked now not only with blood but with sweat too, and Regan knew if something was not done for him soon, he would certainly die.

'Is there no hope of the surgeon recovering?' she asked Charles Maclane when he looked in soon after supper. 'How much did the wretched man drink that he is still abed when he is needed?'

Charles frowned. He had just come from the doctor and he knew he was too shaky and ill-tempered to be the slightest use. 'Just let them try to foist that drunkard onto us again and I'll resign my commission!' he thought, looking at Regan's agonized face and the obvious torment of her father. But aloud he said: 'Zach Casey is better than any doctor. I'll fetch him, Regan.'

He left the cabin, returning a few minutes later with Zach. As the Australian lifted the dressing and probed the wound, Regan winced. The two men muttered together in low voices while she strained her ears to hear and at last Zach turned to her authoritatively.

'The bullet will have to come out and the sooner the better, but the doctor is in no fit state to operate,' he stated. 'Do you wish me to do what I can, Miss Gardner?'

Her eyes went from the dark man to her father and back again. Then she drew a deep, shuddering breath.

'Please do,' she said simply.

He nodded abruptly. 'Charles, visit our drunken friend's cabin and bring me his instruments of surgery. And I shall need the assistance of one other to help me hold him – find someone willing, Miss Gardner – and quickly. Another of the officers will oblige perhaps.'

Regan glanced at her father. How could she leave him to the mercy of strangers now? Willing herself to conceal the uneven beating of her heart, she faced Zach Casey.

'I'll help you,' she offered.

Zach stared for a moment, then turned away. 'One patient is enough for me, Miss Gardner. If you faint away again you will be of no help at all. Among the officers there must be one who has seen this done before.'

Regan's chin wobbled and she bit hard on her lower lip to steady it.

'I shall not faint again, Mr Casey. I have to stay!'

Again Zach's eyes raked her and she held his gaze. Then, as the cabin door opened and Charles Maclane appeared with the doctor's instruments, he nodded sharply.

'Very well. Do just as I tell you, Miss Gardner.'

For Regan, time seemed to stand still then, part of the nightmarish pattern of events that had turned adventure into violent, living hell. In a dream she did as Zach Casey told her, holding instruments for him, staunching the blood which began to flow again and trying all the while to shut herself off from what was happening lest she should faint once more.

She must forget, she told herself, that the man on the bunk was her own dear father. But it was not easy! Oh, it was not easy!

Long minutes ticked by, how many she would never

know, until at last Zach Casey straightened up, covering the wound with a fresh dressing and turning to face her. His dark brows were drawn together into a frown and the tightness of his lips made her blood turn to ice.

'I'm sorry,' he said in a low voice.

'The bullet . . .' she whispered.

He wiped his hands and reached for a coiled bandage. 'It's in too deep,' he murmured to her over his shoulder. 'There's nothing I can do.'

A little sob caught in her throat then and she pressed her hands over her mouth.

'Nothing?' she repeated brokenly. 'But there must be . . . you said . . .'

Zach Casey shook his head, completing the bandaging and turning to her once more. 'I made you no promises,' he said roughly. 'Except that you should have the use of my cabin as long as you need it. But to be brutally frank, judging by the look of your father, that will not be for long.'

Then, leaving Charles Maclane to pack together the borrowed instruments, he turned on his heel and walked out of the cabin.

CHAPTER FOUR

As Zach Casey had predicted, Thomas was dead by morning and as Regan watched the cold grey sky lighten above the cold grey sea the weight of her grief was like a leaden jacket around her heart.

All her tears had been shed now – she felt she could not cry another if she lived to be a hundred – but the dry ache inside her was worse than ever.

They had started on this adventure with such hope in their hearts, she and her father, and now he would be buried at sea, his body going to provide food for the fishes, while she, Regan, would have to go on alone.

What will become of me? she wondered. Supposing Richard hasn't received my letter! If this country is as vast as they say it is, I may never find him!

But even that anxiety seemed shadowy and unreal compared with the knowledge that never again would she sing to Thomas's mournful fiddle, never see the eager smile transform his mobile face, never sit with him to read the plays of William Shakespeare.

Day broke, but the nightmare went on. Captain Barnes summoned her to the chart-room where he broke off from his calculations for long enough to lecture her on 'the will of God', but Regan was only too well aware of his underlying disapproval. Bully Barnes did not like gamblers and he did not like men who tried to start gunfights. Most of all, he did not like scandals aboard his ship – and the unhappy events of the last days had come close to causing a stir on more counts than one.

'I will conduct the funeral service for the departed myself,' he told Regan. 'And may the Lord have mercy on his soul.'

She nodded, unable to equate what was happening with the voyage they had set out on with such hope. It was only when she stood that afternoon on the windswept deck, seeing through tear-blurred eyes the small bundle wrapped in a Union Jack poised above the fathomless grey ocean, that the enormity of it came home to her. That bundle was not *just* a bundle – it was Thomas, her father. And until she reached Australia, and Richard, she was quite, quite alone. Not one of the people gathered here on deck to pay their last respects to her father cared a jot for her. The crew, lined up in their rows, did not know either her or him from Adam, and never would. The emigrants, who had crowded up from the cuddy eager for a breath of fresh air, had had little time for her since she left them to entertain in the first class saloon, while the cabin class passengers themselves looked down on her as being beneath them. Of the officers, Charles Maclane had been kind, but now that Bully Barnes had branded her a troublemaker she could not imagine that would last. And besides, she did not want anyone near her to remind her of the arrogant Zach Casey . . .

Involuntarily she looked around for him, but he was nowhere to be seen.

His conscience keeps him away, she thought bitterly, and her hatred for him twisted a notch tighter. Then, as the service began, she thought of nothing but her father and her need to keep her grief private from all those curious eyes . . .

At last it was over. The crew marched away, the gawking passengers dispersed and she was left alone. For one brief moment she stood looking down into the fathomless ocean and the white-capped waves that had opened to swallow that pitifully small bundle, then, drawing her shawl more tightly around her shoulders, she turned to go back to the privacy of the cabin. She could not stay there now, of course. She would simply collect her things and her father's and vacate it, but at least it would afford her a few moments alone before she had to face the rest of the emigrants again, and their curiosity and pretended pity . . .

The first class saloon was almost empty and for some reason she had expected the cabin to be also, so that when she pushed open the door and saw the tall shadow fall across it she almost cried out in surprise.

'Mr Casey! I didn't think . . .'

'That I would be here? Why not? It is my cabin, Miss Gardner.' How she hated that arrogant drawl! If she never heard it again it would be too soon.

'I have come to collect my things, and my father's.' Her voice cracked a little and she swallowed at the lump that had risen in her throat. 'Have the goodness to leave me in peace for a moment or two.'

Zach Casey moved to one side to allow her in, but made no attempt to leave the cabin. Suddenly the sight of him lounging there was too much for her. Her eyes brimming with angry tears, she turned on him.

'Why must you stand there watching me, you hateful pig? Isn't it enough that my father is dead and it's all your doing?'

Taken by surprise, Zach recoiled a little. 'My dear Regan . . .' he began, but his words only seemed to undo the final catch on the floodgates. All her grief and anger came rushing to the surface like molten lava from a volcano and she faced him furiously.

'Don't "dear Regan" me!' she cried. 'You think yourself such a fine gentleman, Zach Casey, but I'll tell you what you really are – a gambler, just as my poor father was, only you're worse. Money means nothing to you so you play with people's lives. And do you know what that makes you? It makes you a murderer!'

'Regan!' Zach Casey said sharply. 'It was your father who took the gun he was offered, don't forget. It had nothing to do with me.'

'Oh that's what you'd like to to think, wouldn't you? That's what it pleases you to pretend, to hide the truth from yourself. He took the gun, yes, but only because there was no other way he could protect me . . .' Her voice tailed away as a fresh spasm of grief and anger shook her. Then: 'And when you could have saved him, you didn't!' she screamed at him.

Zach's eyes narrowed. 'What do you mean by that?' he demanded.

'If you had taken the bullet out he would be alive now!' Regan sobbed. 'You could have done it – it was all up to you . . .'

'Now wait a minute!' Zach interrupted her. His voice was like thunder now and his fingers shot out to clasp her shoulders in a grip of steel. 'What are you saying, Regan? I did my best for your father – at your request.'

She tried to shake herself free. 'I must have been mad to trust you!' she cried. 'Why should you save him? Why? Oh, I hate you! I despise you! I never want to see you again as long as I live!'

Zach's face darkened and for a second she thought he was going to strike her. Then his fingers released their grip on her shoulder and he pushed her away.

'Really my dear?' he snarled. 'Well that will be a little difficult for you, I fear.'

'What do you mean?' She was shaking, a nameless fear beginning to encroach on her anger.

'Since you are now mine you can hardly avoid seeing me!' he stated coldly. 'Do not look at me with such surprise, Regan. Surely you have not forgotten so soon? I won you, my dear, did I not? Fairly and squarely in a game of dice!'

She opened her mouth to answer him, but no words came. It was as if the whole of her body had turned to ice. He sprawled carelessly against the cabin door, watching her reaction with something akin to amusement, and she thought it might have been the very devil himself who stood there, mocking her.

'You beast!' she managed.

He straightened a little, folding his arms across his waistcoated chest. 'I'm sorry if I've shocked you, my dear, but I cannot allow what is mine to slip so easily through my fingers,' he drawled. 'Your father is dead, it is true, but I must hold you to the debt, I fear.'

Outrage lent Regan courage. How could this man treat her so with her father dead and buried such a short time! Had he no ounce of common decency in his body – no jot of humanity? If he thought she would go with him and submit to his arrogant, bullying ways, he was very much mistaken.

'I'll die before I'll be owned by anyone – least of all you!' she cried.

A muscle tightened in his cheek. Suddenly he looked not only mocking, but dangerous.

'A debt is a debt, my sweet. And there were witnesses.'

'My father lost his money to you – he did not lose me!' she told him spiritedly.

'But I returned all he had lost and more besides in exchange for what I knew to be a much richer prize – you, Regan!'

'And you shall have it back – every last penny – and my mother's ring, too, though it is all I have left of her!' In a frenzy Regan crossed the cabin to where her father's coat lay on the bunk. With trembling fingers she searched for the hidden pocket deep in the tails and extracted his pouch. It hung heavily on its cord and defiantly she held it out to him. 'Here, take it. Do not think you can buy me for a handful of sovereigns.'

Zach raised a questioning eyebrow. 'And what will you do, penniless in a strange land?' he asked mockingly.

Regan lifted her chin. 'Don't worry about me. I shall be taken care of, have no fear. My fiancé, Richard Gammon, will be waiting for me when we berth in Melbourne and . . .'

'Your fiancé?' Zach straightened suddenly and with a small stab of triumph Regan realized she had discomfited him for the first time.

'Yes, Mr Casey, my fiancé,' she affirmed. 'Richard is a gold miner and he has been in Australia a year already. So you see I really do not need my father's sovereigns. You may have them and welcome!'

Again she held the pouch out to him and, when he made no move to take it, she screwed it into a ball between her fingers. So he *had* thought he could buy her and now he had learned he was mistaken he was not too pleased. 'Here, take it!' she cried and with a quick, determined movement she flung the pouch at him and turned away, intending to gather her things together and leave the cabin and his hateful presence. She heard the pouch strike the floor with a dull thud, but it was Zach's exclamation that attracted her attention.

'So you thought to cheat me, Miss Gardner!'

She swung round and the expression on his dark face struck terror to her heart. Shrinking suddenly she followed his eyes to the cabin floor and a gasp escaped her lips. The pouch, when it had fallen, had burst open. But spilling from it were not the sovereigns she had expected, but a pile of pebbles!

Slowly Zach bent and picked them up. Then he crossed to the bunk, emptying the pouch completely onto it. The pebbles clanked together, smooth, even, and worthless. But there was not a single sovereign amongst them – nor the precious ruby ring that meant so much to Regan. She stood for a moment looking down at the pebbles in horrified disbelief and the sea seemed to be roaring inside her head. Above it she heard Zach's voice, hard and unpleasant.

'How did you hope to get away with such a trick, my dear?'

'I didn't . . . I . . .' She swallowed hard, trying to fight down the panic that was rising within her. 'I haven't touched his pouch since the night he was shot! Why should I?'

'Perhaps you hoped I wouldn't look inside until we were off the ship and you could be well away,' Zach suggested. 'I would hardly blame you for that.'

She shook her head wildly. 'I didn't – I swear! Search my things – search all you like. It wasn't me. Someone must have . . .' She broke off, unable to bear the thought that while her father lay dying, someone had rifled through his pockets, a thief, caring only for dishonest gain.

'And supposing I believe you – what then?' Zach asked cuttingly.

Her eyes were puzzled. 'What do you mean?'

With a flick of his brown wrist Zach indicated the worthless pebbles.

'You *will* keep forgetting your debt to me, Regan. The sovereigns are gone, and the ring. How do you think you can pay me now?'

Was there no end to his cruelty? she wondered.

'You're enjoying this, aren't you?' she spat at him. 'You'll have your sovereigns, I promise you – and the value of the ring, too – when we reach Australia. I told you, my fiancé is a gold miner. He will pay you and gladly, just to have you leave me in peace.'

Zach laughed harshly and he looked at her through narrowed eyes.

'You haven't the least idea what you're talking about, my dear,' he said coldly. 'Do you really think your fiancé will be able to pay me one quarter of what I am owed?'

'Why shouldn't he?' she cried. 'He's a gold miner, I tell you, and he's sure to have found wealth by now. Why, in the last letter I received from him before we sailed, he spoke of a new field he was working. He'd knelt on the ground, he told me, and seen the dust run through his fingers . . .'

'Oh Regan, Regan, you are an innocent!' Zach mocked. 'Dust is all he's ever likely to find.'

'But the goldfields . . .' she protested.

'The goldfields are not as romantic as they sound,' he told her. 'Can you imagine it – men scraping in the earth day after day, breaking their backs for a handful of glittering dust that will be but a few grains when they wash the dirt from it? And sleeping beneath the stars is not the fun it sounds, nor eating tasteless beans day after day, with the grog shanties the only shelter or entertainment. They fight, they fall ill, they die – and all because the gold is a fever in their blood, driving them on.'

'But there are fortunes to be made – men have come from all over the world, even from California itself,' Regan argued. 'Richard wrote me of nuggets . . .'

'There is gold, of course,' Zach conceded. 'But the ordinary miner will not find much of it. It's people who can afford decent equipment, like Dickon Trenoweth's brother Jud, who will make their fortunes – if fortunes there are to be made. And men such as your Richard will more likely dig their own graves than mine gold, for the madness will drive them on, whatever the conditions. They see nothing, nothing, except that tomorrow their luck will change, tomorrow will see them rich beyond their wildest dreams.'

Regan shivered. It might almost have been a gambler he was describing. A gambler such as her father . . . With determination she pushed the thought away.

'Not Richard!' she stated forcefully. 'He will have found gold by now, you'll see. And if it takes every penny he has, he'll repay you.' Turning her back on him she folded her father's coat and placed it upon the pile of her own things. 'Now, if you will excuse me, I will leave you.'

'Not so fast!' In one stride Zach reached the cabin door, barring her way, and ignoring the beating of her heart she faced him defiantly.

'Be so good as to let me pass!'

He folded his arms, regarding her through narrowed eyes, and suddenly, disquietingly, she was reminded of the night he had kissed her. As if she could ever forget! Her small mouth hardened and her eyes blazed furiously.

'Let me pass!' she demanded. 'Whatever you may choose to think, you don't own me, Mr Zach Casey, and you never will. I am already promised to someone who is twice the man you will ever be, and I'll die before I let you lay a finger on me again!'

'Indeed!' Her last words were choked off as he took an abrupt step towards her and she felt her arms caught in a grip of steel. His face was close to hers, so that the dark eyes seemed to be boring into hers, and the dangerous twist of his mouth struck terror to her heart. 'We shall see about that, my dear!'

'How dare you!' she cried, but fear made her voice a frightened squeak and he laughed deep in his throat.

'I dare because you belong to me!' he grated harshly. 'I want no trouble over what is rightly mine so I intend to stake my claim now. Do you understand, Regan?'

Then, before she could move or speak, his hand slid up behind her neck as it had done that night in the saloon, holding it so firmly that his fingers bit into the soft flesh like ribs of steel, and his mouth came down to cover hers. For a second she was too startled to struggle, then, as she tried to back away, his free hand slid down her back, closing in beneath her buttocks and pressing her close to his lean body, so that there could be no escape. Her hands, still clutching her father's coat, were pinned between them and fluttered against his broad chest like trapped birds, and as his lips bruised hers she thought she tasted the faint but unmistakable flavour of rum.

He's drunk – he must be! she thought wildly, but the depth of his kiss seemed to leave her no room for thought. His lips were greedily drinking her in, exploring, demanding, and then his tongue was forcing its way into the deepest recesses of her mouth, probing so thoroughly she thought she might choke.

In a panic, she tried once more to push herself free, but his hand pressed her to him more closely still until her hips moulded to his and she felt him growing against her. The sensation took her by surprise and a deep answering pleasure twisted momentarily within her so that briefly she let herself hang there, suspended on a cord of unbearable sweetness.

Then as she felt his hand leave her neck and slide across her back to seek the curve of her breast she knew an uprush of revulsion. How could she enjoy what this beast was doing to her – even for a moment? His fingers reached her breast, squeezing at the soft flesh, and she jerked herself away, dropping the coat she had held and striking out at his face with the flat of her hand.

'You pig!' she spat at him. 'What do you take me for?'

Zach took a step backwards, pressing his fingers to his stinging cheek, but the pain had only served to heighten his awareness of Regan, and he felt his desire harden as he looked at her now. She had been lovely before – now, with her passions aroused, she was beautiful. Her eyes were like emeralds sparkling above her hot cheeks, her lips had been reddened by his kiss, and the tumble of red-gold hair framed her small face. And her body was made for love – the curve of rounded breasts, the tiny waist, the firm buttocks and thighs. Her struggles had served to loosen the neck of her dress – it had been pushed down on one side so that her shoulder and upper arm were exposed to view. He had wanted her before. Now, he was determined to have her – and have her without delay.

Almost lazily he reached out and caught at her dress, pulling it down over her other shoulder. Under the strain the gathering-thread gave and the bodice fell loosely, exposing the swell of her breasts above her chemisette and the edge of the waist-whittling corset that squeezed her already tiny waist to minute proportions. Regan squealed with outrage, desperately trying to retrieve the bodice, but her elbows were trapped in its voluminous frill and before she could do so his arms were around her again, and he was fumbling surely with the back fastening of her dress.

'Stop – stop!' she cried, but it was as if she spoke to a deaf-mute. His hands seemed to be everywhere – as she chased them from one fastening they moved to another, so that her struggles soon became a losing battle. With one last deft yank he pulled her dress down over her hips and the fullness of the skirt, with no petticoats to impede it, finished what he had begun. To Regan's horror it dropped limply from her, leaving her standing in her long white drawers. Desperately she tried to evade the monster who threatened her, but her foot caught in the heap of material around her ankles and she fell, unwittingly pulling the surprised Zach over with her.

For a moment shock robbed her of her senses but Zach, devil that he was, turned the mishap to his advantage. As they landed together on the cabin floor his two hands caught hers, yanking them above her head so that she lay spreadeagled and helpless. Then her cry of outrage became one of pain as he twisted her left arm to meet her right, holding them both prisoner with one strong hand while he used the other to lever himself to his knees and unbutton the front fastening of his trousers.

His intention was now clear to Regan if it had not been before, and sobbing with fear she began to thresh about wildly. But it was useless. She was trapped beneath him like a butterfly on a pin and every move was such agony for her poor stretched shoulder that momentarily she could think of nothing else. She opened her mouth to scream, but he covered it with his own, his teeth sinking viciously into her soft lower lip while his free hand tore at her drawers. They gave, and as his weight descended on her once more she felt his manhood forcing its way between her thighs.

Somehow she twisted her mouth away from his, but she could not raise her head and a tangle of hair covered her face as she writhed helplessly. He was probing her now, his hard body searching hers for the orifice that was hidden in her most secret virgin places, and as he entered that first little bit the pain in her shoulder was forgotten in a new, sharp hurt. Again she twisted and turned in a frenzy, her heels kicking impotently against the floor and for a second his weight on her seemed to lessen. Pushing on her heels she arched away, but as she did so his body descended, thrusting once more between her soft thighs, and thrusting deep and sure. The pain was like a knife within her, sharp-edged yet spreading to a deep, burning pool, and her scream made him pause, looking at her through dark narrowed eyes.

Her head was turned to one side, but although her face was half-hidden in the tangle of her hair he could see that her eyes were tight closed and her features contorted with pain. Tenderness engulfed him and he released her hands, brushing her curls away from her face and stroking the softness of her flushed cheek. But she only twisted her head away from his touch, and the tightness of her body enfolding his manhood stirred him to a new fever of desire. He had been too long without a woman – and he had wanted Regan too much to stop now. The feverish demands of his body reclaimed his attentions and he thrust into her with long, satisfying strokes that permeated all his senses with delight whilst they seemed to tear her apart.

As the storm reached its climax a cry came from his lips and it seemed his desire burst within her like molten rain. For a few moments more he worked, unwilling to let the sensation ebb, but it was a lazy movement now, more contented than urgent, with the heat of passion cooled to comfortable warmth, and tenderness began to return for the woman who had given him so much pleasure.

He rolled from her, trying to pull her into his arms, but she turned away from him and lay sobbing on the hard cabin floor. Concern joined his other emotions and he raised himself on one elbow, looking down at the lovely body that had so recently been his. Her struggles and his own efforts had left her naked except for the corset, still laced tightly around her tiny waist. Above it her shoulders and back were smooth and curved and her breasts firm and creamy, their rose-coloured tips rising from the paler aureolas. Appreciatively, his eyes ran the length of her body, taking in the rounded buttocks and thighs resting on the pile of torn clothing. Then breath caught in his throat as he noticed for the first time the tell-tale specks of blood.

So she was a virgin! That was something he had not expected. From the start he had known she was no loose woman, but he was surprised, to say the least, that a girl in her profession had not fallen prey to the charms of some gentleman, even if it was only the fiancé she had mentioned.

At the thought something strangely painful twisted within Zach and he stood up abruptly, rearranging his own clothing and looking down at the sobbing girl.

They came to his country with such hope, these emigrants, and they had so little idea of what lay in store for them. Because they had heard of gold in the earth, and land for the taking, they imagined they were going to the land of milk and honey, where all their troubles would be over. He had watched them often enough from the comfortable security of his father's sheep station and wondered at their courage and the hope that would not die in them in spite of the hardships they had to endure. Most of them would never be any better off than they had been in the countries they had left behind. The miners still squabbled over their licences and men who had not the first idea how to farm squabbled over land. And the best of it was taken, anyway, and had been half a century before by squatters like his own father.

A sudden wave of something like guilt cut through Zach's composure and he bent to cover Regan's naked body with her shawl. Then he crossed the cabin, pouring himself a tot of rum and swallowing it in one healthy gulp. The thought of his father at such a time was a strangely uncomfortable one – it was as if he had violated the girl and her kind twice – once by the demands of his body and once by his father's prior occupation of the land that could never now be theirs. But that was ridiculous. Australia was a vast country, with thousands of miles of interior as yet untaken – unexplored, even – and it took a special kind of man to build an empire from a wilderness as Seamus Casey had done. It was nearly forty years since, as mate on a convict transport, he had first seen the new country and fallen in love with the idea of making it his home, and his shipmates had called him insane. But Seamus had a will of his own, as Zach, his son, knew to his cost, and he had taken as little notice of their warnings as he had taken of the warnings of his parents when he had first run away to sea at the age of eleven. When the ship left Sydney it had left without him and he had tramped his way south-west until he found some land to his liking. There he had laid the rough foundations of the house that was to become Ballymena, and started to farm with his first few Merino sheep.

It was not easy now, thought Zach, to imagine those first humble beginnings, though if he cast his mind back he could remember hard times when he had been a child. But now he was five-and-thirty and his acceptance of life as it was lived had grown to maturity with him. The Caseys were now a breed apart from the humble emigrants who came in on their poor assisted passages. They were wealthy squatter-sheepmasters, the aristocracy of the new land. And as such they did as they pleased.

With a quick, impatient movement Zach put down his glass and crossed the cabin. The girl, Regan, lay where he had left her, huddled beneath her shawl, but she was no longer sobbing. Instead, she lay in exhausted slumber, and the sight of her moved him strangely. She had probably had no sleep since her father's accident, he guessed, and now not even her tears had been able to keep her awake. There, on the hard cabin floor, she had cried herself to sleep.

Zach bent over her and the warmth of her sleeping body stirred his senses again. But for the moment he was satiated and his concern was for her. Gently, so as not to wake her, he lifted her onto one of the bunks and pulled the blanket over her. Then he quietly crossed the cabin, opened the door and went out, leaving her in peace.

CHAPTER FIVE

It was dark when Regan stirred. She lay for a moment, puzzled by the quiet in the cabin that took the place of the whispering cuddy, for here there was only the swell of the waves outside the window to break the calm. Then, as she came fully awake, she felt the smouldering pain between her legs and memory returned in a horrific rush.

Swiftly she sat up, the blanket falling from her, and as she did so, a crack of light appeared around the cabin door and widened to allow a full beam to enter. So that was what had disturbed her – the door being opened softly! In a panic she snatched at the blanket and was just in time to cover herself before Zach's tall form was silhouetted in the doorway, carrying a lamp.

Mutely she watched as he came in and as he closed the door behind him and set the lamp down on the table she shrank back against the wall.

'So you're awake.' His voice was deep and rough; it struck terror to her heart and reminded her too sharply of the things he had done to her. She shifted closer to the wall and the harsh blanket rasped on her bare skin.

'Here – I brought you something to drink.' He was bending over the bunk, pushing a cup towards her. She could not take it – if she let go of the blanket it would expose her nakedness once more, yet until she did he would go on leaning over her, making her stomach turn with the smell of rum on his breath and his nearness.

Somehow she folded one arm across the blanket to hold it about her, and extended the other to take the cup. What was in it? she wondered fearfully.

Gently he guided it to her lips. 'Drink it!' he ordered. 'It'll do you good.'

The smell reached her nostrils and she recognized it as broth. Nervously she parted her lips to allow access to the cup, and as the warm liquid ran into her mouth she shivered violently and heaved on it.

'I don't want it!' She pushed it away and he guided it back again, just as her mother had done when she had been sick as a child.

'Try to drink it, sweet. You've had nothing all day.'

Obediently she opened her lips again and this time she managed to swallow some of the broth. But when it was gone she began to shiver again so violently that he had to take the cup from her.

'You're cold. I'll fetch you another blanket,' he told her and she lay impassively hugging herself with her arms while he did as he said.

For a moment or two he paced the cabin wondering what he should do with his newest possession. She must stay here, of course, and when it was light he would send to the cuddy for the rest of her belongings. But should he leave her here alone for the moment to cry out her grief and shock, and forget his own aching desire for her over a game of dice in the saloon, or should he stay and do what he could to comfort her?

He could still hear her shivering so much that her teeth chattered together and impulsively he crossed to the bunk, climbing onto it and taking her in his arms. After her first startled withdrawal from him she lay like a dummy, shuddering in violent spasms while he tried to warm her with the heat of his own body and murmured to her as if to a child.

'Easy love, easy. I won't hurt you. Easy now.'

Little by little her shuddering lessened until there was only the occasional tremor to bear witness to her state of a few minutes earlier, and as she grew calmer, so the nearness of her body began to have its effect on Zach.

At first, lying there beside her, he tried to control the hardening of his manhood. He had frightened her enough already, he thought, and close as they were there was no way he could conceal his growing desire. But her warming sweetness was too much for him and as the demands of his body became more urgent, he began to see the situation in a new light.

She had been a virgin and the first time had been a painful shock for her. If he wanted her for his own, he must show her it need not always be like that.

Zach, the bachelor, was far from being inexperienced with women. In spite of their scarcity in the new country, his good looks and the standing of his family among the 'squattocracy' had meant he was never short of a bed mate and more than one girl in the townships within reach of Ballymena had had designs on him – something that had afforded him plenty of opportunity to learn the ways of love-making. Now, faced for the first time in his life with a girl who was not only unwilling to submit to his overtures, but positively rejected them, he summoned up all the tenderest tricks he had learned, running his fingers over her body and caressing the most intimate points and caverns in a way that had driven his former lovers to a frenzy of distraction.

But although the feel of her firm, sweet body under his hands increased his own desire to fever pitch, Regan still lay wooden and unresponsive to his touch. It was as if she could not feel him at all, he thought, except that she recoiled as his fingers tweaked at the point of her breast, raising the nipple from its soft bed and feeling it harden between his fingers.

'Regan, you're so beautiful,' he whispered, burying his face in the base of her neck and letting his tongue circle gently on her smooth, slightly salt-flavoured skin.

But she lay unyielding as his hands slid over the tightly-laced corset that still encased her waist, her stomach rigid to his touch, and when his hands reached the valley beneath the soft tuft of maiden hair her thighs tightened against them, the muscles taut and hard under the baby-soft skin.

'Regan!' he whispered again, easing his fingers between them and searching for the hidden orifice. But when she winced and pulled away, he did not press her, withdrawing his hand and sliding it back up her belly to begin unlacing the corset.

A small whimper escaped her and he stroked her gently as his hands did their work.

'I hurt you before, love, and I'm sorry. But I will not hurt you again,' he promised her. 'We'll find such heights together, you and I, and you'll see what love can really be like. Wait now, while I rid myself of these clothes.'

She inhaled sharply, half gasp, half sob, but lay still as if afraid to move while he slid from the bunk and divested himself swiftly of his shirt and trousers. Then he slipped back under the rough blanket, curling his hard body round hers and cupping her breasts with his hands.

As his manhood slipped between her buttocks he felt her stiffen and he pulled away, rolling her onto her back and towards him. The unlaced corset fell away and he eased her onto her side.

'Turn over, love, so we can be really close,' he urged her, his voice low and throaty with desire, and he moved towards her so that her nude breasts lay pressed against the matted hair of his chest and the length of their bodies found one another.

For a moment her breathing seemed suspended and he could have sworn she arched her body towards his. Then her breath came out on a sob and she lay inert, her thighs tightening once more against him.

Softly he swore to himself. His body was aching with

wanting her here and now, but he was determined to show her the way it could be if only she would respond to his caresses.

He turned her again onto her back, cupping one breast between his hands and burying his face in it. As his tongue teased the tip to a fresh arousal, he heard her moan low in her throat and the sound made the blood pound in his veins. His hands slid down her hips to her thighs, with one swift movement he parted them and levered himself between them.

'Gently, love, open to me,' he whispered, and for a moment, as he entered the soft moist place he thought she had done just that. Then he felt her stiffen once more and he withdrew so that only the tip of him breached her.

'Easy, now, relax!' he urged her, and was startled when the ball of her fist caught him full in the face and the nails of her free hand drew a searing pattern down the soft flesh of his underarm.

'No!' she screamed in sudden fury. 'No! No! No!'

He had not withdrawn from her under the attack, now he lunged onto her, pinning her fighting arms down against the bunk and driving home into the depths of her. He heard her gasp and anger and desire devoured him. So much for gentling her! Much good had it done them! She was a beautiful girl, but she needed to be broken like a mettlesome horse. And if he had to keep her locked in his cabin from here to Australia, by God he would do it!

A few deep stokes and it was over and as he grew soft within her remorse flooded through him. He'd done it again – taken her violently when he had simply meant to show her what they could share if she would only allow him to. Now, she lay trembling beneath him once more, and a hatred for himself and for her began to creep through his veins.

With a violent push he rolled away from her. Why was he doing this? he asked himself. Why was he bothering with her? Had the voyage crazed him so that he was reduced to raping an unwilling victim and carrying her off? Why was he so intent on holding her to her father's gambling debt – surely she had suffered enough and it would be a kindness to her now to refill her father's empty pouch with sovereigns and turn her loose. It would not be long until the ship berthed in Melbourne and he would be able to pick up where he had left off with one of the Australian girls who would be waiting for him – perhaps even Adelaide Jackson, who knew better than most how to make a man feel good.

But, strangely, the thought of Adelaide, whom he had known since he was a boy, only highlighted the attractions of the girl who lay sobbing softly beside him. Adelaide was beautiful in her own bold way, but she had never stirred him as Regan's freshness did. And never, for all her tricks of love, had he felt the same uprush of delight that he had experienced that afternoon on the cabin floor with Regan – nor for that matter, a few minutes ago, though that satisfaction had been marred by anger with himself for his lack of self-control. But that was the way she affected him, damn her! She was like a fever with him, turning him into something no better than an animal.

'A dog after a bitch in season could control himself better than I with her!' he thought in self-disgust. 'I promise to be gentle with her, then I take her in a fury because she offends my pride. You must do better, Zach Casey, if you wish to win her heart as well as her body.'

With an oath he levered himself from the bunk, crossed the cabin and lit himself a cigar. Then, drawing only a robe around his naked body, he stood at the window with his back towards Regan, staring out at the dark sea and thinking it was scarcely less violent than the storm within him.

As she lay beneath his working body for the second time in hours, Regan had thought she would never sleep again, but so exhausted was she by the events of the last few days that while Zach stood smoking his cigar at the cabin window, merciful oblivion claimed her and the tortured mesh of her thoughts were relegated to fitful, nightmarish dreams that only occasionally broke into her heavy slumber.

It was light when she awoke, a cold grey dawn that crept into the cabin to paint it in sombre hues, and Regan lay stock still and afraid to move, numbering the aches in her body – and in her heart. She was warm now at least. The weight of the blankets seemed more than they had last night, folding in around her nude body, and although they were rough, there was comfort in the feel of them. But her shoulder ached and so did her back. And between her legs was a burning soreness that would have reminded her, even if she had needed reminding, of the man who had brought her here and used her heartlessly for his own pleasure.

At the thought she closed her eyes tightly again, but there was no way she could shut out the memory of his hands on her body or the painful thrusting of his manhood deep within her; no way she could wipe out the feeling of being used and dirty, or the anguish of knowing he had stolen her virginity with the same devil-may-care arrogance that he had shown throwing the dice to make her father a pauper.

And now her father was dead and she was alone – alone at the mercy of this monster . . .

A small sound in the cabin brought her fully awake and her eyes flew open. What was that – could it be someone breathing? Had all this been a nightmare after all and was Thomas still with her and not in a watery grave? The tiny hairs pricked on the back of her neck and, half-afraid, she turned her head on the pillow. Then disappointment flooded through her and the tears started to her eyes.

It was not Thomas. How could it have been? It was the monster himself – Zach – sleeping in the bunk on the opposite side of the cabin and she cursed herself for not having known it must be. Yet somehow she had thought, even after all he had done to her, that he would have the decency to leave her alone. Oh, there had not been one night on this terrible voyage which she had spent on her own, but not even the company of the other hundred and eighty passengers in the cuddy had intruded on her privacy as he was doing, simply by being there.

Hate welled up in her as she looked at him, his hair jet black against the pillow, one brown arm lying carelessly across his broad, furred chest. Then as her eyes travelled down the length of him she gasped in surprise to see that he was covered not by a blanket but by his cloak, his bare feet sticking out from beneath it. Could it be that he had slept cold to give her warmth? She could hardly believe it, yet the rough cloth that covered her was proof enough and she felt a tiny spark of gratitude before the hatred snuffed it out once more.

So he had given her his blanket. Surely after the way he had treated her, it was the least he could do. A blanket was a miserly exchange for her father's life and her own virginity. Everything she had loved, everything she had possessed he had taken. Now she had nothing to take with her to the new land – nothing to give the man she was to marry . . .

At the thought of Richard, her heart seemed to stop beating and a new despair began to flood through her. How could she bear to face him, knowing that the one precious gift she had preserved for him was no longer hers to give? How could she tell him that, when he came to her bed, he would not be the first? He had always been so gentle with her, and so patient, never pressing her for more than she was ready to give. There had been times when she had wished that he would – when she had wondered if she might want him the more if he treated her more forcefully and showed her who was master. But it was not his way, and now her heart cried in anticipation of his hurt. Would he believe her when she told him she had not parted willingly with her virginity – that she had fought for it with every ounce of her strength? She did not know. But even if he did, things could never be the same between them – never be as they should be. Always, it would be there, a shadow on their happiness . . .

I ought to kill you, Zach Casey! she thought. I ought to take a knife and stab you through your black heart. And I could do it, too, while you sleep . . .

Carefully she pushed back the blankets and swung her legs over the edge of the bunk. The boards were cold beneath her bare feet but she hardly noticed. Like a thing demented she crossed to his clothes, dropped in an untidy pile on the cabin floor, and began to rifle through them, looking for something with which to attack him. But her hands were trembling too much to find the pockets and after a moment she thew the garments aside impatiently.

She couldn't do it. Even if she found a knife, she couldn't do it. Nice, satisfying idea it might be, but that was all. And even if she did have the courage to do something like that – where would it get her? Shipped around the coast to Western Australia, maybe, where they still accepted thieves and murderers. Or hung from a yardarm if Bully Barnes took the law into his own hands.

But there was something she could do while Zach Casey slept – she could try to escape! Once she was back in the emigrants' quarters, perhaps he would forget her and leave her alone. The thought had occurred to her last night, just before sleep had claimed her, but she had not known then how to set about it. With Zach standing guard over her she had been a virtual prisoner. And besides, her clothes were all scattered and in ribbons after his vicious attack. In the dark she could never have covered herself sufficiently to brave the saloon and the eyes of the men who would certainly have been sitting there. But now – in daylight – she might be able to pull them together. If only Zach slept a little longer . . .

Casting one nervous look at him over her shoulder, she moved about the cabin collecting her scattered garments. Her corset, at least, was undamaged, and her chemisette was presentable. As for her drawers, if she took a ribbon from her dress to tie around them, she could most likely keep them up while she dashed for the safety of the cuddy. It was her dress that had suffered most, her lovely white dress whose bodice now sagged limply like the broken wings of a butterfly . . .

Sadly she held it against her. How could she keep it up? she wondered, unless she was to tie her shawl around it for support . . .

'Good morning, my love!'

At the sound of his voice she whirled round, holding the dress in front of her nude body. How long had he been awake and watching her in that lazy fashion, with his eyes narrowed and his head propped up on his bent forearm?

'What are you doing?' he asked.

She opened her mouth to answer but no sound came and he stretched out a strong brown arm. 'Come here, sweet.'

Briefly she stood regarding him like a rabbit caught in a beam of lamplight, then slowly, because there seemed nothing else to do, she crossed the cabin. When she was within his reach his fingers closed over her arm and she gasped softly, but still her feet moved her obediently towards him as if she was mesmerized by the narrowed eyes, dark with desire, that held hers.

'Sit down beside me, Regan,' he said softly, drawing her down onto his bunk and slipping his arm around her hips so that his hand lay between her firm thighs.

At his touch she withdrew, the whole of her insides seeming to contract. Surely he did not want to take her again! He was insatiable! But if he did, he would have her. It was useless to fight. It only prolonged the agony. Her heart beating within her like a frightened bird, she sat taut and erect while his fingers stroked her firm flesh and he raised his head to press kisses on her breast and stomach.

'Allow yourself to relax, love,' he murmured to her. 'There will be no pain again. That was yesterday. It can never be like that again.'

Because I am no longer a virgin! she thought bitterly. But for all her hatred of him, there was something strangely sweet about the touch of his fingers on the soft insides of her thighs and involuntarily she parted them slightly.

The tiny acceptance was enough for Zach. Levering himself up, he slipped a hand beneath her knees to lift her onto the bunk beside him. Then he covered her body with his, letting his manhood move between her legs with an insistent rhythm that started strange sensations deep in her loins. Breath left her throat in a moan and he parted her thighs with his hands, penetrating her with fierce gentleness and driving into her with slow, even strokes.

'You see?' he whispered at her throat. 'You see how it can be?'

But she lay stiff and unresponsive once more. From the moment he penetrated her, the sensation of sharp sweetness was gone and she felt only revulsion for this man who used her again and again, and for herself that she had momentarily come close to enjoying his repulsive attentions. This time she did not fight him, fighting was useless.

Instead, she lay quite still and detached from him, so that she could note every move that he made as if it were someone quite separate from herself who lay on the bunk. For what seemed a lifetime it went on, while he squeezed her breasts and kissed her unresponsive lips, until at length his breathing grew harder and the movement within her became faster and more urgent. And then it was over, he had softened within her and there was the wetness between her legs that she found so loathsome, yet which touched the depths of her conscious in a way she could not understand . . .

He rolled away from her, but his hands still lingered on her breasts and belly and suddenly she could bear his touch no more. It was as if every nerve ending in her skin was shrieking a protest and she struck out at his hands.

'Leave me alone, you pig! Haven't you had enough even now?'

His face changed, his dark brows coming together and his mouth hardening after the softness of passion.

'Still the wildcat then,' he observed.

'I have a good teacher,' she grated at him. 'If you take what you want over and over again, you must expect to feel the sharpness of my claws.'

With an abrupt movement he levered himself up and away from her, swinging himself to a standing position and towering over her naked so that she found herself staring in awe at his majestic body, with its furred chest, narrow hips, and rippling muscles. But he seemed unaware of her gaze.

'Don't worry, my dear, I shan't take you by force again. I promised myself last night that I wouldn't, but when I saw you there this morning looking so beautiful, I was tempted. I thought I could teach you to enjoy my love-making. Now, I see I deluded myself.'

She was hunched up, glaring at him, and with a stride or two he crossed the cabin, picked up her dress from where it had fallen and tossed it to her.

'Get dressed, for the love of heaven!' he ordered her.

She clutched the garment, covering herself with it, and the scant decency gave her the courage to defy him.

'And what am I to wear?' she demanded. 'Thanks to

you, my dress is ruined and it is the only one I have.'

He raised a sardonic eyebrow. 'I am sure you will find some ingenious way to hide the damage. And when we reach Melbourne you'll have gowns aplenty – though not so revealing as that one. I don't like the charms of my woman displayed for all the world to see.'

'What do you mean?' she cried, though the coldness deep inside her confirmed that she already knew. This madman was going through with his wager! He actually intended to keep her for his pleasure!

'I mean what I say, my dear.' He was pulling on his trousers as he spoke. 'And have no fear – the dresses I shall buy for you will be fashionable. I intend to treat you well, sweet Regan.'

She sat bolt upright, her eyes blazing fire at him.

'I won't go with you!' she cried. 'How many times do I have to tell you – I have a fiancé waiting for me, and he'll see you in hell first!'

'We shall see about that,' Zach said with an infuriating shrug. 'In the meantime I am sending to your quarters for the rest of your things. You will stay here, in my cabin, until we reach Melbourne.'

'So you can rape me time and again, I suppose!' Regan threw at him.

He turned towards her, buttoning his waistcoat over his pleated shirt. There was no hint of a smile on his face now – it was all dangerous lines and narrows.

'I told you once and I tell you once more, Regan: I shall not take you by force again. It is not my way. The next time we make love, my dear, it will be because we both want it.'

'Then that will be never!' she cried spiritedly. 'If you think I could ever want you to do those terrible things to me – you of all people – you are much mistaken.'

Zach took his coat up from where it lay, putting it on and smoothing the tails while he looked at her with grim amusement in his dark eyes.

'Would you like to make a wager on that, my dear? I think you will find that you will be as much the loser as your father was. The time will come when you will want me, right enough. At the moment you are shocked and grieving, but that will not always be uppermost in your mind. The time will come when you will beg me to take you – you will see.'

'Never!' she spat at him. 'Never, never, never!'

'You say that now, Regan, but I believe I know your sensual nature better than you know it yourself.' He smiled. 'Get dressed now, my dear, for both our sakes. I have promised not to touch you again, but be so good as to play your part. If you are to flaunt yourself before me like this in the privacy of my cabin, you will test my self-control too severely. Now, I will have breakfast sent to you and I advise you to be covered by then if you do not want to be set upon by whoever brings it to you. But do not leave the cabin, my Regan.'

With that he turned on his heel and as the door closed after him Regan let out a howl of fury. Who did he think he was, this unbearable Australian! What did he want with her? And why, if he did not intend to rape her again, was he intent on keeping her prisoner?

Regan did not know. Of only one thing she was quite sure. Never, as long as she lived, did she want him to touch her again. Never, if she lived like a nun for the rest of her life, would she willingly allow him into her body. And if he thought differently, he was very, very much mistaken.

CHAPTER SIX

For the remainder of the voyage, Zach was as good as his word. Although he had Regan's few belongings brought up from the cuddy and installed in the cabin, he spent little time there himself.

At first Regan was too relieved to be left alone to wonder very much where he was, but after a few days, bored with her own company, she ventured into the saloon and found him sitting at his usual table with his old friends, drinking a tot of rum, smoking and laughing as if he had not a care in the world.

When he saw her he waved to her to join him, but when she turned on her heel and returned to the cabin he did not bother to follow and she flounced about for a while in a high huff, oddly piqued that he should show such obvious disinterest in her after his recent over-attentiveness.

I suppose now he has had me I have lost my attraction for him, she thought angrily.

But if that was so, then why did he keep her in his cabin? Why not return her to the cuddy, used and forgotten?

I declare he's mad! she informed her own image as she brushed her hair before his dressing mirror. And what his friends must think of him – and of me – I dare not even imagine! They probably look upon me as his paramour, but little do they know I am not even that! Why, there are some nights when he does not return to the cabin at all, and when he does, he barely glances in my direction.

Strangely enough, she was hardly sure which nights she liked the least – those when she was alone in the cabin, wondering if and when he would return, or those when he slept in the opposite bunk to hers. There was something deeply offensive about the way he turned his back on her, lying with his bare brown shoulders rigid above the harsh blanket, and she hated him more than ever and longed to cross the cabin and strike out at him with her fists, expressing her hatred and her frustration at being kept a virtual prisoner. But she dared not do that lest his lean, hard hands should catch her and pull her down onto the bunk with him where his thrusting body could take her once more. That she could not risk – her stomach turned at the thought of it – so she controlled her emotions with difficulty and turned her back on him with the same nonchalance to which he treated her.

She remembered, too, his warning that she should not try his self-control too far and she slept each night in her chemisette and drawers, changing them only when he was out of the cabin, and contriving to slip in and out of her dress while under cover of the blanket. Once, when he turned and caught her doing this, she thought for a moment that he was on the point of laughing at her, then his face tightened and he turned away so abruptly that she knew she had been mistaken. But for the most part he treated her with supreme indifference and her confusion grew with every passing day.

Once, Charles Maclane came to the cabin looking for Zach and she asked him in, glad to have someone to talk to for a few minutes. She had got over her first dislike of the young officer – now that he seemed to look on her as Zach's property he made no improper overtures to her and she found him pleasant, undemanding company. But when Zach returned he was unreasonably snappish, and her temper rose to match his own.

How dare he act as if he owned her, and even try to dictate to whom she may or may not talk? Why should he, who had raped her, be disparaging to the young officer who merely treated her with civility? It was too much! But then, that was Zach, utterly unbearable – and a puzzle into the bargain.

Just what did he intend to do with her? she wondered. Surely he could not intend to keep her prisoner for ever! Perhaps it was just an exercise to save face whilst they were at sea. He was a proud man and all his friends had been there when he had made the bargain with her father – expecting her, no doubt, to fall into his arms with gratifying haste. When he had found she had not, he was too committed to give up easily and be made a laughing stock. No doubt, when they reached Australia, and the witnesses to the deal were scattered, he would let her go, she consoled herself. But for all that she tried to believe that this would be the case, she remained unconvinced.

There was a hard core of steel in Zach that was frighteningly unmovable. He was a man of his word, if ever there was one. And she was uncomfortably sure that he would expect his gambling debts to be honoured.

That thought brought her mind full circle to the missing sovereigns and for the hundredth time she mused over what had become of them – and her mother's ring.

It hardly seemed possible that anyone could have been so wicked as to slip into the cabin while her father lay dying, take the pouch from his pocket and substitute the worthless pebbles – but someone had. And they had got clean away. When she had discovered the loss, Zach had reported it to Bully Barnes, but there had been little he could do. Sovereigns were sovereigns – quite unidentifiable – and although Bully instigated a cursory search, no trace was found of the ring.

Not that it was likely to be, Regan thought. Something so small would be the easiest thing in the world to hide. No, it was the original theft that seemed so impossible. Why, she had hardly left Thomas's side in the whole time he lay wounded. But someone – some heartless, wicked thief – must have been watching and waiting his opportunity. Was it a fellow passenger who knew the sovereigns were there? Or had they been discovered by chance by a sneak thief who had crept in to rifle the cabin, perhaps, while she and most of the passengers and crew were on deck for the burial. Whoever it was would have been certain then of finding the cabin empty and unlikely to be missed amongst all those gathered on deck.

But whatever the explanation, one thing was virtually certain: the stolen sovereigns would never be recovered now and she would remain in Zach's power for as long as he wished to keep her – or at least until they reached Melbourne and Richard could pay the debt for her.

One afternoon, unable to stand her confinement in the cabin a moment longer, Regan ventured out. She had used the long hours when she had been alone to effect what repairs she could to her dress, and now, with her shawl drawn tightly about the offending neckline, she thought it respectable enough to save her embarrassment.

In the saloon she looked around for Zach. It was hours since she had seen him and then he had left without a word as to where he was going or when he would be back.

So let him find me gone! she thought defiantly. He can think I have jumped overboard for all I care, for he knows very well whilst we are on board this wretched ship it is the only way I could escape him!

She crossed the saloon, ignoring the overtly curious stares of the few passengers who sat there, and climbed the steps to the door. As she opened it she was surprised at the warmth of the wind that greeted her. She had seen from the cabin below that the sun was shining and the sky blue, now, as she stepped out onto the companionway, she tasted the air that was fresh and spring-like, though still salt, and involuntarily her heart lifted. Who could be downcast on such a beautiful day?

She walked to the rail, holding tightly to her shawl so that the wind should not blow it away, and stood looking back at the deep white furrows they had cut in the waves. Above her, the sails billowed gracefully against the blue skies, and the wind whistled in them so loudly that she did not hear the footsteps approaching her until a man's voice at her elbow made her start.

'Forgive me! I didn't mean to frighten you.'

It was Dickon Trenoweth. He stood smiling at her uncertainly, his light eyes flickering over her face.

She drew herself up, refusing to return his smile. All too clearly she was remembering that it had been his gun which had been responsible for her father's death; evil though Zach Casey might be, the terrible chain of events could not have been set in motion had it not been for Dickon Trenoweth.

As if he had read her mind, his smile faded slightly and he spread his hands helplessly in front of him. They were soft and white, she noticed, quite different from Zach's lean brown ones.

'Miss Gardner, I must speak with you,' Dickon began placatingly. 'I cannot leave the ship without expressing to you my deep regret for the unfortunate happenings . . .'

'Please, Mr Trenoweth, I'd rather not talk about it,' she said sharply.

'I do understand, my dear Miss Gardner. Truly I do. But I have to speak. That night in the saloon, I jested when I offered your father my revolver. I never imagined for one moment that he would take it. Oh, I see now it was unforgivable folly on my part. I have had long days and nights to ponder on what I did and regret it. And I have prayed for an opportunity to make my peace with you.'

Regan did not reply. She could not. Was she to tell this stupid man who had brought about her father's death that it did not matter? Did he think she would absolve him from blame and give his conscience a clean bill of health? Oh, they were insufferable, these landed gentry with their soft words and their hard hearts . . .

'Zach Casey is taking good care of you, I hope.' The tone was bland but she swung round defensively, expecting to see knowing amusement in his eyes. But it was not there. He merely looked concerned.

'Yes,' she replied shortly. 'He has allowed me the use of his cabin and I take most of my meals there.'

'Admirable. Admirable.' Dickon was leaning on the rail beside her now, clearly relieved to put the subject of that unfortunate evening behind him. 'He is a most unusual man, would you not agree?'

Regan almost choked on the exclamation that rose to her lips. Unusual! Well, that was certainly one way to describe Mr Zach Casey, though she could have chosen a stronger word, herself.

'No doubt it is his breeding that makes him so,' Dickon continued silkily. 'The native blood that runs in his veins.'

Regan started. '*Native*?' she repeated involuntarily.

'His mother is, I believe, an aboriginal.' Dickon's mouth twisted in a superior smile. 'According to my brother Jud, she and some of her people worked for old Seamus Casey when he first settled in Ballymena. For the most part, he tells me, the natives are unreliable labour. The others moved on, taking what they could with them, no doubt, but the girl stayed to share his bed and bear him a son – Zach – sole heir to his father's empire.'

Regan did not answer. She stood staring out to sea while a turmoil of thoughts chased themselves around her head. So Zach was half aboriginal! That explained the darkness of his hair and skin, the jet-like quality of his eyes. And it explained too the wildness of his behaviour. No wonder he acted like a savage! It was because he *was* one!

'Yes, even in a country like Australia it must have caused quite a stir at the time,' Dickon went on conversationally. 'To continue to give house room to a native woman and her child must have set tongues wagging wherever settlers met. But of course she did not stay long. The aboriginals are nomads. He woke one day to find she had abandoned the child and gone – something the neighbours had long predicted. And I dare say he was well rid of her, though by all accounts he went wild for days when he found her missing. The Caseys do not like to lose what they consider as theirs.'

Involuntarily, Regan's hands tightened on the rail.

Had Seamus Casey treated his aboriginal the way his son had treated her, she wondered – taking her by force and then keeping her prisoner on his homestead until at last she had found her opportunity to escape? How desperate she must have been, to go and leave her son behind – desperate to return to her own people, who cared about her when he did not. For a moment Regan felt a spirit of kinship with the unknown native woman who had borne the hateful Zach. She had not been broken by the iron will of the Caseys – nor by their indefatigable lust.

And neither will I be! thought Regan fiercely.

'I am surprised, Miss Gardner, that Zach did not engage a cabin for you instead of cramping you into his own,' Dickon, having exhausted one line of conversation, had turned to another. 'There are several vacant ones, I believe, on your own side of the saloon.'

Colour rose in Regan's cheeks and she turned her head slightly so as to hide it from him.

'I suppose he thought there was no need,' she said tartly.

Dickon Trenoweth smiled. 'You are likely correct. Even a man of Zach's wealth no doubt baulks at paying the rate for a whole passage when there is so little of it left. We should, after all, be sighting Melbourne very soon.'

'We should?' Regan's eyes widened.

'Indeed, and most welcome it will be to set foot on dry land again, would you not agree?' Dickon glanced at his watch that hung on a gold chain across his chest. 'And now, my dear, it would appear to be time for dinner. Will you be joining us in the dining room this afternoon?'

Regan shook her head. 'No, thank you. I'm not hungry. I may have supper in the cabin later.'

Dickon's mouth twisted again into its peculiar smile

and with a nod, he moved off along the companionway. As he went, Regan realized suddenly how chilled she was. The brightness of the day had made it easy to forget that here at sea a wind could easily cut through thicker garments than her woollen shawl, and now she pulled it around her as she turned away from the rail herself.

As she had told Dickon, she did not want to join the first class passengers for dinner any more than she wanted to return to Zach's cabin. But where else could she go to be out of the wind – and not have to see Zach? Oh, if only they were not at sea – if only there was a way of escaping from him so that she need *never* see him again!

It was in that moment that the idea occurred to her – an idea so enormous in its audacity that it almost took her breath away. Supposing she did not return to the cabin – supposing she hid herself somewhere! If she could stay concealed somewhere until they berthed at Melbourne – not long, according to Dickon, perhaps she would be able to slip off the ship and away, especially if . . .

Her own earlier thought of the impossibility of escape came back to her then – that on a ship the only route was overboard. If he could not find me, that would be what he would be bound to think she told herself excitedly. Why, even Dickon would testify that he had last seen me on deck, and they would all think I was unhinged and had gone to join my father!

Excitement brought a tight knot to her throat and she stood for a moment regaining control of herself. It was a bold idea and it might just work. But where could she hide? Where?

The empty cabins! Dickon's words came back to her in a flash and she blessed him for his sly remarks. There were several on her side of the ship, he had said. Well, perhaps if she could discover which one of them was empty and slip into it, she could hide there!

Her mind was alert now, working at a rate of knots. If her plan was to succeed, no one must see her enter the cabin – no one must see her in the quarters under the poop deck at all. And the best time to slip unnoticed through the saloon would be whilst the first class passengers were at dinner. If she allowed them another five or ten minutes to settle themselves for the meal she might just be able to do it.

Braving the wind, she leaned once more against the rail. Oh, it was bitterly cold now, but that was so much the better. People would think she was mad to stand in the cold with nothing but a thin dress and shawl – when she was reported as missing they would look back and say: 'Oh yes, poor thing, we saw her standing at the rail looking at the sea. Her father's death was too much for her.'

At last Regan decided it was safe to make a move. Every nerve in her body was alive and tingling with tension and with each minute that passed she expected to hear Zach's voice, bidding her to return to the cabin with him. But he did not.

It shows how little regard he has for me, she thought bitterly.

But there was no time for regrets and hatred. With a quick look around to make certain she was unobserved, she crossed the deck and hurried along the companionway. If only there was some other route to the cabins than through the saloon! But as she had hoped, it was empty, and she passed through it at a run.

Now came the real gamble. Which of those doors that faced her hid an empty cabin? If she should burst in and find herself in one that was occupied, it would be the end of her escape bid. Why, she could hear the lady's outraged screams already, or the gentleman's amused authority as he returned her to Zach.

But there was no time for dallying. To delay here might be to invite discovery. Offering up a quick prayer, Regan tried one of the doors and when it opened she was amazed to see she had been answered. An empty cabin indeed! Swiftly she stepped aside, closing the door behind her and leaning against it while her breath came in harsh gasps and she trembled from relief and the release of tension.

As her breathing grew steadier again, elation began to fill her. She had done it, she told herself! She had actually concealed herself – and in a place where no one would think to look for her. Why, if he searched at all it would be the emigrant quarters where Zach would think to find her, hiding from him amongst the packed bodies of her own people . . .

Remembering the squalid discomfort in the cuddy, Regan felt a small spasm of indignation. How unfair it was that these cabins should lie empty while below the emigrants were packed together like herded cattle! The divisions of life were too sharp, too cruel. But she would return to her own class without a single backward glance at the more leisured life she had seen here in the quarters of the moneyed passengers. At least when she had been an emigrant lass she had had her pride and self-respect. And what did being poor matter if you were also happy?

A step in the passageway outside made her tense suddenly and she stood, hardly daring to breathe, as it came closer. There's no reason why anyone should come into this cabin, she told herself, but the self-assurance did nothing to still the irregular beating of her heart and she looked around for somewhere she could conceal herself should the door open.

There was a space between bunk and floor, storage room for a trunk if the cabin had been occupied, and she crossed to it at a run, falling onto her knees and trying to scramble into it. It was a tight fit and in her haste she caught her dress on a nail in the wooden framework above. She stopped as she felt it rip, trying to disengage it without getting out again, and as she did so there came a thunderous knocking on the door.

Regan jumped so violently she caught her head on the bunk above and almost cried out. Then, heedless of the dress that was still attached to the nail, she wriggled hastily into the hiding place. The knock came again and she held her breath, stuffing her fists against her mouth as if to shut off every possibility of sound. She heard the click of the door opening but her back was towards it and she could see nothing. She lay, wide-eyed with fear, and the few moments silence that followed gave her hope that she would be undetected.

Then, close by her ear, an all-too-recognizable voice spoke.

'I should come out of there if I were you, my dear,

before you get a cramp, or a spider spins a web in your hair.'

'Oh!' she squealed, her hands going to her head, and behind her the man laughed, low and mocking.

'What do you think you are doing down there, Regan?'

Because there was nothing else for it, she wriggled backwards out of the hiding place. Behind her, Zach had straightened, now he looked down at her with a mixture of annoyance and amusement on his dark features.

'Did you really think you could escape me so easily?' he asked.

'How did you find me?' she choked, brushing the dust from her dress.

'I followed you,' he told her simply. 'When I saw you creeping through the saloon I knew you were up to something.'

'But the saloon was empty!' she protested.

He smiled. 'You did not look closely enough, I fear. Those deep chairs conceal a multitude of indiscretions. I had little sleep last night, and I was catching up on my slumber when you disturbed me.'

'Oh you're impossible! I hate you!' she cried.

A muscle quirked in his cheek and he held out his hand to her.

'Never mind that now. If you want to catch your first glimpse of the country that is to be your home, you had better come on deck with me – but put on a thicker cloak than that one, or you'll die of pneumonia.'

'But I haven't one . . .' She broke off as his earlier words came home to her. 'The new country! You mean – We're near enough to *see* it?'

He nodded. 'Yes. A distant blur on the horizon, pehaps, but unmistakably there all the same. And if you have no cloak, then you had better take my coat.'

With a smooth, unhurried movement he divested himself of a heavy woollen overcoat and put it about her shoulders. Then he led her to the cabin door and back on the deck.

CHAPTER SEVEN

The *Maid of Morne* dropped anchor in Port Melbourne the following morning and Regan stood at her vantage point by the rail scanning the faces of the people who jostled on the wharf for the one she would instantly recognize even after all these months.

Her heart was beating an uneven tattoo and she hung halfway between hope and fear. Richard would rescue her from the monstrous Zach. He must! Yet Zach would not let her go easily, she was sure of it. He was stubborn enough to try to keep her even though he no longer seemed to want her, and even though she had made it plain she did not want him. And what would happen then? Already one man she loved had died because of his arrogant possession of her. She could not bear the thought of the same thing happening again . . .

'Come, Regan, it is time to disembark.'

The hated voice interrupted her thoughts and she turned to see Zach standing behind her.

'I – I don't want to leave yet!' In a panic she scanned the wharf again, but there was no sign of Richard amongst those who bustled about or stood and waited and Zach seemed to read her mind.

'He is not there, your fiancé?' he asked mockingly.

'No, but . . .' Regan's chin lifted a shade. 'He soon will be, I'm sure. When he hears the ship has berthed . . .'

Zach smiled ironically. 'Your faith is touching. But I would be willing to lay odds that you will be disappointed.'

'Oh, you never think of anything but gambling!' she burst out.

Ignoring her he went on, 'What makes you think he has even received your letter, Regan? If he is at the diggings, he could be anywhere. And in any case, when the madness of gold gets into a man's blood, he forgets all else.'

Her lips tightened. 'Richard would never forget me. He'll be here, you'll see.'

Zach shrugged. 'Very well, we will wait a little longer, until the emigrants have disembarked. I'm in no hurry. I should hate you to think I had stolen you away before you had the opportunity of bidding "Hail and farewell" to your old love.'

She jerked her head around, refusing to look at him, but his words had rekindled the sick despair within her. He was so confident that Richard would not come! So arrogantly sure he was a worthless idiot, too besotted with the lust for gold to care what happened to the woman who loved him.

'Oh, prove him wrong, Richard! Please prove him wrong!' she whispered through gritted teeth.

But the minutes passed and though the wharf became awash with emigrants, herding like cattle out of the 'tween decks, there was no sign of a familiar figure rushing forward to search amongst them for the girl he had left behind.

As the wharf cleared a little Zach touched her arm with authority.

'Are you satisfied now? Shall we disembark?'

Hopeless tears stung her eyes and throat but she could not give up so easily. She had crossed the world to rejoin Richard – when she left the *Maid of Morne* she would be leaving the one place in this vast country where he would know where to find her.

'Please – a little longer!' she begged.

'My dear girl, we shall be put to sea again if we delay much longer!' Zach told her, then laughed mockingly at her downcast expression. 'I'll tell you what I'll do. I'll leave messages as to our whereabouts so that if your long-lost lover does arrive at last he'll be able to find us. I'd hate to miss the opportunity of meeting the man who commands your heart!'

'And where *will* we be?' she asked spiritedly.

'The Imperial Hotel in Collins Street. I have some business to attend to in Melbourne and there is the little matter of getting you fitted for some new dresses. And in any case, we could not leave today if we wanted to – we shall have to wait until tomorrow for the coach.'

'The coach,' she repeated dully.

'To take us to Ballymena. Don't look so worried, my sweet. Cobb & Co will take good care of you.' He laid a hand beneath her elbow. 'Now we will go ashore and find a buggy to take us into the city.'

In a stupor of misery she went with him, but all the while her eyes were darting about in the hope of seeing Richard. He must be here – he must be! Surely when that man turned around, or that one, it would be him! But it never was, and by the time they were installed in a buggy with Zach's trunk and her own few poor possessions she was close to despair. She saw the bustling streets, where bullock carts ran axle to axle with the horse-drawn buggies as if through a haze of tears, and though Zach pointed out various places of interest, from the new buildings under construction to the old red gum 'Separation Tree' so named to commemorate the separation of the colony five years earlier, her ears buzzed too loudly to allow her to hear much of what he said.

At last the buggy drew up before the Imperial Hotel and Zach handed her down into the street.

'My room here is already booked,' he explained as they went through the swing doors. 'And I'm afraid I shall have to ask you to share it. But after the confines of our cabin on board ship, it is certain to seem spacious.'

She ignored him, too unhappy for such things to make any impression on her, but when they were shown up the wooden staircase and a door was flung open to reveal a room where a double bed took pride of place, she recoiled, breath catching in her throat.

But Zach's hand was on her waist, his fingers bit into it like steel ribs as he pushed her before him, and unless she wished to make a spectacle of herself she had no choice but to precede him in.

As he had said, after the cramped cabin the room seemed spacious. Besides the bed there was a wooden chest and a washstand equipped with a prettily decorated china jug and basin, and there was still room to spare. As her eyes fell on the jug and basin Regan let out a small gasp of pleasure, and Zach turned to the man who had shown them upstairs.

'We have been at sea for three months, and I'm sure the lady is anxious for a bath. Have a tub and plenty of hot water sent up at once, will you?'

The man nodded, a smirk twisting his ugly little face, and Regan felt the colour rise in her cheeks. She would love a bath, of course. To be able to soak away the sweat and dirt of the voyage and feel fresh and clean again would be heaven. But how could she take off her clothes with Zach here in the same room?

As if reading her thoughts, when the man had gone, he turned to her.

'I have business to attend to in Melbourne as I told you. I'll leave you in peace for an hour or two and you can enjoy the luxury of a hot tub. Or you can spend the time hanging out of the window, if you prefer, searching the crowds below for your sweetheart. Collins Street is the main thoroughfare of Melbourne; all the world will pass by beneath your window if you watch long enough. But don't think of escaping, my little chicken. That wouldn't be wise.'

Her chin came up. 'Oh, and why not?'

'Because I should quickly find you and bring you back and it would be the worse for you.' He smiled cruelly. 'However, since I do not want the bother of hunting for you, nor the expense of bribing those in the know to tell me where you are, I shall take a few elementary precautions to ensure you remain here.'

'You mean – you'll have me locked in?' she asked in a whisper.

He laughed. 'Oh no, nothing so crude. The last thing I want is to draw attention to the fact that you are an unwilling guest. I think it will suffice if I remove certain of your garments from your reach while I'm away. They may be poor enough, but I don't think you would wish to venture into the street, or endeavour to start a new life without them.'

'You devil!' she cried, outraged. But he only laughed at her.

'When I return, and you are bathed and fresh, I'll take

you to visit a dressmaker. But don't fall over yourself to thank me. I shall be doing it as much for myself as for you. I should hate to present you to my father and the others at Ballymena looking like a scarecrow from the outback. You are too beautiful for that, and I want them to see you at your best.'

She stared at him open-mouthed, but before she could formulate a reply, a tap on the door announced the arrival of the tub. As it was filled, steam rose from it in a warm cloud and not even the conditions Zach intended to impose upon her could detract from Regan's pleasurable anticipation as she watched.

When the servant left the room, Zach stood looking at her with amusement on his dark features.

'Well? Don't you want to take your bath while it is good and hot?' he demanded.

Regan flushed. 'But I . . . you . . .' Her hands went protectively to her breasts and he laughed aloud.

'I told you I am not leaving unless I take with me the most necessary of your garments,' he told her. 'I will not crumple your dress more than it is already by stuffing it into your bag. But I don't think you would go far wearing only that and no undergarments. The neckline is revealing enough when worn with your chemisette. Without it . . .' He broke off, smiling as his imagination ran riot, and for a moment Regan regarded him with pure hatred in her eyes. Then she lifted her chin a shade.

'If you insist on humiliating me in this way, at least have the goodness to turn your back while I undress,' she said stiffly.

'Very well. Though why you should be so coy with me after all we have shared, I don't know,' he mocked. 'I have only to close my eyes to visualize every curve of your lovely body. But still, if it pleases you . . .'

With exaggerated chivalry he turned away and Regan slipped out of her dress, wondering wildly if there was any way she could conceal some of her undergarments where he would not see them, and thus have them still when he had gone. Perhaps if she pretended to put them into her bag herself, but in fact threw them into the deep shadow beneath the bed . . .

Clutching her dress about her, she bent over the bag, but he was too quick for her.

'You wouldn't be thinking of cheating me by any chance?' he admonished her, taking the garments from her and stuffing them into the bag himself. 'My, but I must watch you like a hawk if I am to prevent you from being so foolish as to try and run away from me. Now, I will take these, and you can enjoy your tub in peace.'

With a mocking bow, he picked up the bag and went out, leaving Regan to fume helplessly.

The hateful man she thought! He knows I can no more go into the street with no chemisette and drawers than I could go stark naked as the day I was born! Why, even if I were to find Richard, how would I explain to him? I'd die of shame that he should see me so humiliated!

She crossed to the window, holding the dress in front of her while she peeped out. The street below was alive with people, some prosperous-looking, some sun-bronzed but clad only in dirty rags. Bullock carts laden with wool, meat and hides rolled by. But Regan could see no sign of anyone she recognized – not even Zach – among the milling crowds. With a sigh she turned away, folding her dress and setting it down on the bed, and testing the water in the tub with one toe.

At first it made her shiver, it was so hot. Then, as she braved it little by little, her skin began to glow wherever the water touched and she sat down, knees drawn up to her chin, back resting against the cold copper rim.

Oh, but it was heaven! It was so long, so long, since she had been able to take a bath and now all her bad temper melted away as the steam rose around her in a warm, wet mist. With a small sigh of delight she reached for the soap, lathering herself all over and feeling the sweat and grime of the voyage dissolve into the scalding water.

It was making her drowsy, that water, giving a langorous feel to her limbs and tugging at her eyelids. She leaned back against the tub, closing her eyes and floating in the warmth. It was beautiful – so beautiful – she wished she could stay here forever . . .

The click of the door catch sounded loud as a pistol shot as it cut through her dream and she jerked upright, eyes flying open, hands gripping the rim of the tub for support. Then, as the door opened and Zach was framed there, a cry of shock was forced from her lips and she tried to cover her nude breasts with her hands.

'What are you doing here?' she squeaked. 'You said you had business to attend to!'

'Unfortunately the associate I wished to see is otherwise engaged until this afternoon.' Zach came into the room, closing the door behind him and looking at her through narrowed eyes. 'Though why I should say "unfortunately" I don't know. To see you so can be nothing if not fortunate!'

'Oh, you beast!' she cried, quite unaware of the picture she made, or the effect she was having on Zach.

As he looked at her sitting there in the tub, her hair falling in damp ringlets about her face, her skin rosy from the warmth, desire was stirring in him until his body ached with it. He wanted nothing more than to take her in his arms and kiss every inch of her lovely body from her creamy throat and rose-tipped breasts to her slender thighs and the softly curling maiden hair where the bath water would still cling in crystal droplets when he carried her to the bed. But he was determined not to give way to his insatiable passion for her so easily. She thought him no better than an animal – he was determined to show her she was wrong if it killed him. And that conceit of hers needed to be taught a lesson, too. From the look on her face it was clear she thought he wanted her, and the fact that he did was irrelevant. It was time Miss Regan Gardner learned she was not so irresistible as she thought herself! No, the next time he touched her it would be because she wanted him too, and if she had to beg him for it, so much the better.

He turned away from her abruptly.

'Get out and get dressed,' he ordered her roughly.

She glared at him, her eyes sparkling angrily in her flushed face. 'And what am I supposed to get dressed in?' she demanded.

'This will do for the time being.' He tossed a brown paper parcel he had been carrying onto the bed with a careless gesture. 'I thought it might suit you and the fit cannot matter too much.'

Forgetting her nudity, she scrambled to her feet, then, as he laughed aloud she blushed furiously and made a grab for the towel the servant had left beside the tub. Winding it around herself, she ran to the bed and tore open the paper with almost child-like eagerness. Then she gasped with delight as she shook out a silk wrapper, as green as her eyes.

'Oh!' she whispered as her fingers slid over the smooth fabric that was finer than anything she had ever owned. 'Oh, it's beautiful!'

'You like it?' he asked. There was a strange, husky note in his voice, but she did not notice. She dropped the towel and slipped into the wrapper, and her body, flushed from the bath, was exposed for a moment before she pulled it around her, relishing the feel of it against her damp skin. Then she pirouetted while it clung tantalizingly to her curves.

His breath came harsh in his throat as he watched her. 'You see?' he said roughly. 'I told you I would treat you well.'

She stopped in mid-pirouette, the smile froze on her face, and her mouth hardened.

'So you still think you can buy me!' she spat at him. 'You think your money can compensate for taking me by force. Well, you're wrong. I still hate you, Mr Zach Casey.'

Zach's face, too, hardened. He turned abruptly, went to the door and shouted something down the stairs. Then, returning, he closed the door and began unfastening the buttons of his shirt.

Suddenly afraid, Regan watched him, holding the wrapper tightly around her. Did he intend to take her again here and now, despite his promises? She had made him angry, and when he was angry he was dangerous. But she was determined not to let him see she was afraid.

'What do you want with me now?' she cried, facing him boldly though the curl of his lip was making her tremble inside as if she were stricken with palsy.

He finished unbuttoning his shirt and tossed it onto the bed and as he did so she saw the way his muscles rippled beneath the brown skin of his shoulders and back. Then, to her horror, his hands moved to the fastenings of his trousers and a moment later he was stepping out of them to stand naked before her.

In all her life she had never before seen a man so shamelessly unclothed. He had been naked in the cabin when he had made love to her, it was true, but she had caught no more than a glimpse of him before turning awkwardly away, and the magnificence of his body had been distorted by the angle from which she had seen it. Now there were no such distractions, and she found herself quite unable to tear her eyes away from him. For what seemed like a lifetime she looked, taking in his broad chest with its mat of dark hair, his flat stomach and slim hips, his strong thighs. And between them, rising from another mat of hair, the manhood that had taken her virginity. Her eyes round as saucers, she stood as if transfixed and it was only when a knocking came at the door that the hot colour began to flood her cheeks.

'Come in!' Zach called and she watched, mortified, as the servant entered.

He'll know I'm here with Zach and him naked! she thought in horror, and turned away to hide her embarrassment. Then, as she heard a splashing, she could not resist peeping to see what was going on, and she saw the man had brought another bath tub and was filling it with hot water.

Seeing the expression on her face, Zach laughed aloud.

'Why should I not bathe too, my love?' he asked mockingly. 'I, too, was too long at sea. And you can help me.'

'Help you?' she squealed.

'Why not? I would like someone to wash my back for me.'

She stared at him, speechless; then as the servant left the room, casting a knowing look at her over his shoulder, she flew at Zach.

'Never! I'll never wash your filthy back for you! I'm not your servant!'

'We'll see about that,' he sneered. 'Now, come here.'

For a long moment, she resisted. Then, as if compelled by his voice and his hypnotic dark eyes she moved slowly towards the tub. Amused, he watched her, excited by her curves beneath the sensuous green silk, yet controlling his urge to catch her and pull her into the water with him. Then, with a leisurely movement, he handed her the cake of soap.

'Don't be afraid to scrub me hard,' he instructed her.

And with a sob that signified her capitulation to his mastery, she pushed the sleeves of her robe up her arms and thrust her hands into the steaming water.

The day passed on heavy wings. His toilet completed, Zach dressed in fresh pleated shirt, silk waistcoat and grey trousers, so that he looked for all the world like a gentleman once more. Then he bade Regan make herself as respectable as she could in her battered white gown and shawl and, after a late lunch, he took her to a dressmaker's shop in Bourke Street where he ordered her so many fine gowns her head spun.

'We leave on the Cobb coach in the morning,' he told the dressmaker. 'We shall want one of the dresses ready by then if it takes you and your assistants all night to finish it.'

The dressmaker, who had done her best to conceal her surprise at Regan's rags, nodded dutifully.

'Which one would you like, Mr Casey? May I suggest the French blue silk? Or the promenade dress in pink and black?'

Zach considered for a moment. Have I no say in the matter? Regan wondered, irritated momentarily in spite of her excitement over the dresses. Does he even expect to tell me what I am to wear?

'For ease of travel, I think Miss Gardner should have one of the carriage dresses,' he replied at last. 'Which one can be her choice.'

In spite of herself, Regan's eyes sparkled. Of all the fabrics and designs, her own favourite was the dark green silk which the dressmaker had promised to edge in magenta velvet and which was to have an overskirt and yoke of plaid taffeta. She knew it would be one of the most complicated dresses to make, and the dressmaker would indeed most likely have to sew all night if it was to be finished in time. But the order was a good one – worth a great deal to a seamstress in a new country where fashion was not as important as it was back home in England. And if she was really to be taken off to Heaven knew where on a Cobb's coach in the morning, she thought she might feel the better able to face it in the green silk.

She said as much and the dressmaker nodded her agreement. 'A wise choice! Madam has a talent for clothes, I'm sure,' she murmured.

'And we shall want a bonnet to match. And gloves,' Zach added. 'I will leave Miss Gardner here to choose them if I may. I have a little business to attend to, but I'll be back within the hour.'

Regan stared in disbelief. He was actually leaving her here unguarded! Did he think he had now bought her with a dozen gowns, and she would never run away without them? How shallow he must consider her! Beautiful though the dresses might be, she would be better off with her freedom!

Impatiently she ran through the motions of choosing two or three bonnets with one eye on the door, because she half-expected Zach to return at any moment. Then, making some excuse about going after him, she took her leave of a surprised dressmaker and hurried out into the street.

It was alive with people. They jostled her this way and that, but she only laughed. Free! It was such a wonderful feeling and it made her believe for the moment that anything was possible – even finding Richard! Eagerly she scanned the crowds as she hurried along, but nowhere could she see a friendly face. On and on she went, sometimes running, sometimes walking, across the busy teeming streets that intersected each other so neatly, putting as much distance as she could between herself and the dressmaker's where Zach had left her.

It was only when she came to a crossroads where a large new building was being constructed that she stopped, looking around uncertainly, and the first glorious intoxication of freedom began to fade. Where was she? She didn't know. And what was she to do? She was lost in a strange country, and no nearer to finding Richard than she ever had been.

A group of men she took for miners approached her along the narrow pavement, laughing and singing – obviously drunk. Perhaps they had struck gold and come into town to spend their new-found riches, she thought. As they reached her, they began catcalling and when she tried to hurry by one of them caught her, spinning her round so that she almost fell.

'A wench – and a pretty one, too!' one of them cried, grabbing at her with eager hands, and the look on his face both revolted and terrified her. These men were crazy for a woman – any woman – and she suddenly found herself remembering how Zach had said they would use her, one after the other, time and again. Twisting free she began to run, and after a few moments they gave up the chase and let her go. But her heart was beating unevenly against her ribs and now every strange face she saw seemed to hold menace.

They were men, all men, hardly a woman anywhere. And she had learned to her cost what animals men could be!

A sob caught in her throat and she turned wildly this way and that. Already dusk was beginning to fall – soon the spring afternoon would turn cold and it would be dark. What would she do then? Where would she go? The few women who were on the streets would disappear – or all the decent ones would, anyway – and the men would become more drunken, rowdy and lecherous than ever. And she would be at their mercy, with no roof over her head and no money to buy one . . .

Tears started to her eyes as the realization of her plight came home to her. She had run away from Zach – to what? She would never find Richard. And if he *had* gone to the wharf looking for her, Zach's message would send him to the hotel in Collins Street – only she would not be there. Zach would tell him she had gone – been swallowed up by the teeming streets of Melbourne.

I wouldn't even know how to find my way back there now, she thought. And I wouldn't dare approach any of these men in case they thought . . .

At the hand on her shoulder she froze, everything in her seeming to turn to ice. Only her thoughts ran riot. What could she do? How could she save herself? Her fear was so intense she felt her knees begin to buckle and as they did so a voice she knew cut through the mists.

'And where do you think you are going, you foolish woman?'

She turned, her head swimming from hunger and fear.

'Zach!' she murmured. Then the darkness closed in so that it was all she could do to keep from swooning.

CHAPTER EIGHT

Zach had a buggy waiting at the kerb. He half-carried Regan to it, set her in and climbed up to sit beside her and support her. He hardly spoke until they were back in his room at the hotel. Then he turned on her furiously.

'You little fool! What were you thinking of to go wandering off on your own? I had the devil's own job to find you.'

She stared at him miserably and he went on: 'You disappoint me, Regan. I gave you credit for more common sense. Don't you know what would have happened to you if I hadn't found you?'

His anger suddenly struck her as being almost comic. Since when had Zach Casey been concerned for her moral welfare?

'Much the same as will happen to me now that you have, I imagine,' she replied tartly.

'You think so?' A muscle worked in his cheek as he controlled his fury. 'Then let me tell you that you are much mistaken. In the first place, I doubt you can have any idea of the way those love-starved drunken animals would use you. And in the second, I have already told you, you have no more to fear from me. You will be quite safe tonight and every other night.'

'Then why keep me?' she sobbed. 'I don't understand!'

He smiled enigmatically.

'Do you know, I asked myself that self-same question when I found you gone. "Let her go, Zach", I told myself. "She is an ill-tempered, conceited wench who brings you nothing but trouble and expense. If she wishes to become a saloon girl or a queen of the diggings, then let her do so." But it isn't so easy. For one thing, I don't like to give up so readily what is mine – and you are mine, whether you like to admit it or not – won fairly and squarely at a game of dice. And for another thing. . . I feel responsible for you.'

'Then please don't!' she said sharply.

A strange expression crossed his face.

'Where would you have spent the night?' he asked gently. When she did not reply, he went on, 'You have no money, no friends, you took no possessions with you. Wildcat you may be, Regan. Self-sufficient you are not.'

She turned away, remembering all too clearly the fear and isolation she had felt in the street when she had realized she was lost. But she did not want Zach to know it had been almost a relief when he had found her – the devil she knew – whilst around her the deep blue sea she did not know had lapped hungrily.

'And now that I am here, where am I to sleep?' she asked haughtily in an effort to change the subject. 'Surely you don't expect me to share the bed with you?'

He smiled ruefully. 'I'm afraid that is exactly what I expect. Had I been able to trust you, I might perhaps have booked you a room of your own. But now that I have been reminded once again that the moment I leave you alone you intend making your escape, no matter what the consequences, I dare not risk such a thing. You will sleep on the bed beside me.'

'And what is to stop me creeping out when you are asleep?' she demanded.

He crossed the room, locking the door and swinging the key tantalizingly before her.

'You will first have to take the key from me,' he informed her. 'And that, sweet Regan, will be in a place that I do not think you will attempt to raid – if you are the lady you pretend to be!'

In fascinated horror she watched as he turned his back

on her, divesting himself of his trousers and tucking the key into the front pocket of his underpants.

'I should advise you to prepare for bed now,' he suggested calmly. 'We have several long days travelling before us and the accommodation along the way may not be so comfortable.'

There seemed little for it but to undress herself to her chemisette and drawers and climb into the big bed. But when Zach climbed in beside her he was as good as his word. In spite of being so close that she could feel the warmth of his body enveloping her, he did not attempt to touch her, and before long exhaustion overcame her and she drifted into a deep and dreamless sleep.

Next day Zach was already up and dressed when Regan awoke and there was an enormous dress box on the chair beside the window, together with a hatbox and various assorted parcels.

Unable to contain her excitement, Regan jumped out of bed to look inside, and moments later was shaking the dress free of the tissue paper that held it.

It was beautiful – even better than she had pictured it when she and Zach had selected the fabric and the design!

'Oh, may I try it on?' she begged and Zach laughed at her eagerness.

'Of course. And woe betide the dressmaker if it is not a perfect fit.'

'But she had no time to do it – none at all . . .' Regan was struggling to lace her corset and she was too excited even to complain when Zach came to her aid, drawing it tightly around her to achieve the tiny waist the dress demanded.

She hoisted the dress over her head. There seemed to be yards of it. Then she caught her breath and she looked down at the sweeping skirt and Zach stood back to admire the picture she made. The green silk set off her colouring to perfection and the plaid taffeta overskirt added fullness that made her waist appear smaller than ever. Beneath the wide bell sleeves he caught a glimpse of the spotless lace undersleeves, and around the yoke tassels of black, white and magenta danced enticingly.

With an effort he choked back the longing to take her in his arms and kiss her face, still rosy from sleep.

'I hope you chose a bonnet to match before making your bid for freedom yesterday,' he observed drily.

She coloured slightly.

'Yes, I . . .' she could not finish, knowing as she did that she had scarcely noticed the bonnets in her eagerness to escape. Nervously, she opened the hatbox and lifted out the bonnet – a concoction of green crepe, trimmed with velvet ribbons and roses – and immediately blessed the dressmaker. It was perfect with the dress – perfect! Happily she settled it on her red-gold curls and peered into the mirror above the washstand.

'Well, and aren't you glad you waited for your dress before deserting me?' Zach drawled from behind her and she straightened up, her pleasure melting like snow in summer.

If he expected her to be grateful, he was going to be disappointed. It was a beautiful dress. No doubt he had spent a small fortune on her. But she would have exchanged it all if only she could have turned back the clock and had her father and Richard back again . . .

After an early breakfast, Zach informed Regan it was time to board the coach and with a heavy heart she left the hotel. She did not want to go with him – to leave Melbourne was to give up all hope of meeting up with Richard – but after last night's terrifying excursion, Regan was forced to accept that she had little choice.

Zach was right – she could not survive here in a strange country alone and penniless. Perhaps she could sing in the bars for her keep, but with no one to protect her she would be fair game for the first band of ruffians who took a fancy to her – and from past experience, Regan knew that when she sold herself in this way there would be plenty who would assume far more than just her voice was on offer. No, quite apart from the gaming debt, which she would turn her back on without a second thought, she was bound to Zach by necessity.

Even so: 'I won't stay with him a moment longer than I have to!' she promised herself.

The coach was drawn by four horses, with seating for nine passengers, and when they climbed aboard, Regan was dismayed to see that Dickon Trenoweth was to be one of their fellow travellers. He wished them good day politely enough, but she could not help seeing the smirk on his face as he turned away, and shrank from the thought of his company for the next two or three days. Even the most objectionable of the other passengers, smoking his Bengal twist and spitting onto the floor of the coach uncomfortably close to the hem of her dress, was preferable to Dickon, who knew too much about her, Regan thought.

As the coach skimmed through the die-straight streets of Melbourne, past green parks and stores, and along the bank of the Yarra Yarra river, Regan kept scanning the faces of the people they passed in the faint hope that even now, at this late stage, she might see Richard. But it was useless. All too soon the town was left behind and the coach was bowling along a road that was little more than a dirt track, skimming over potholes and hillocks with a swaying motion that Regan found more nauseating than the swell of the ocean. To take her mind off the quaking of her stomach, she looked around her at the country through which they were passing, and Zach, noticing her interest, began pointing out and naming the majestic eucalyptus trees that towered above the track, the red stringybarks and the ghost gums with their strange grey trunks.

'The natives have a story about them,' he told her. 'They say the ghost gums are occupied by the souls of the dead.'

Regan nodded silently, but she found herself wondering if Zach had learned that story at his mother's knee. After all, she had been a native . . .

It was a beautiful spring morning and as the Australian countryside unfolded around them Regan felt her spirits lifting. Who could be downcast when the air was full of the scent of the wattle flowers and the whistling of birds? Who could fail to feel elated at the sight of a flock of galahs rising in a flush of pink and grey against the blue sky? But as the track became more and more obscure, hardly discernible except as dust and stones in the middle of the bush, she bagan to feel a little apprehensive. They might be miles from anywhere – they *were* miles from anywhere. And on a road such as this the coach could be overturned all too easily and all of them with it, and what would happen to them then?

The queasiness was returning, too, and Regan was almost relieved when one of the wheels became wedged in a pothole and she and the other passengers had to get out and push. To see her skirts dragging in the dust was irritating, but at least while she was on foot she knew she would not vomit. Zach, too, noticed the look of her, though typically he made a joke of it.

'Your face is a good match for your dress, my love!' he murmured to her as he heaved at the coach with careless ease. 'Perhaps you would have preferred the old days before Freeman Cobb brought in the American Concords. The coaches were English and steel-sprung until then, but though they might have jerked you to flinderjigs, at least they would never have made you seasick!'

The journey went on and as the first novelty of the strange countryside and the dangerous interludes passed, it seemed to be interminable to Regan. After a while, the rocky surfaces, the creeks and the potholes all began to merge into one, in spite of regular stops to change horses, and when dusk fell and the coach drew up outside a bush pub – The Star and Garter – Regan fell from it gratefully on legs that felt shaky and unwilling to support her.

In spite of its English sounding name, the *Star and Garter* was a primitive, single-storied building constructed of bark and logs, but for all that it provided an excellent dinner of mutton pie, which the travellers ate hungrily. But as the men lingered over their cigars and the inevitable rum, Regan felt her eyelids growing heavy and it was all she could do to keep from nodding over the table.

Zach, who had been discussing with Dickon the likely duration of the journey, glanced across and noticed her, and immediately got to his feet.

'You're tired, my love. Excuse me, gentlemen, I will see her to our room.'

There was a murmuring as they exchanged knowing

looks, and instantly Regan was wide awake once more.

'Thank you, I can find my own way!' she said haughtily, but Zach was not to be deterred.

'I would not think of letting you wander about on your own,' he told her, placing a hand beneath her elbow to guide her to the door. As they passed out of earshot of the others, he continued softly, 'Not without a word of warning, anyway. Don't try to run away from me here, Regan. If you do, you will only lose yourself in the bush – a fate I wouldn't wish on anyone. This is wild country, and it is cruel to those who treat it without respect.'

She raised her chin. 'I can see that. Do you take me for a fool?'

He smiled. 'Sometimes, yes. Now, I suggest you try to get a good night's sleep. We have another long day before us tomorrow.'

'Shall we reach your farm then?' she aked hesitantly.

'Not tomorrow. If we get by without mishap we should arrive at the township of Robertson by nightfall and we can expect a little more comfort at the inn there – it is kept by a friend of mine. Then another half-day will bring us to Ballymena.'

She nodded, too tired suddenly to talk any more. They had reached the room they were to share, but to her surprise, Zach only stood in the doorway when she went in.

'Aren't you coming to bed?' she asked.

'Not yet.' In the lamplight his face was all lines and shadows. 'I shall play a hand of poker with my friends first. I think I can take the risk of leaving you now that I have pointed out the dangers should you think of escaping. Even you would not, I think, be that foolish.'

'Oh!' she fumed, but when he had gone she undressed and climbed into the hard bed without even considering escape. Once again, Zach was right. The bush was a far more efficient gaoler than he could ever have been.

For just a few moments she lay listening to the unfamiliar sounds of the Australian night. Then her eyes grew heavy again as sleep claimed her.

The second day's travelling was much the same as the first. Once or twice the passengers had to climb down and help right the coach when it left the road, but for the most part the journey was uneventful if far from smooth. During the morning they came upon a gold miners' camp, where the trees had been cut down to form a clearing and dirty, straggly-looking men scrubbed about in the earth or straightened their bent backs to watch the coach pass by. There were even a few women, struggling with their billy cans over a camp fire, and a handful of grimy children ran along after the coach.

At the sight of the miners, Regan's heart had come into her mouth and she sat forward eagerly, peering about in case she could catch a glimpse of Richard. But nowhere was there a face she recognized, nor anyone that might be him, though she had to admit that in their dirt-streaked rags, with their shoulders bowed from too many hours spent digging and cradling, they were almost indistinguishable one from the other.

'You see, Regan?' Zach murmured as they left the clearing behind them. 'That could easily have been your future home. You wouldn't have cared for it very much, I think. You're too fond of the little luxuries of life for that.'

She closed her lips tightly over the retort that had sprung to them, but for all that she could not help feeling there might be some truth in what Zach said. The women had looked such sorry souls, the men like things obsessed, and the children . . . what future was there for the children? In spite of the warmth of the sun, which was now high in the sky, Regan shivered.

Night was falling and Regan was just beginning to believe they would go on travelling for ever when they saw the first shacks that signified the outskirts of the township. The horses, as if they knew they were almost home, put on an extra spurt, and within a few minutes they were reining to a halt outside a square, stone building whose awning proudly proclaimed Commercial Hotel.

Was this the place owned by Zach's friend? She supposed it must be. Zach had not mentioned him again during the day's gruelling journey and now she found herself wondering if he would be as arrogantly hateful as Zach himself, or Dickon Trenoweth, who had spent the last hour or more listing the properties in this township, Robertson, owned by his brother Jud.

As the passengers climbed down from the coach, stretching themselves gratefully and heading towards the hotel, the door opened and a woman came out.

She stood on the top step, a strikingly beautiful figure in a scarlet dress. Her black hair was caught up on the top of her well-shaped head before falling into glossy ringlets, her shoulders were white and smooth above the flounced neck of her dress, and her complexion was enhanced with more rouge than Regan would ever have dared wear.

Behind her Regan could hear the male passengers grunting their appreciation, and her pleasure at seeing another woman dimmed. She must be a saloon girl, she supposed, there to provide entertainment for the miners who came into town to spend their new-found wealth, and travellers alike. Without Zach's protection she might be in the same position herself. But she could see no sign of the woman's beauty being marred yet in the way Zach had warned, though she was obviously older than first appearances had led Regan to believe. Perhaps it was not such a bad life, after all!

Zach handed her up the steps, but the woman made no attempt to move. She stood there, smiling at Zach, so that Regan had the strange illusion that she might have become invisible. Then, as they drew level, the woman opened her arms, kissing Zach on the cheek.

'It's good to see you back!' Her voice was heavy with the accent Regan had begun to grow used to since she had landed in Melbourne and her tone was a strange mixture of warmth and sarcasm.

'Hello, Adelaide. It's good to *be* back,' Zach returned, and he, too, lapsed into the Australian drawl.

Regan bristled slightly at the familiarity. It was obvious Zach knew this woman and knew her well, and for some reason the knowledge hurt her. Of course it was inconceivable that he should have lived all his life until now like a monk; the way he had treated her had shown considerable experience. But all the same, to have this painted dance girl greeting him as her equal . . .

'Adelaide, I'd like you to meet Miss Regan Gardner.

Regan, this is Adelaide Jackson, owner of the Commercial Hotel.'

Regan was so surprised she almost gasped aloud. *Owner*? Then this woman was the friend Zach had spoken of! But how did a woman come to be the owner of a hotel? And why did she dress in this rather common way?

Why, I believe she's no better than she should be! Regan thought indignantly. *Owner* indeed! She's just a common whore!

The woman was regarding her through narrowed eyes and Regan fancied the smile had frozen on her scarlet lips. She nodded coolly, anxious to get away from that bold stare – and to show Miss Adelaide Jackson that, hotel owner or not, she had no wish to be classed with her.

'We're hungry and thirsty, Adelaide,' Zach said with a smile that seemed to deny the existence of the sudden chill in the air. 'I hope your hospitality awaits us.'

'Since when have you had reason to complain of my hospitality?' Adelaide asked archly and Regan's irritation twisted a notch tighter.

There were few people she disliked on sight – but this woman was certainly one of them. A fitting friend for Zach! She thought bitterly. In her own way she's every bit as hateful as he is. Why, these Australians are a detestable bunch! And I am going to have to live with them until I can somehow find the wherewithal to escape back to England . . .

The saloon was full of the delicious aroma of roast meat, wafting in from the kitchen, and if Regan had not been fuming so, it would have set her mouth watering. As it was, she barely noticed.

'Did you say that despicable woman was the owner of this place?' she demanded of Zach.

He laughed. 'Now, now, put away your claws, wildcat. Adelaide is not a woman for you to tangle with. She'd gobble you up and spit you out before you knew what was happening. But all the same, I don't think you should describe her as being despicable. She's an attractive woman – and a very shrewd one.'

'Ha' Regan exploded, further annoyed by Zach's obvious admiration. 'I can think of another word for her sort! How did she come to own a hotel like this one, I'd like to know.'

Zach smiled. 'By dint of sheer hard work – though there are those who'd like to think differently. She began here as a saloon girl, it's true, but she became so indispensable to the man who owned it, old Jock Mackenzie, that when he died he left it to her. Since then, she's run the place single-handed.'

'I knew it!' Regan said triumphantly. 'I knew what she was the moment I set eyes on her!'

'Careful, Regan!' Zach cautioned. 'Adelaide is a good friend, but she could also be a dangerous enemy. There's wild blood in her veins. Her mother was a convict, you know.'

'*What*?' Regan exploded.

Zach smiled at her surprise. 'Hers is an interesting story. Remind me to tell you about it sometime. But now I think we should endeavour to be a little sociable. Dinner will soon be served, and we shall be expected to eat with our travelling companions.'

Whilst they had been talking, the other travellers had drifted into the saloon and Adelaide, following them in, crossed to an oak desk and opened a heavy bound register to allocate the accommodation they required. When it was their turn Regan felt her face grow hot with embarrassment, but to her surprise Zach casually booked them single rooms.

'Next to one another if you have them,' he added.

'Why are you suddenly ready to trust me?' Regan hissed at him as they followed the porter up the stairs.

'Because I don't think there's a single place you could run away to,' he replied softly. 'And besides, I would not like you to begin your life here with a bad reputation.'

'So that's it!' Regan retorted furiously. 'You don't want to upset that woman, I suppose!'

Zach smiled, but his eyes were dangerously dark and he nodded towards the bulky figure of the porter.

'I'd keep your voice down if I was you, my sweet. Matt Jordan has been with Adelaide as many years as she has been here and he's devoted to her. It wouldn't be a good idea to let him hear you refer to her in those tones.'

The room was small but, as the door closed after her, Regan forgot her annoyance in the delight of actually being alone. She luxuriated as she freshened up, and by the time she returned downstairs for the evening meal she was more than ready to do justice to the mutton, vegetables and gravy that were put before them. Oh, but there was something about the fresh clear air of this country that sharpened the appetite, and after weeks at sea with fare that tasted of nothing but salt it was heaven to be able to eat so well!

It was quite late when the meal was done and Regan was more than ready to retire to the longed-for privacy of her own room. But before she could escape, Adelaide Jackson approached the table, drawing up a chair.

'And how did you find the old country?' she asked Zach. 'Were the merchants as eager to buy your wool as you hoped they would be?'

Zach nodded, drawing on his cigar. 'They would take all I could send them. I have orders in my book that will keep Ballymena fully extended for some time to come. It was a long trip, Adelaide, but well worthwhile.'

'And it was not all work and no play, I hope? You broke a good many hearts, I dare say.' The Australian woman's eyes, narrowed like a cat's, flickered to Regan's face. 'He is a charmer, is he not? But oh, the things I could tell you about him if I cared to . . .'

And the things I could tell you! Regan thought, colour rising in her cheeks. But aloud she said:

'I am sure you two have a great deal to talk about and I should hate to interrupt you. If you'll excuse me, I think I'll retire.'

'Oh, what a very great shame!' Adelaide murmured, but her eyes were shining with triumph. 'We have only just met and I so wanted to discover what brings you to Robertson and whether you'll be staying long?'

'I . . .' Regan broke off, at a loss how to answer, but Zach, who had risen to help her from her chair, slipped an arm about her waist.

'I can answer that one, Adelaide. Regan will be staying a very long while, I hope. And the reason she is here is because she has agreed to be my wife. As soon as I have introduced her to my father, we shall make an official announcement. There will be a wedding at Ballymena before the summer, and you are the first to know.'

CHAPTER NINE

The silence around the table seemed to go on forever. Though if anyone had spoken, Regan doubted whether she would have heard it above the ringing in her ears.

Wife – wedding – was it possible she had heard aright, and Zach actually intended to marry her? Holy Mary, such a thing had simply never entered her head, no, not even when he had said he intended her to stay with him. She had thought he wanted her as a plaything – an acquisition – and when he tired of her she would be able to make her escape. But it was not to be. He planned to make her his wife!

'Well, well, Zach, so you've been cornered by a foreigner!' Adelaide's voice was hard. 'You work fast, Miss Gardner. I congratulate you on your conquest.'

'Adelaide!' Zach cut in, his tone sharp and warning, and the older woman shrugged.

'You can hardly blame me for being taken by surprise, Zach. I find it hard to believe my own ears. I had thought you to be wedded to the sheep station – and your own liking for the freedom of a bachelor.'

'One cannot be a bachelor forever, Adelaide,' Zach returned easily.

'No, I dare say you are right to look to the future,' Adelaide snapped. 'You will want heirs for Ballymena and there are few hereabouts you would consider fit to supply them, though you are ready enough to take them to your bed.'

'Your tongue runs away with you, Adelaide,' Zach said darkly. 'I thought you would be pleased to be the first to hear the news and be glad for me. Since it is not to be, I will bid you goodnight.'

She rose, her eyes sparkling dangerously.

'Goodnight, Zach. I would wish you happiness, but I don't think it's likely you'll find it. You need a woman with a spirit to match your own.'

Zach's mouth curved briefly.

'And I happen to think I have found her. Do not let appearances deceive you. Were Regan not so tired by her journey, I have no doubt you would see the sharpness of her claws.' His arm tightened around Regan's waist. 'Are you ready, my sweet?' he asked with deliberate chivalry. 'I will see you to your room.'

Somehow Regan contained herself until the door had closed after them, then she turned furiously to Zach.

'How dare that woman speak of me so – as if I were not even there! And you – I don't need you to defend me! It's not that I'm tired! It's just that I'm dumbfounded by your audacity!'

'But not dumbfounded for long, it seems,' Zach murmured wryly. 'I'm sorry I had to break the news to you so publicly, but I had no idea it would come as such a shock to you. Surely you knew I had every intention of marrying you?'

'I certainly did not!' she cried. 'Why should you want to marry me? You don't love me! I don't think you even like me!'

He turned her to him. In the lamplight his face was all lines and shadows. 'You're wrong there, Regan. Very, very wrong,' he said softly.

For a moment she stared at him, half comprehending. Then her anger towards him returned in a rush. Was there no end to what this man intended to extract from her as payment for her father's debt?

'I hate you – I despise you!' she cried. 'And I won't marry you! You can't make me!'

His face hardened. She saw a muscle work in his jaw and a flicker of fear ran through her.

'Can't I, Regan?' he asked, his voice low and dangerous. 'Well, we'll see about that. But I think it would be the better for you if you accept my offer gracefully. Think of the embarrassment it will cause us both if the whole of Ballymena knows how I came by you. Surely you would rather they knew you as a willing bride? But whichever way you play, it will make no difference in the long run. I will have you, Regan. My mind is made up on that score.'

With that, he turned on his heel and left her to fume helplessly.

That night Regan slept little. All night she lay tossing and turning as she explored every facet of her plight and when the first golden rays of morning began to slant through the window she had come to a decision.

For the moment there was nothing for it but to go along with Zach. However little she might like it, she had really no choice in the matter. And Zach was right – it would be humiliating if the whole of Ballymena knew the truth of their relationship. It was bad enough Dickon Trenoweth knowing.

Dickon! Her heart took a leap into her throat. Would *he* tell the neighbourhood what had happened on the *Maid of Morne*? Or had Zach already secured his promise of silence? She did not know. But somehow she had the feeling that if Zach wanted something taken care of, he would see to it, and the thought was strangely comforting. Zach was immovable, indestructible. Why, even his beastliness could be relied upon!

Regan rose, washing herself in the fine china jug and basin that reminded her nostalgically of England, and trying to pinch some colour into her pale cheeks. If she was to face Zach's family today, she would have liked to look her best, and she knew she did not.

At last it was time to go down for breakfast and, summoning all her courage, Regan left her room. Zach was already up and in the dining room. Did he never sleep? she wondered. But she was strangely glad to see him, all the same. Hateful he might be, but their shared secret was a bond, and Regan felt Adelaide Jackson would be less likely to fall upon her and attack her if Zach were there.

Breakfast was a strained meal, but although Adelaide treated them coolly, she said no more about the betrothal, and as soon as they had done the coachman expressed his readiness to leave. Zach and Regan might have only another half-day's travelling before them, he did not, and he was anxious to make the good time the line expected from him.

As they left Robertson behind, the track seemed to become more primitive than ever and in order to take her mind off the bumps, ruts, and the frightening way the ground fell away from the track in places, so that they seemed to teeter along the very edge, Regan asked Zach about Adelaide. 'Tell me why you said she had an interesting background,' she pressed him.

'Well, there's her name for a start,' Zach began. 'She was named Adelaide after King William's consort, who came to the English throne the year she was born, and the "Jackson" is taken from Port Jackson, a settlement near Sydney where her mother had been landed.'

'But why? Why didn't she take her mother's name?' Regan asked, interested in spite of herself.

'Her mother died when she was born,' Zach explained. 'She had been transported, as I told you, and when she arrived in the colony, she was assigned to a family of immigrants. That often happened in those days. Convict labour was cheap and plentiful – in fact if my father and others like him had their way, we would be accepting convicts still and putting them to work as we once did. But Adelaide's mother must have found time for other things besides hard labour. When she discovered her activities were to bear fruit, she concealed the fact as long as she could – too long for her own safety. She died giving birth.'

'And what happened to the baby?' Regan asked.

'The immigrant family raised her and they gave her her new name thinking she would have a fresh start in life,' Zach explained. 'They were God-fearing people, good staunch Scottish Presbyterians, and they tried to make Adelaide the same way. But the blood in her veins was too wild to be satisfied with the life they could give her. She ran off to become a saloon girl as soon as she was old enough – and you know the rest.'

'Yes.' Regan's lips tightened as she recalled the bold hotel owner. In spite of her dislike for Adelaide there was something oddly fascinating about a woman who lived such a life – carrying on a man's business in a man's world, yet retaining all the appearance of a lady of pleasure. She was hard, she was cheap, and she had a tongue as sharp as a razor, yet for all that, Zach appeared to admire her.

As for Adelaide herself, she seemed to reciprocate the feeling and Regan was uncomfortably sure that the two of them knew one another a great deal better than was so far apparent. Was there something between them? Certainly Adelaide had reacted violently when she had learned of Zach's intention to marry her, Regan. But if she had wanted him, then why had they not made a match of it? If it was true that Zach admired her, and if he had known she was waiting for him, then why had he found it necessary to force himself upon a girl who despised him?

No, Regan thought, the truth was most likely that Adelaide was a dog in a manger. She liked having men dancing attendance on her and felt slighted when a rich and attractive one, such as Zach Casey, decided to take a wife . . .

'It's hardly surprising she is so rude if her mother was a convict,' Regan remarked, giving vent to a sudden spark of irritation, and an amused look crossed Zach's face.

'I wouldn't say such things in Dickon's presence,' he murmured, putting his mouth close to her ear.

'Why not?' she asked, startled.

'Remember, in this country many people have a convict as an ancestor or a relative,' he informed her. 'Dickon Trenoweth is no exception. His brother, Jud, came here as a convicted criminal too.'

Regan's cheeks flamed and she glanced quickly at the man who lounged in the opposite corner of the coach.

'Dickon's brother? But he . . . he . . .'

'You see, it's not a good thing to question a person's past here,' Zach went on. 'We judge a man by what he is, not what he once was. And however he began, Jud is now a very wealthy man, and one who has spread his net wide. Why, he even has a stake in a goldfield.'

'But I thought you said there was no money to be made out of gold,' Regan protested.

Zach shrugged. 'I said there was nothing in it for the small miner, working alone or with a mate. But it could be different for Jud. He has a way of making things work for him. There's gold in the ground, all right, and for those who are able to afford to prospect and mine it in the right way, anything is possible.'

'Money, money, money!' Regan snapped fiercely. 'That's what it comes back to, time and again. With money you think you can buy anything – or anyone!'

A strange smile twisted Zach's mouth.

'You could be right,' he said softly.

The sun was high in the noonday sky when Regan heard the jingle of the reins and the coachman's voice calling to the horses to 'Whoa, my beauties,' and her heart came into her mouth.

Zach had told her he had persuaded the driver to go several miles out of his way to take them direct to Ballymena, and although she had been glad at the time that they would not have a long wait in Robertson until someone came to collect them, now she wished heartily that something – anything – would occur to prevent their arrival.

What sort of reception could she expect from Zach's family? Not a very warm one, she thought. In the first place she was not expected. And besides . . .

They aren't likely to want him to marry a stranger, she thought nervously. They will be as rude and unfriendly as Adelaide, as like as not, when they discover Zach's plans.

Almost before the coach had come to a stop, Zach was on his feet and leaping down into the road. Then he stopped, turning back to help her down, but her legs were trembling so that when she landed on the road beside him they almost gave way beneath her and she stumbled.

At once, his arms went around her and for a moment her cheek was pressed against the rock-like strength of his chest, while his arm, lean and muscled, held her firmly. She gasped, half in fear, half in shock, and blushing furiously pushed herself away from him. For a moment more he held her, and she almost panicked. Was he going to snatch the opportunity and kiss her again, here in front of all the coach passengers and perhaps within view of his family too? If he did, there was nothing she could do to prevent him. Nothing. After all, was he not going to be her husband?

Then, abruptly, he released her, leaving her standing dizzily in the road whilst he unloaded his baggage and her own poor holdall from the coach. Ridiculous tears stung her eyes, though what caused them she had no idea, unless it was lack of sleep the previous night. As she blinked them away, Zach touched her arm.

'Come, Regan. I am anxious to show you your new home.'

She turned nervously. She had been almost afraid to look before, but now as the dust that the coach had raised on the dirt track began to clear she shaded her eyes and found herself looking at a grand, pillared house not unlike an English mansion. It was built of a yellowish stone that seemed to reflect the sunshine, with cool green shutters at each of the windows, and fronted with lush lawns, flower-beds and trees, some the strange grey ghost gums she recognized, others pale-green and shady.

Behind the house she caught a glimpse of other, single-storied buildings in the same yellow stone, all linked to the main house and shaded by more of the pale green trees; but before she could even wonder what they were, the front door of the house flew open and a child of nine or ten came running out, almost falling down the steps in her haste.

Zach set down the bags and the child ran straight to him, throwing herself into his arms with a sob of delight.

'Oh you're back! You're home! I thought you'd never come!'

Zach laughed, holding her away.

'Steady now, Queenie! D'you want to knock me over?' he asked, but there was a note in his voice Regan had not heard before and she looked at him in surprise. She had not expected a hard man like Zach to be fond of children, but the bond between him and this one was clear to see.

As he released her, the child seemed to notice Regan

for the first time and her freckled nose wrinkled in perplexity.

'Who's this?' she asked.

'This is Regan. She's coming to stay with us,' Zach told her with a smile.

The child's face fell and she scowled at Regan.

'Why?' she asked bluntly.

Regan glanced uncomfortably at Zach but he seemed unperturbed by the child's forthright manner.

'You ask too many questions, Queenie,' he told her, gently tweaking a strand of her gingery hair. 'If you don't stop it, I won't show you what I have for you.'

Her hazel eyes became round as saucers. 'What? Oh, what have you got for me?'

Zach reached into his pocket and pulled out a small, flat package.

'Open it and see,' he instructed.

All fingers and thumbs she fumbled eagerly with the wrapping, then extracted a box of home-made chocolates, each topped with a tiny sugar sweet in mauve or green.

'Oh Zach!' she squealed, her annoyance with him for bringing Regan forgotten, and he gave her hair another gentle tug.

'Off you go then, Queenie. Just don't eat them all at once, or you'll be sick and I shall have your mother after me. Understand?'

She nodded, then skipped happily off towards the house, presumably anxious to show someone the present Zach had brought her.

'Who is she?' Regan asked as she watched her go around the side of the house.

'Her parents work for us,' Zach informed her. 'Her father is our head stockman and her mother . . . her mother has been our housekeeper for more years than I care to remember.'

Since your own mother ran away to her own people, perhaps, Regan thought, remembering the story Dickon had told her on the *Maid of Morne*.

As they neared the house a shadow darkened the door, which still stood open, and framed in it Regan saw a man, as tall as Zach and broad, with a mane of snowy white hair above a face tanned to a leathery brown and eyes as piercingly blue as periwinkles. She knew him at once, without any introduction, and her heart seemed to stand still.

She wondered what he would be like, this man who had run away to sea at eleven years old and later left his ship with the same adventurous spirit to cross the Blue Mountains and become a 'squatter' sheepmaster. Knowing her own misgivings about coming to a new land even now, forty years later, when towns had been built and the land colonized, she had asked herself what calibre of man could start as he had done from nothing, and build an empire from a wilderness. But now, as she came face to face with the Irishman who had married an aboriginal girl and fathered Zach, she could see it all. Seamus Casey was every bit as imposing as her wildest imaginings had told her he would be, and she quaked inwardly at the thought of meeting him.

Zach's hand was on her wrist, however, urging her forward, and Regan's fierce pride came to her rescue. She wouldn't let him see she was afraid, this indomitable man who had conquered a harsh land and made a fortune from it. She took a small, steadying breath, squaring her shoulders and lifting her chin a fraction higher. And when the man came down the steps from the verandah she managed not to flinch, not even when she saw his arm raised towards them.

'Zach – Zach, it's good to see you, son!' It was a moment before Regan realized the arm had fallen about Zach's shoulders in a gesture of affectionate greeting that took her completely by surprise, and before she had time to recover, the piercingly blue eyes were on her, shrewd, yet oddly welcoming.

'And who is this colleen you've brought with you?' he asked in his broad Irish brogue.

Zach's arm tightened about her waist; to Regan it seemed to burn through the silk of her dress like a branding iron.

'This is Regan, Father. I met her on the ship and persuaded her to come home with me.'

The blue eyes scanned her face and caught and held her own emerald ones. Then a smile creased the leathery cheeks and he took her hands in his.

'Sure I brought you up to have good taste didn't I, my boy!' he exclaimed with a twinkle. 'She's as pretty as all the angels in Heaven. Welcome to Ballymena, Regan.'

Regan smiled, light-headed from relief. She had not expected to find a friend here in the outback, but now all her instincts warmed to this man. Adventurer he might be, hard-headed sheepmaster he certainly was. But there was kindness behind those shrewd blue eyes, as real as the feeling of strength and power that emanated from him.

'And what brought you to Australia, child, if it was not this good-for-nothing son of mine?' Seamus asked.

Regan bit her lip. 'I was emigrating with my father,' she said hesitantly.

'Your father?' Seamus looked around expectantly and Regan felt her chin quiver suddenly.

'Unfortunately he did not survive the voyage,' Zach said swiftly. 'Regan was left quite alone.'

'And so you brought her here. Well, my son, I'm glad you did. It will be good to have a pretty woman about the place.' Seamus smiled at her and Regan felt the foolish knot of tears growing in her throat. It seemed to her like a lifetime since anyone had been kind to her.

The older man led the way up the steps to the verandah, where Zach deposited the luggage, and into a spacious hall. For just a moment Regan hesitated in the doorway, gazing in awe at the marble-tiled floor and the magnificent sweeping staircase. In all her life she had never known a home of her own. Always it had been inn rooms and shared accommodation as they travelled with the players from place to place. But this majestic house had been built by Zach's father and would one day be his – and he accepted it without a second thought.

That is the difference between his world and mine, thought Regan.

A small, ginger-haired woman appeared in one of the doorways and Regan was immediately aware of the likeness to the child who had greeted them. This must be her mother, the Caseys' housekeeper, she guessed, and a moment later she was proved correct as Seamus turned to beckon her in.

'Mary – Zach has brought a guest home with him. Will you see to it a room is prepared for her and an extra place set at table.'

The woman nodded, treating Zach to a tight smile of welcome and casting a narrow, suspicious look at Regan.

'The Blue Room is always kept aired,' she offered. 'And as for food, if they're hungry after their long journey, I've some soup ready that I can make hot in ten minutes.'

'Fine – I'm ravenous!' Zach approved. 'But I expect Regan would like to freshen up first. Show her to the Blue Room, Mary, and I'll have a jug of hot water and her bag sent up.'

Regan followed the housekeeper up the sweeping staircase, wondering uncomfortably what the servants would make of her poor holdall. They would no doubt expect her to change out of the dusty travelling dress, too, but apart from her tattered white gown and the wrap Zach had purchased for her, she had nothing until the dressmaker sent out the other clothes they had ordered in Melbourne.

Oh well, they'll have to think what they please! Regan thought.

On the broad landing that overlooked the hall below, the housekeeper stopped, opening a white-painted door, and Regan found herself in a large, sunny room, tastefully furnished with solid wood and blue drapes.

'This will be your room while you're here,' the housekeeper told her shortly and once more Regan sensed the underlying hostility. Why should this woman dislike her so, she wondered, after such a brief acquaintance? She was unpopular with everyone but Seamus, it seemed.

Left alone, Regan crossed to the window. From here she could look out across the broad paddock and the drive up which they had come, to the road. And beyond it was nothing but open country, stretching as far as the eye could see. The sheer expanse of it frightened her; it trapped her just as the sea had trapped her on the *Maid of Morne*, or the bush that had closed in around the pub where she and Zach had spent the first night of their journey.

A tap at the door announced the arrival of a maid with the hot water and Regan stripped to her chemisette and drawers to wash herself and shake the dust of travel from her green tartan dress as best she could. Then, feeling more presentable, she went back down the sweeping staircase.

The hall was empty now, but she could hear voices coming from one of the adjoining rooms. She crossed the floor, her slippers making no sound on the marble tiles, then paused, looking through the half-open door at the two men. They stood together by a huge carved fireplace, each with a drink in his hand, talking earnestly together, and Regan was suddenly struck by the similarity between them. Though one had snow white hair and the other jet black, yet the family likeness was there in their bearing, too clear to be ignored, and for some reason it disturbed her oddly.

As she hesitated, her hand on the brass doorknob, Seamus looked up and saw her. At once he broke off his conversation, beckoning to her to enter.

'Don't be shy, m'voreen! Come along in and let an old man feast his eyes on you!'

'I didn't mean to interrupt,' she said, blushing. 'You must have a lot of business to discuss.'

'Sure nothing that cannot wait a little longer, for if what I hear is correct, you'll have more important things on your mind than Merino sheep, wool markets and droughts.' He smiled at her, his blue eyes very bright in his suntanned face and she stared at him, uncomprehending.

'Father!' There was a warning note in Zach's tone. But the older man was not to be deterred.

'I dare say the time will come when you'll hear more than enough of the farm business to fill your pretty head – when we begin treating you as one of the family instead of a guest,' he informed her with a twinkle. 'Now don't look so surprised. Zach has told me that he's hoping to persuade you to become his wife, and there's no mistaking I'm delighted to hear it.'

Breath caught in Regan's throat and her wide eyes flew

from Seamus to Zach. He had not moved from his careless pose by the fireplace, but it seemed to her his long
body was no longer relaxed. Since entering the house he
had removed his jacket, now she had the impression that
every muscle was taut beneath the fine linen of his shirt.
For a timeless moment his eyes held hers and her legs
seemed to turn to jelly beneath her.

So he had told his father that she was to be his bride –
no, not quite that – that he hoped to persuade her! To *per-*
suade her, after taking her by force and dragging her unwil-
ingly a hundred miles into the outback – two hundred,
maybe! Why, it was the most ironic thing she had ever
heard and she would have laughed aloud had she not been
certain that her laughter would quickly turn to tears.

As the hysteria bubbled inside her, she tore her eyes
away from Zach's and looked once more at Seamus. He
was smiling at her, quite unaware of the tumult within
her, and suddenly she was completely calm. Seamus was a
good man, strong and warm-hearted. She knew it instinctively – had done from the moment she had met him.
Supposing she was to tell him the truth of what had
happened – surely he would not stand by and see Zach
force her into marriage against her will?

Desperately she swallowed at the lump in her throat.

'Mr Casey . . .'

'Yes, m'voreen?'

She looked from father to son and back again, her heart
beating painfully. The fear of what might happen if she
spoke seemed to freeze her. She couldn't tell him – she
dared not! Who knew what kind of temper was concealed
behind that leathery countenance? Who could say how
he – or Zach – would react?

Silently she shook her head. Then, hating herself for
her cowardice, she whispered: 'I'm glad he told you.
That's all.'

The figure of the housekeeper appeared suddenly in the
doorway. How long had she stood there listening? Regan
wondered.

'Soup's ready,' she informed them briskly.

At once the tableau shattered. With an unreadable
smile, Zach levered himself away from the fireplace, refil-

ling his glass, and as if oblivious of any tension, Seamus tucked a hand beneath Regan's elbow.

'I do hope you'll accept his proposal, my dear,' he told her solemnly. 'As sole heir to this property, it's more than time that Zach settled down, so it is!'

CHAPTER TEN

A week after Regan arrived at Ballymena the bullocky delivered the rest of the dresses which Zach had ordered for her in Melbourne, and to her relief she was able to change out of the green plaid carriage dress. Zach had explained away the absence of any baggage by saying it had been lost on the voyage and Regan was grateful to him, though she doubted that anyone but Mary Mitchell, the housekeeper, would even have noticed.

Considering the size of the homestead, Regan had been surprised to find that apart from Zach and Seamus, the only other occupants were the Mitchells and two servants, Maggie and Kathy, who kept to their own quarters. The stockmen and the other workers, it seemed, lived in the single-storied dwellings at the back of the main house and Regan rarely set eyes on them in those first few days when she revelled in the luxury of a room of her own, a soft feather bed, and as much hot water for bathing as she could wish for – providing no drought came to lower the water level in the huge storage tanks so much as to force economy on her.

'Think yourself lucky we had some rain this winter,' Mary Mitchell told her shortly. 'It isn't always like this, you know. In this country you seldom get just what you need of a thing – it's more often too little or too much.'

'I suppose you could say that of a lot of things,' Regan suggested, but the housekeeper only pulled an ill-tempered face.

'If you say so,' she returned, 'but I don't think you'll

find Australia the bed of roses you expected it to be.'

Regan, brushing her hair in front of the mirror, bit hard at her lips but said nothing.

Why does she have to be so unpleasant all the time? she wondered. It's as if she thinks she'd do herself a mischief by smiling or speaking a friendly word.

But a moment or two later, she was given an insight into Mary's hostility.

'Being mistress here won't be as easy as you think, either,' Mary said nastily, and with a shock Regan realized what lay behind the housekeeper's resentment.

As the only woman in the house she had virtually been mistress herself since Zach's mother had 'gone walkabout', living in the homestead with her family and running things with next to no interference from the Casey men. But now that Regan had come, she feared things would change.

She doesn't know I've less right than her to decide anything here, Regan thought bitterly. She doesn't know I'm worth no more than a pile of sovereigns to Zach – or a saloon girl to be on hand when he needs a little light relief. And I suppose I should be grateful that she doesn't . . .

'Have you decided yet when the wedding's to be?' Mary asked, somehow managing to make the question sound like an accusation, and Regan swallowed at the lump of nervousness that rose in her throat at the very mention of the word.

Since the night she had arrived, neither Zach nor Seamus had raised the subject of the marriage and she did not know why. In fact, in a strange way the silence worried her.

It was as though they were playing cat and mouse with her, she thought, and again she cursed herself for not having spoken up and thrown herself on Seamus's mercy. He had been so kind that night – and still was, though he seemed to have little time for talking with her now. The only time she saw him was at dinner and in the hour afterwards and then he had other things on his mind. Business came first with him, for all his remarks about enjoying the company of a woman, and she guessed the habit of years was too strong for him to break.

Besides, Zach had been away from Ballymena for a long time and there was much for him to catch up on, as well as reporting back to his father regarding all the business deals he had arranged in England with those who wanted to buy their wool.

Regan also found herself wondering if Zach had suggested to Seamus that it would be unwise to question her about her past, for he never mentioned the subject at all, though she guessed he must be full of curiosity as to what sort of girl his son intended taking for a wife. Although she was glad not to have to talk about Thomas and the nightmare happenings aboard the *Maid of Morne*, it meant she got no further opportunity to brave Zach's anger and beg Seamus not to allow her to be forced into a marriage she did not want.

It's like being a caged bird, thought Regan. Physically I'm better off than ever before. I'm well-fed, well-clothed and comfortable. But the door of the cage is firmly closed, there's no escape, and knowing it makes all the luxury seem tawdry.

Another week went by. Still no mention had been made of setting a wedding date and Regan began to wonder if Zach had given up the idea just as she had been forced to abandon the vain hope that Richard might have eventually arrived in Melbourne and found the messages Zach had left for him. At first she had jumped every time she heard the galloping hooves of an approaching horse, running to the window and half-expecting to see Richard's slim figure in the saddle. Even when the bullocky brought the dresses, her first thought had been that he might have some mail too, and her pleasure in opening the boxes had been somewhat marred because he had not. But at the end of two weeks she was forced to the conclusion it was hopeless. If Richard had not come looking for her by now, he never would. The realization was like a lead weight inside her and, coming as it did at just the same time as the novelty of having nothing to do was beginning to pall, it was almost more than she could bear. Regan decided that if she did not get out of the house for a time she would go crazy.

It was a fine spring afternoon when the sun turned the

grey bark of the ghost gums to liquid silver and dappled the lush lawns that were never starved of water from the big tanks, even in the harshest drought.

As she went downstairs from her room the house seemed silent and empty. For once there was no sight of Mary Mitchell bustling about, no tuneless singing coming from the kitchen as Maggie and Kathy went about their work, no buzz of business talk from the study or the laughter of young Queenie and the other workers' children who were her friends.

She pushed open the door and stood for a moment on the verandah, looking out at all the space that awed her so. Then, unnoticed by anyone from the house, she went down the steps and around the corner of the building.

The stables must be here somewhere, she knew, and she was filled with a longing for the company of a creature that would neither judge her nor try to own her. Once, long ago, she and Thomas had lodged at a farm, and she could still remember the comforting smells, the still-warm fresh eggs and the way a wet nose could push into you with rough friendliness. The memory was a comfortable one and it seemed to her, oddly, that if she could recapture it she could once again feel as she had done as a child.

At the rear of the house was a dusty yard and there, sure enough, were the stables. Feeling like an intruder she began to cross to them, but she had gone but a few steps when Zach's voice arrested her, making her jump from both shock and sudden, irrational guilt.

'Regan! You're not thinking of trying to run away again, I hope!' he shot at her.

She turned quickly, colour flooding her cheeks. He looked so arrogant standing there, hands on hips, and a faintly amused expression on his dark face! But for all that she could not deny he was very handsome. The open-necked shirt and buckskin breeches he wore instead of a suit at Ballymena accented the rippling power of his lithe body and noticing it made her suddenly shy in his presence.

'I – I was just looking around . . .' she faltered.

He nodded brusquely, but his black eyes were still suspicious.

'Just as long as you're aware of the dangers of taking a horse out alone here. This isn't England, you know.'

Her chin came up. Why did he always make her so defensively defiant, she wondered.

'I wouldn't dream of it. I can hardly ride at all. But I wish I could! I'm bored out of my mind sitting in my room all day with nothing to do.'

A surprised expression crossed Zach's face.

'My apologies, Regan,' he said. 'My days have been so full of business since our return I hadn't stopped to think that yours were empty. Would you like to learn to ride? It would be very useful to you, living here.'

In the stables she could hear the horses jostling together, as anxious to be out as she was, and excitement bubbled in her.

'Oh I'd love to!' she cried, her eyes shining. 'I've always wanted to ride! But we were never in one place long enough for me to learn – and we usually stayed in towns anyway, where the cobbles are hard for a beginner to fall on!'

Zach smiled, enjoying her pleasure. She was always a pretty picture, but when she was happy her face seemed to glow, making her truly beautiful.

'Then learn you shall,' he promised. 'I'll teach you myself. But you'll need a riding habit and boots. We'll send to Melbourne for them. The dressmaker will still have your measurements. What colour would take your fancy?'

'Oh, green!' She clapped her hands together, picturing it in her mind's eye. 'Rich green velvet!'

He laughed. 'It's all green with you, isn't it, my sweet? It's no wonder Father took to you at once – you remind him of the Emerald Isle he left behind. But it does suit your colouring, I must admit. Now.' He took a small leather pouch from his pocket and drew out his watch – a heavy gold timepiece with the most unusual markings on the face that Regan had ever seen. 'I've an hour to spare before dinner – perhaps it's time I showed you around a little. We'll take a buggy out, if you'd like that.'

'Oh, yes!' She could no more conceal her eagerness than she could have grown wings, and he strode into the yard calling to Tommy, the stable lad, to harness a horse to the buggy.

Hardly had the instruction been issued than it was done – Regan had noticed already how the servants leapt into action when one of the Caseys spoke. Then Zach handed her up into the buggy, took the reins, and they were off, through the grounds of the house, past kitchen gardens already being planted with spring vegetables, and through sweeping orchards where orange and fig trees grew alongside the more familiar apple trees.

'Is all this yours?' she asked before she could stop herself.

Zach laughed, but there was pride in his voice as he replied.

'This is only a tiny part of it. My father's land stretches as far as you can see.'

She caught her breath, and not only at the vastness of the land. There were so many things to see, more startling even than the first sights she had glimpsed from the coach – a lyre bird perched on a tree fern, displaying his beautiful tail while he mimicked the cries of other birds one after the other; an emu, almost as tall as she herself, running as fast as its spindly legs would carry it; a kangaroo, baby in pouch, sitting on its haunches at the roadside and watching the buggy pass with alert curiosity. Zach pointed them all out to her, gratified by her interest in the land he loved. When they reached a thick grove of eucalypts he reined in the horse.

'Well, Regan, and what do you think of this new country?' he asked.

She shook her head, unable to find words to express her wonder. After the days of being confined to the homestead it was like being turned loose suddenly in paradise.

'You like it?' he pressed her, jumping down to secure the reins to a dead tree trunk. 'Come down then, and set foot on a little bit of the real Australia!'

She laughed, giving him her hand, and as he swung her down the nearness of her suddenly made his senses swim. Her hair, sweet-smelling as new-mown hay, brushed his chin, and beneath his steadying hand her waist was taut and neat, making him ache to crush her to him.

For a moment he stood there holding her and his breath came hard as he fought to control the urge to throw her down on the brush and cover her body with his, discovering and possessing as he had done aboard the *Maid of Morne*. The blood sang within him as each muscle and nerve remembered the curve of breast and buttock, the soft thighs and the way her sweetness had enfolded him. And her face, laughing up at him now, seemed to taunt him with a vision of how it could be if only she would come to him willingly.

But even as he looked down at her, feeling the desire mount within him, he knew this was not the time or the place. That last time he had taken her by force he had vowed to himself that never again would it be so, and it was a vow he intended to keep. There had been a reason behind his bringing her here and it was not to fall upon her again and ravish her – as he would do if she did not soon remove her hand from his chest, or if he did not remove it for her . . .

Abruptly he turned away, only keeping her other hand in his, and as the spell shattered it seemed she suddenly became aware of him as he was of her. She stiffened, drawing back slightly, so that her fingers tugged at his hand, and her voice was full of apprehension.

'Why have we got down?'

He looked round at her, and as he saw the naked fear in her face his desire was suddenly laced with anger, irrational and destructive. It was his own fault that she feared him so and he knew it. Yet it was at her that he struck out blindly.

'I wanted to talk to you about the arrangements for our wedding,' he said harshly. 'I thought it best we should discuss it away from prying ears.'

Her heart seemed to stop. He had not given up the idea then!

'So you can try to *persuade* me, no doubt!' she flashed at him. 'That was a beautiful touch for your father's benefit, I thought. *You* should have been an actor, Zach, not me. My admiration for your gift of pretence is unbounded!'

A muscle tightened in his cheek, but he left the charges go unanswered.

'Father has been pressing me to set the date,' he went on smoothly. 'He's most anxious it should be soon.'

To her annoyance, she felt foolish tears pricking behind her eyes.

'And you want it to be soon, too, I suppose.'

His gaze held hers; if he had noticed the tears, he gave no sign.

'Yes, Regan, I do,' he said softly.

For a moment she stared back at him, disconcerted by the depth of his look, and emotions she could hardly understand flooded and ebbed within her. She was trembling with the strength of them – her hands and her legs, her throat and her stomach. Even her spine felt as if it had turned to liquid. Somehow she controlled herself and her voice, when it came, was low and harsh from the effort.

'And I suppose what I want doesn't matter at all.'

His other hand caught hers and he swung her round to face him.

'You're wrong, Regan,' he said urgently. 'Very, very wrong. What you want matters a great deal to me.'

The tears stung more sharply. Angrily she blinked them away.

'The only reason you're interested in what I want, Zach Casey, is because it hurts your pride that I *don't* want you. You can't bear to take me knowing I care for someone else. You can't stand to have me despise you. Well, I'll tell you something. If you really care what I want, you'll let me go!'

'Regan . . .' There was a strange expression on Zach's dark face, and if she had not known better, she might almost have taken it for one of uncertainty. But that, she knew, was ridiculous. Zach was never uncertain, never less than confident in everything he did. With supreme arrogance he had changed the whole course of her life and now . . . now, she wanted only to hurt him as she had been hurt.

'What would your father say if he knew the way you've used me?' she demanded. 'He'd never stand for it, I'm sure. I almost told him the truth about his precious son the first night we came here!'

'Then why didn't you?' Zach asked coldly.

She stared at him, taken aback. It was the same question she had asked herself over and over again, and as yet she had found no answer to it.

'Why didn't you?' he repeated harshly and when she did not reply, his hands slid to her wrists, pulling her so close to him that he could feel the uneven, rapid beat of her heart through the fine fabric of his shirt. 'I'll tell you why not, my sweet. You didn't say anything because you didn't choose to say anything. Because whether you know it or not, you want me as much as I want you.'

She could not answer. Breath seemed trapped in her lungs and she was frozen by fear. Yet within the ice it seemed something stirred – something sharp and exciting like a fine-honed sword with a point of fire at the tip of its tempered blade . . .

For endless moments it seemed she hung, suspended in time, and the only realities were his hands on her wrists, holding them so tightly she feared they would snap, and the hard muscles of his stomach and thighs pressing against her and bringing the nerves of her own body to strange, tingling awareness. If her pulse quickened and the blood ran faster through her veins she did not notice it, any more than she noticed the horse pawing impatiently at its tether. For Regan, it seemed that the world outside the circle of his arms ceased to exist – even the air about them was still and heavy with the sounds of the bush muted into an indistinguishable symphony.

Then, suddenly, the silence was shattered by a mocking laugh. Shocked and horrified, Regan tore herself away, and Zach, though his first instinct had been to swear roundly at the interruption, could not help laughing at her obvious embarrassment.

'Who is it?' she cried. 'Why are you laughing?'

'Oh Regan, did you think someone was spying on us?' he chuckled. 'It was only a kookaburra.'

'A kookaburrah?' she repeated.

'A bird.'

'Oh!' She felt foolish suddenly – and something more

than that. A few moments ago her senses had reeled beneath an onslaught of strange emotions and Zach had been at the centre of them – Zach, who had caused her father's untimely death, who had taken her virginity with cold arrogance, and who still believed he owned her. How could she, even for a single second, have felt anything but hatred for him? To do so was to betray both her father and herself – and renege on the vow she had made at Thomas's deathbed. Zach Casey was conceited, cruel and despicable – he might be the devil himself, and she must never forget it.

'Don't worry, you'll get used to the bush in time,' Zach continued, seemingly unaware of the turmoil of her thoughts. 'And now tell me, Regan, what am I to say to my father? That he will get his wish for a wedding before shearing?'

She stared at him, unable to answer, and he put an arm around her shoulders.

'For sheep farmers, the time when we take the wool is the busiest period of our year. Can I say we will be married by then?'

She caught her lip between her teeth. The tears were unbearably close now – she felt they would choke her. But the last thing she wanted was that he would know it.

'Oh, do as you please!' she cried. Then, with a swish of her skirts, she turned and climbed back into the buggy.

The drive back to the homestead was a silent one, as different from the joyous ride out as anything could be. Zach used the whip on the horse a good deal more than Regan thought necessary, and as soon as they drew up in the yard she climbed down, not waiting for Zach to help her, and hurried back into the house.

In her room, she threw herself down on her bed, but the tears had been kept back for too long. Though she now longed for release they refused to flow and the hot anger burned within her more brightly than ever. To give vent to her feelings, she crossed to the heavy oak wardrobe, threw open the door and took down the beautiful dresses Zach had bought her, one by one, tossing them into a pile

on the floor. The hats followed, and the gloves and petticoats. Suddenly it seemed they symbolized his possession of her, and had it not been for some tiny barb of
warning within, she would have stamped on them and
torn them into shreds. As it was, she satisfied her burst of
defiance by taking off the dress she was wearing and
adding it to the pile. Then, instead, she put on the white
gown she had owned before she had ever known Zach.

It was grimy now. It had not been put away as carefully
as the others and the dust of the outback seemed to have
settled into its frills and flounces. But she did not care.

Let them think what they like – tonight I'll show them
no one owns me! she thought furiously.

She shook the dress out and slipped into it, pinning the
shoulder that Zach had ripped well enough to hide the
tear from those who did not know what had happened to
it, yet not so much that it could fail to remind Zach. Then
she brushed her hair into tantalizing ringlets and pinched
more colour into her already flushed cheeks.

At last she was ready. With one last contemptuous kick
at the pile of dresses, she swept out of the room and down
the stairs.

Zach and Seamus were already in the dining room, she
could hear their voices clearly. For a moment her courage almost failed her, then lifting her head high she
marched in to join them. There was a moment's stunned
silence, and she knew she had achieved the effect she
desired. She caught a glimpse of Zach's face, dark and
furious, and heard the clink of crystal on wood as he set
down his glass of rum abruptly. Then he was blotted out of
her line of vision as Seamus came towards her.

'Zach's told me the news, m'voreen, and you look like a
bride already, see if you don't!' His arms were open and
the smile on his face brought her heart into her throat.
'You know, don't you, that you've made an old man very
happy?'

And suddenly the tears were there again, aching in her
throat. She stood helplessly, ashamed of the spectacle she
had made of herself, wishing desperately that she could
run back upstairs and pick up all her dresses before one of
the maids should find them, and put one of them on so as

to face Zach and his father with dignity if not defiance. But it was too late. To run from the room now would be an admission of defeat so enormous it would be worse than to stay and brazen it out.

'Zach said it would please you,' she murmured stiffly.

Dinner was a miserable meal. She could feel Zach's accusing eyes on her and every mouthful seemed to stick in her throat. When it was over she longed to escape, but Zach had not finished with her yet. He sat back easily in his chair, rum glass in hand, eyes narrowed to slits behind the smoke that curled upwards from his cigar.

'Seeing Regan in the dress she wore the first time I set eyes on her has reminded me what a fine singer she is,' he drawled. 'Will you not favour us with a song or two to mark the day for the special one it is, my sweet?'

Regan stiffened, the last thing she wanted was to sing tonight.

'You forget, I have no one to accompany me,' she protested.

From behind the screen of cigar smoke, Zach's gaze held hers.

'I'll buy you a piano for a wedding present and you can learn to accompany yourself,' he offered. 'But for the moment, I'm sure there's no need for anything but your own sweet voice.'

She bit her lip. 'I – I don't think I could . . .'

'Come now, we are not a critical audience,' Seamus urged her. 'You need not feel shy.'

'Oh, Regan is not shy.' Zach's voice was hard, but she knew why. She had hurt him and now he was hurting her in return. 'She sang to a saloon full of passengers on the *Maid of Morne*. Come now Regan, do not disappoint us!'

She lifted her chin. There was nothing for it – she would have to sing. Though if her voice came out through the tightness of her throat, it would be nothing short of a miracle.

'What shall I sing?' she asked in a whisper.

'Anything,' Seamus urged her, but Zach interrupted.

'I have a special request. The first time I heard you sing, it was a folk song, telling a story of how faint heart never won the fair lady. I thought it most . . . apt.'

Her lips felt dry as autumn leaves. Nervously she moistened them.

'You mean "The Flowers in the Valley".'

He smiled, but it was not a nice smile. 'Yes. That's it.'

Slowly Regan got to her feet and moved to the centre of the room. Her dress dragged limply behind her and one of the carelessly pinned ringlets escaped to hang loosely on her cheek. But she was aware of nothing but Zach's eyes watching her, driving her on. Then, taking a deep breath, she began to sing.

Nervousness had done nothing to mar her sweet voice. It rose clear and bell-like in the quiet room:

Oh there was a woman and she was a widow
Fair are the flowers in the valley
With a daughter as fair as a fresh, sunny
meadow
The Red, the Green and the Yellow . . . .

On and on she sang, memory taking her back to that other night when she and her father had been together for almost the last time. On and on, while recollections of all that had befallen her since then flashed into her mind like pictures in a magic lantern show. At last she stopped, and Seamus began to appluad, but Zach did not join in. Instead his voice cut into the daze of her thoughts, harsh and domineering.

'You haven't finished yet, Regan. The verses you have sung are about the knights who failed to win the lady because of their weak-kneed indecision. There is another – do you not know it?'

'I . . .' she faltered, dumbstruck by his cruelty, and he uncurled his long form from the chair and crossed to where she stood.

'I can see I shall have to teach it to you, so that you can sing the song in its entirety,' he sneered. Then, laying his hand about her shaking shoulders, he began to sing in a fine, baritone voice:

There came a Knight, in yellow was he
Fair are the flowers in the valley.
'My bride, my queen, thou must with me!'

The Red, the Green and the Yellow.
The Harp, the Lute, the Pipe, the Flute, the Cymbal
Sweet goes the treble Violin.
With blushes red: 'I come,' she said,
'Farewell to the flowers of the valley.

CHAPTER ELEVEN

For all Seamus's hopes and plans, it was not possible for the marriage to take place before shearing time.

Father Peter O'Rourke, who would have to conduct the ceremony, was laid up with a severe bout of the fever that recurred time and again since he had first contracted it from convicts in Parramatta in his early days in the colony, and could not hope to stand the day and a half's journey to Ballymena.

'But at least it gives us time to arrange a decent wedding for you, my child,' Seamus told her. 'Sure, it's the most important day of your life, and you won't be wanting to see it slip away with nothing special to mark it for you.'

Regan said nothing, and he took her silence for acquiescence, turning to Zach with a list of instructions so long it made her head spin.

In the short time that was left before the sheds came alive for the wool taking that was the climax of a year's work on Ballymena, invitations were issued to the few neighbours Regan had met and many she had not, a wedding dress was ordered from the Melbourne dressmaker along with the riding habit Zach had promised her, and Mary Mitchell was placed in charge of overseeing the arrangements.

Mary was still as short with Regan as she had been when she first arrived, treating her with the same suspicion as she did the sun-downers who called at the homestead looking for work in the shearing sheds, and young Queenie, too, was sullen and unfriendly in her presence, though Regan suspected that might be because she had put an end to the little girl's own childish dreams of Zach.

The two seemed very close, in fact, in Regan's eyes, almost the only time Zach appeared human was when he was with the child, treating her with an endless patience and good humour that was lacking in his dealing with the rest of the household.

The waiting period was a strange, unreal time for Regan, when her body moved in obedience to Seamus and Zach's commands while her mind searched helplessly for a way to escape the inevitable.

If only I could ride! she thought. I'd take my chances with the outback in spite of what Zach said. If I followed the track I'd be bound to reach *somewhere* eventually.

And then what? The unanswerable question. What could a girl alone do in a strange country – a girl trained for nothing but the stage?

Unless . . .

Unless we were not the only ones to think of trying to form a theatrical company here, thought Regan. If I could get to a city maybe there would be a troupe playing there and I could join them.

But still she came back to the same insurmountable barrier. She was miles from a city, and with no way of getting to one. The nearest town was Robertson, a half day's drive away, and it would be a pretty poor company who played in such a place, she imagined. On the two occasions Zach had taken her back there, shopping for various provisions, she had been struck by the rowdy, lawless feel in its streets, and she was sure that when gold miners were in town, brawls would be two-a-penny and nobody willing or able to stop them, with the possible exception of Adelaide Jackson. She might be more than a match for any drunken lout, Regan suspected, and there was a story passed from mouth to mouth concerning an infamous night at the hotel when a group of men had set upon a barman they thought was cheating them.

By the time Adelaide came on the scene they had half-killed the unfortunate man, so the story went, and the Commercial Hotel was in uproar. But she had fired her revolver into the air until the fighting stopped, and then stood at the top of the steps like a tight-lipped schoolmarm while they shuffled, shame-faced, past her.

Yes, she was a hard woman, Regan thought, and in some ways a fascinating one. But, most of all, she was not a woman to tangle with lightly.

The days passed, and Regan's lethargy grew. Now that shearing had begun she hardly saw Zach or Seamus, so busy were they, and she was glad when Mary Mitchell suggested she should help her in the kitchen with the preparation of meals for the men who were working from dawn to dusk in the sheds. At least it meant her days were occupied, and when she fell into bed at night she was exhausted enough for sleep to come easily. But however tired she was, nothing seemed to stop the nightmares that came too often now – nightmares when she relived in ghastly detail the night Thomas had been shot, and all that had followed.

Strangely enough the nightmares came more frequently now than they had at the time – as if then she had been numbed and only now could her subconscious mind go over and over the dreadful sequence of events, as if it were a long-running drama in which she was forced to play the leading role again and again.

It's ever since he made me sing that song, she thought, lying in bed one night with the tears still wet on her cheeks after waking, sobbing, from the nightmare. Standing to sing 'The Flowers in the Valley' that evening when she had foolishly worn her old white dress had somehow brought it all to the surface and now she seemed unable to forget.

As the shearing progressed, the days were already growing longer and warmer, so that sometimes as she worked in the big kitchen the heat from the oven was almost more than Regan could bear. And it was not yet high summer!

'It'll be strange to have a hot Christmas,' she commented to Mary Mitchell, but the housekeeper merely shrugged.

'It's usual here,' she said shortly, and Regan was forced to bite back the comment that rose to her lips.

Would Mary treat her so if she knew how little she wanted to be her mistress? She doubted it. But better that she should take her for grabbing adventuress than that she should know the truth. That would be a savage blow to Regan's pride indeed and she was grateful to Zach for allowing her to retain her dignity, if nothing else.

But still, in the quiet of the night, she wished feverishly that there was some way she could escape before the inevitable happened and she was bound to him forever.

When his fever had passed, Father Peter rode out to the homestead to make arrangements for the ceremony and as he talked with her in the shade of the pepper trees, Regan wondered if she dare confide in him. He seemed a kindly man and not as unworldly as some of the priests she had known back home in England. But what could he do to help her? He would refuse to conduct the marriage service, she supposed, but if Seamus and Zach then threw her out of Ballymena she would be without a roof over her head as surely as the gold miners in their pathetic camps. Just remembering the one she had caught sight of from the coach was enough to set her shivering in spite of the heat of the sun.

So once more she bit back the words and it was only when Father Peter had gone again that she gave vent to her feelings, running up to her room and beating at the pillows on her bed as if by pummelling them she was somehow pummelling the hateful Zach Casey, who kept her prisoner here, yet hardly seemed to have the time to so much as speak to her.

But it'll be a different story when we're married, she thought, and a shiver of dread ran through her as she remembered the way he had taken her on the *Maid of Morne* and would doubtless take her again and again once the law was on his side. Then, it had been rape. With a ring on her finger and the marriage lines in a drawer beside the bed, it would be wifely duty. But to Regan it seemed there was little difference.

The wedding took place a week after shearing was done on a warm November day when bees hummed in the wistaria that covered the verandah and the house was full of the scent of a thousand flowers.

The big, sunny drawing room where the ceremony was

to take place had been decked with roses and when the windows that opened onto the verandah were thrown wide, the perfume of wallflowers wafted in to mingle with them and form a heady pot-pourri.

Guests began arriving from early morning on – the Daveys, a family from a neighbouring property who had come in spite of Mrs Davey's advanced pregnancy; Adelaide Jackson, driving herself out in her neat little buggy, and the Trenoweths, Dickon and Jud.

It was the first time Regan had set eyes on Jud and knowing him to be a former convict she could not help but be curious. When she heard their horses trot up the drive she went to the window to look out and saw a man as different to Dickon as two brothers could be. His face was heavier than Dickon's, and harder, and he did not have Dickon's everlasting smile. His body was thicker, too, but perhaps the difference in their ages accounted for that. The only similarity they shared was the colour of their hair and their eyes – and from this distance colour of eyes was not something Regan could have been sure of.

They stood beneath her window, talking to Zach, and once Jud looked up suddenly almost as if he had sensed she was watching them. She drew back sharply, but not before she had noticed a scar on his face running from the highest point of his cheekbone to the corner of his mouth. Yes, Jud looked a dangerous man right enough, and she found herself wondering just what his crime had been. For all that Zach had said it was not the thing to question a man's past here, Regan thought she would prefer to know what manner of company she was expected to keep; for although it was twenty years or so since he had been transported, she could not believe any man could change his nature that much.

Though not all criminals are caught and punished, she thought, viciously tugging a comb through the tangle of her red-gold hair. There will be those in the same room guilty of acts for which they will never be brought to justice! Dickon, whose revolver had been the cause of her father's death, would be one. And there would be another, even more guilty than he . . .

At last it was time to prepare for the ceremony. The

bullocky had delivered Regan's wedding gown, made by
the seamstress in Melbourne, just a few days before, and
when she was bathed, Maggie came to help her dress in it.
So excited was the maid she would willingly have bathed
her mistress too, but the weeks aboard the *Maid of Morne*
when she had been denied any privacy had left their mark
on Regan and now she was her own mistress she lost no
time in sending the disgruntled Maggie away while she let
the warm water ease some of the tension out of her body.

Usually this was one of the luxuries she enjoyed most,
pampering herself with the scented soap and gaining a
sensuous enjoyment from the feel of the water trickling
over her skin, but today it was marred by the knowledge
that the preparation was not only for herself, but also for
Zach. Tonight her freshly washed body would be his
pleasure. His hands would linger on the delicately
perfumed curves and explore her most secret places. Tonight, he truly would possess her, body and soul.

But no, she thought sharply. *Not* soul. Never that. He
could take her body, but he could not make her love him.

The thought gave her courage and she stood up abruptly, towelling her rosy body dry and slipping into clean
undergarments before summoning Maggie again. Then,
when the maid had brushed her hair into shining ringlets,
she helped her into the ivory silk dress and stood back to
admire her mistress, eyes shining with excitement.

'Oh you look lovely, Mum!' she murmured, and as
Regan moved around so as to see herself in the looking
glass, she too was forced to catch her breath.

Could this really be her, decked as a bride? Not even
the lack of radiance in her face could detract from the look
of her.

She was ready with just a few minutes to spare before
Seamus came up, tapping on the door.

'Since you have no father to give you away, sure I'll do
it myself,' he had told her when arrangements were being
made, and she had been able to think only of the irony of
his words.

But now, unexpectedly, she was glad to see him. He
was the one person in this God-forsaken place who had
treated her with kindness. If she had to go down the stairs

and marry Zach at all, then she would be glad to have the arm of the snowy-maned Irishman to lean on.

When Maggie opened the door to him he stood for a moment looking at Regan, his blue eyes very bright in his weathered face.

'My, but it's a picture you are!' he told her at last. 'This is not the first time I've been thinking that if I was a younger man, Zach would have to fight for you, and that's a fact. As it is, I can only say I'll be the proudest father in all Australia today, with a daughter such as you coming into my family.'

Regan swallowed at the lump that rose in her throat. What she would have given to have her own dear father here! But then, if that were possible, she would not be here at all . . .

'Thank you,' she said quietly to Seamus.

He smiled. 'Sure, it's my pleasure. Now, if you're ready, we'd best go down. The priest is all ready for you, the guests are waiting, and so is your bridegroom. As for young Queenie, it's all we can do to stop her turning the house upside down with her excitement. She'd a child's notion that Zach would be waiting to wed her when she was grown, and I thought it would be a while before she'd forgive you for stealing him from her. But sure, the thought of a wedding was more than she could resist!'

Regan returned his smile. His cheerful chatter had eased the emotion of the moment for her and she was able to take his arm with dignity. But as they went together down the sweeping staircase and she saw Zach's dark figure waiting for her, it all returned in a rush so that her legs seemed to falter beneath her.

I can't go through with it! she thought in panic. But Seamus's hand was beneath her elbow, urging her on and automatically, like one in a dream, she took the last few steps.

Heads turned to look at her and Father Peter cleared his throat in readiness to begin. But to Regan the only reality in this unreal world was Zach, waiting for her in the centre of the room. As she drew level he turned to look at her and the expression on his lean face was guarded. But the black eyes held hers, seeming to bore into the very depths of her, and she felt the hot colour rising in her cheeks.

Why must he look at her like that – why? Was it not enough that he had what he wanted – forcing her into a corner so that he could not only possess her, but deceive all his friends and neighbours into thinking she was a willing bride?

Bitterness rose in her throat like gall. But Father Peter had begun the words of the marriage service and as she listened to them the feeling of unreality washed over her again, swamping her senses. The voices seemed to her as indistinct as the humming of the bees in the wistaria outside the window – Father Peter's light and melodious, as if he was constantly singing with some unseen choir; Zach's deep, low and firm. And it was only when the silence had stretched into long seconds and a gentle hand touched her arm that she realized it was her turn, and they were waiting for her to make her vows.

Panic began again and she wished she could turn and run. But instead she heard her own voice echoing the priest's, reciting after him the phrases that had made girls into wives for hundreds of years. Then her hand was between Zach's and he was easing a ring onto her finger – a narrow golden band that slid comfortably over the knuckle. In a daze she looked down at it, symbol of her slavery, and around her the room swam once more.

Voices, faces, heat and scent merged into one dizzying whole, lapping at her consciousness like the waves of the ocean. A sudden chill shivered across her skin and she felt her legs begin to tremble. As if from a long way off she heard Father Peter pronouncing them man and wife, but the mists were rising to envelop her.

I mustn't swoon – not here, not now! she thought, and her trembling fingers caught in desperation at Zach's sleeve. Then her knees buckled beneath her and she was falling, falling into the dark depths, aware only dimly of the gasps of the assembled company and the strength of the arms that came round her, catching her up and holding her. The room moved again, not swaying now, but jolting, as if it had grown legs, and then she was lying on something soft but firm and fingers were moving at her throat. Even in her semi-conscious state she knew it was Zach and she tried to raise a hand to stop him. She couldn't let him undress her here and now – there were people about – she could hear the muttering swell of their voices! But her hand refused to answer her command. It lay lifeless beside her and the fingers went relentlessly on, loosening the neck of her dress. She felt a cold, wet pressure on her forehead and a woman's voice rang through her ears like a bell muffled for a peal of mourning.

'She's fainted, that's all. Your English rose can't put up with the heat like we natural-born Australians, Zach.'

It was Adelaide, even half-conscious as she was Regan knew that, and recognized the sarcasm in her tone. With a tremendous effort she opened her eyes and saw them towering above her, but for the moment they were looking not at her but at each other, so that she had the strangest impression that she did not exist for them.

'Careful, Adelaide!' Zach's voice was heavy. 'Regan is my wife now, remember.'

'How could I forget? But I am afraid *you'll* wish to before long. She's not the one for you, Zach.'

'And you think you are? Adelaide, we've been over this before. It would never have worked. You have the saloon and I . . .'

Breath caught in Regan's throat and the small sound was enough. Zach broke off in mid-sentence, looking sharply down at her. His dark eyes were narrowed, his expression unreadable. Even if she had been in full possession of all her senses she would not have been able to tell what his words had meant.

Drunkenly she struggled to sit up and he eased her back again.

'Lie still, now. Maggie's fetching smelling salts – if she can find any. They'll help you.'

'I'm sorry I can't be of assistance, but smelling salts are not a thing I have any use for,' Adelaide remarked in a hard, superior tone, and Regan wished heartily she had the strength to get up and slap her beautiful painted face. She was impossible, this woman, as arrogant and hateful as Zach. Weak tears filled Regan's eyes, though she hated herself for them.

'I'm sorry,' she whispered, and Zach bent over her, brushing a ringlet off her cheek.

'Hush now, love. There's not a thing to worry about. Ah, here's Maggie now. Have you got the salts, Maggie?'

'No, Sir, there's not a bottle in the house. But the master sent this. He said t'would do Miss Regan more good than all the smelling salts in the world.' She produced a spirit bottle from the folds of her apron, and Regan's stomach turned at the very thought.

Brandy! The smell of it instantly took her back to the night her father had been shot, with all its attendant horrors, and the taste – it was like liquid fire in her empty stomach. But she sipped it as he told her to, listening all the while to Maggie's senseless chatter.

"Twas the water too hot for you, Miss Regan. I should've cooled it more. The moment I saw the flush of your skin I knew you'd overdone it. And the heat and the excitement . . .'

With an effort Regan raised herself. She was uncomfortably conscious now of Adelaide's scornful gaze and she wondered if it was being echoed by the other guests. Were they thinking as she was that Zach had taken a bride unworthy of him? Unwilling she might be, but her fierce pride shrank from being thought a weak-kneed ninny.

'I'll be all right now,' she said firmly and summoning all her willpower to control her still-wobbly legs she insisted on returning to the big, sunny drawing room and the anxious assembled guests.

The remainder of the day passed in a blur of sound, colour and scent, and it was evening before the guests left and an exhausted Regan was able to escape their congratulations and advice. But as she went up the broad curving staircase, leaving Zach to drink a last glass of rum with Seamus, she was all too aware that the greatest ordeal was only just beginning.

While the wedding party had been in progress, Maggie had moved Regan's things from the Blue Room to the large bedroom she was to share with Zach, and now the maid stood waiting at the head of the stairs, unable to conceal her delight in being the one to help Regan prepare for her wedding night.

'Here we are, Mum!' she announced, throwing open a door to reveal a light, airy room in the centre of which stood a big, four-poster bed. 'I've set everything out ready for you and I ironed every crease from your nightgown myself. By the time I've finished with you, you'll be every bit as beautiful as you were this morning.'

Regan managed a wary smile. More than anything she wanted to be left alone, but she knew Maggie would never forgive her if she dismissed her immediately, and she allowed the maid to unfasten her dress, help her out of it and her undergarments and slip the nightgown over her head. Then she forced herself to sit still on the low stool while Maggie combed and curled her hair before the dressing table mirror. But it was not her own lovely image she looked at while Maggie's deft fingers twisted the red-gold ringlets. Instead her eyes were drawn and held by the reflection of the huge bed that seemed to dominate the room, and her mouth became dry with fear as she thought of the night that lay before her and the indignities she would suffer at Zach's hands.

Dear God, what had it come to, that she was bound to submit time and again to a man she despised – and not only tonight, but every other night for the rest of her life if he so chose. And not only nights, if his wild explosion of passion on the *Maid of Morne* was any yardstick, but morning, noon and evening too.

Well, at least I won't give him the satisfaction of knowing how afraid of him I am, she thought rebelliously. If he is licking his lips at the prospect of taking me by force again, then he will be disappointed. I'll steel myself to submit and I'll hide every bit of emotion. I'll show him he might as well make love to a block of wood as to me.

At last Maggie was satisfied with her work.

'I'll tell Mr Zach you're ready,' she giggled.

Left alone, Regan stood for a moment at the window, looking out at the vast acres that formed an insurmountable barrier between her and the outside world, then, with resgination, she crossed to the bed, pulled back the covers and slid between the sheets. They felt cool to her burning skin and behind her shoulders the pillows were soft as swansdown.

No luxury spared, she thought, a little surprised. Zach did not seem a man who would concern himself with luxury.

With a little wriggle of pleasure she eased herself back against the pillows, forgetting for the moment the reason she was here in the delight of finding comfort at the end of a long and tiring day. Then a small sound made her turn sharply towards the door and a gasp of surprise escaped her lips.

Zach stood there looking at her, his eyes narrowed in his dark face. She recognized his expression at once – the same brooding desire she had witnessed aboard the *Maid of Morne* – and fear shot her through. She lay still, the sheets drawn taut above the curve of her breasts, her eyes round and terrified in her pale face.

'I didn't hear you come in,' she whispered hoarsely.

Without replying, Zach slammed the door behind him and crossed the room in two huge strides, lowering himself to a sitting position on the bed beside her. In spite of her resolve not to show her fear, she could not keep herself from pressing back into the pillows as far as she was able, and as his hand moved around the nape of her neck she held herself stiffly beneath his touch.

'Regan . . .' His fingers moved to trace the outline of her chin and her lips and she lay like an alabaster statue, moving not a muscle. Only her eyes followed his, held as if by a magnet. Then he lowered his face slowly until she saw it as nothing but a blur and his lips covered hers. They were gentle now, with nothing of the brutality she remembered, moving against hers with a rhythmic pressure that stirred some deep answering chord within her. Tenderly his fingers ran on up the line of her jaw to cup her ear and as his lips followed them, kissing the spots his fingertips had stroked, a sharp sweetness ran through her body. Surprised by it, she lay even more still than before, if that were possible, while his tongue explored her ear and his free hand smoothed the ringlets away from her face. Small needles of fire flickered in her loins and she suddenly felt as if every nerve in her body had been honed to sharp awareness. Frightened more even by the strange sensations of her own body than by his exploring mouth and gentling hands she jerked her head away from him, so that her face was half buried in the feather pillow.

'Regan.' His hand sought her chin again, turning it towards him, and his voice was low and full of the emotion that struck terror to her heart. 'Regan, you're my wife now.'

Her mouth trembled. The fires had gone now and suddenly, inexplicably, she was on the verge of tears.

'Yes, God help me!' she whispered throatily.

He released her, standing up. She felt the bed bounce as he removed his weight from its edge and turning her head again saw he was standing with his back towards her.

'Oh, stop playing with me!' she cried suddenly. 'I'm your wife now, as you so rightly state. Take me and have done with it!'

For a long, timeless moment he did not move and something about the stillness of his figure struck a new chill to her heart. Then with a contemptuous movement he straightened her shoulders and turned to look at her.

There was no gentleness in his face now, and no desire. It was as hard as granite.

'I told you a long while ago I would not take you again until you wanted me to,' he said and his tone was ice cold. 'I intend to stand by that. You're my wife now, but until you know yourself it will be a marriage in name only. I shall not force my way into your bed again, my sweet.'

She stared at him, a new fear taking the place of the old one.

'I intend to make up a bed for myself in my dressing room,' he went on. 'I can close the dividing door and leave you with all the privacy you hunger for. In fact, Regan, you will have privacy and more privacy until you are sick of it.'

'But – what will the servants think – and your father?' she gasped before she could stop herself.

Zach laughed, a loud humourless guffaw that echoed around the room.

'Oh Regan, always the hypocrite! Always concerned

with what others think of you! Personally it's of the least importance to me. But if you wish them to think we're sharing a bed of marital bliss, there's no reason for them to know differently. I shan't be the one to tell them. Though if you wish the deception to continue, I would be inclined to rumple the sheets a little and at least make the bed look roughly used.'

'Oh!' she cried furiously. But he did not give her the opportunity to recover any further. Without more ado he crossed to his dressing room, slamming the door behind him, and Regan was left alone.

'He's hateful! He's hateful!' she wept, pummelling the pillow with her hands.

But as the tears ran down her cheeks, even she was not quite sure why she was weeping.

CHAPTER TWELVE

Next morning Zach had already risen and left the adjoining room before Regan awoke. She guessed it was so from the stillness and from the height the sun had already reached in the sky, and when at last she summoned up the courage to pad across the floor and peep into the dressing room, she found it empty.

She stood for a moment staring into the room where he had spent his wedding night and wondering at the feeling of desolation that seemed to weigh down her limbs.

She had dreaded finding herself his plaything again, but at least she had been prepared for it. What she was not prepared for was this feeling of shame and rejection, as if she had been sampled and found wanting to such a degree that he preferred to sleep on a hard couch in his dressing room rather than share a bed with her.

Why, she wondered, should he treat her so? Why did he want her if not for the pleasure he could derive from her body? Not for her company, that much was certain. She had already seen how little he valued that. And this latest twist of the screw only proved what she already knew. He could scarcely be bothered to give her the time of day. Yet yesterday he had forced her to go through the mockery of a marriage ceremony – yesterday he had placed a ring on her finger and allowed the priest to pronounce them man and wife . . .

She turned back to the bedroom, noticing with a twinge of embarrassment its all-too-obvious tidiness and remembering Zach's suggestion that she should rumple the bed if she wanted to hide the fact that she had slept in it alone. He had been jeering at her, she knew, for her concern over what the servants would think, but she couldn't help that. Gentle jokes about a wedding night might be irritating, especially when the bride wanted a husband's attentions as little as she wanted Zach's. But if they knew there had been no wedding night at all, her humiliation would be complete.

Hating herself for her weakness she crossed to the bed, pulling the sheets awry and punching dents into the soft feather pillows. Then she stood back to inspect her work, and to her unpractised eye it appeared she had made some semblance of a love-nest that would deceive a servant, at least.

The sound of horse's hooves on the path beneath the window caught her attention and she crossed the room, drawing back the curtains so that she could look out. Already the air was singing with heat and the dust particles raised by horse and rider seemed to shimmer around them in a silver haze.

It was Zach, saddled up on Tarquin, his fine, jet-black gelding, and her throat seemed to close as she looked down at him. Hate him she might, but he cut an impressive figure there astride the great black horse; shirt skimming the rippling muscles of shoulders and chest and open at the neck to reveal the mat of dark hair, buckskin breeches taut over hard thighs. He sat the horse easily, with the reins gathered in one lean brown hand, though Regan had heard in her visits to the stables that the gelding was the wildest on Ballymena and it was only Zach who ever ventured onto his back. But now Tarquin stood still for him as if acknowledging his mastery, with

only a cocked ear and a swishing tail to tell the observer of
the impatient strength within the sixteen hands of horse-
flesh.

Regan leaned over to throw the window open wider
and the movement caught Zach's attention. He looked up
and when he saw her he raised his hat while a sardonic
smile twisted his mouth.

'Good morning, love,' he called to her. 'You slept well,
I trust?'

Colour flamed in her cheeks and she cast around to see
if there was anyone within earshot. Seeing her embarrassment he laughed aloud.

'I'm glad you're awake in time to bid me goodbye.'

'Goodbye?' she squeaked in spite of herself.

'For a day or two only.' From here it was not possible to
see the mocking light in his eyes, but his tone told her it
was there all the same. 'I'm sorry to leave you so soon and
so unexpectedly, but business calls. I have to ride to
Robertson and I may not be back until tomorrow.'

'Oh!' she said, piqued without really knowing why, and
it was only as she watched him ride away up the drive,
leaving her feeling even more desolate than before, that
she realized.

She would have liked to go to Robertson with Zach.
Out here at Ballymena she missed the bustle of a town and
the opportunity to browse around a store more than she
knew. Robertson was not Melbourne, but at least it was a
centre where the coach passed through, and its main
street boasted two or three stores as well as the hotel. If
only she could ride, *she* could have gone along too. But
Zach had done nothing more towards his promise to teach
her. He had ordered the riding habit. It had arrived at the
same time as her wedding dress and it was every bit as
beautiful as she had pictured it – rich green velvet trimmed with ribbons. But not one word had he said about
taking out a horse. There had been the shearing, of
course. That had occupied almost every waking moment
for the last weeks. But Regan could not help the sudden
niggling thought that perhaps Zach could have found the
time to teach her if he had really wanted to.

Perhaps it suited him better that she should be confined

to Ballymena, she thought. Perhaps when he rode off to Robertson, he did not want her to be able to go along.

A tap on the door interrupted her thoughts and she tried to compose herself as Maggie's grinning face appeared.

'I heard you talking to Mister Zach, so I knowed you was awake,' she offered. 'It's a shame he has to go off today, and you only newly wed too!'

Regan could think of no reply and taking her silence for sadness at the unexpected parting, the maid burbled on: 'Don't upset yourself, now. He'll soon be back again. And you may depend he'll be well looked after while he's in Robertson. Miss Adelaide and the folks at the Commercial Hotel know all his likes and dislikes – they'll see to it he's comfortable, don't you fret.'

'I'm sure they will,' Regan murmured, but her quiet words masked the sudden torrent of anger that the maid's words had unleashed in her.

Adelaide Jackson – of course! Why hadn't she thought of it herself? If Zach stayed overnight in Robertson, he would be putting up at the Commercial Hotel – with Adelaide Jackson to offer him hospitality!

Too clearly for comfort Regan could picture the scene with Adelaide greeting him at the end of the steps as she had done when they had rolled in on the coach, greeting him with warmth and far too much familiarity. And she heard too, as if were all happening again, the tone the hotel owner had used to Zach when she had thought Regan was in a faint and unable to hear her. There was something between them, Regan was certain of it, though exactly what she was not sure, nor did she want to know for certain. It was enough to sense the tension in the air when they were together, enough to take note of Adelaide's dislike for her and the barbed remarks she made.

She exhibited all the hallmarks of a jealous woman, Regan thought, though did she but know it she had little to be jealous of! But if that were so, why had they not made a match of it? Zach clearly liked and admired her, and while she stood in the wings there seemed little point in his press-ganging an unwilling English girl to be his bride. It made no sense, unless . . .

Suddenly Regan found herself remembering Zach's words to Adelaide on their wedding day as she, Regan, lay semi-conscious on the couch.

'It would never have worked,' he had said. 'You have the saloon and I . . .' He had broken off there, interrupted by Regan herself. But what was it he had been going to say? Could it have been that he had been pointing out that as the son of a wealthy squatter/sheepmaster it would be neither convenient nor proper that he should take an unconventional saloon girl turned hotel owner for his wife?

In all likelihood, that was it. But it did not mean because he was unwilling to marry her that they were not lovers. Everything pointed to them having been more than usually close. And perhaps they still were.

'Perhaps his marriage to me is just a red herring to draw attention away from his affair with Adelaide,' Regan thought, wincing as Maggie tugged at her corset laces. The idea, once planted, began to grow and spread.

It would explain so much if it were so – Adelaide's jealousy where none need exist, Zach's lack of interest in making love to his new bride, even his unexpected trip to Robertson.

'Very convenient,' she thought with a sudden flash of hatred for both Zach and the beautifully-rouged Adelaide, and it occurred to her with a jolt that perhaps this was the reason Zach had avoided teaching her to ride. As long as she was tied to the homestead, he was free to ride off and visit Adelaide as often as he wished. It was a dreadful thought, and it made her feel more degraded than ever.

Regan went on fuming silently as she completed her toilet and went down to breakfast. To her relief Seamus, too, was out, riding to the boundaries of the property with Jim Mitchell, Mary's husband, and there was no need for her to have to make polite conversation or parry references to her wedding night and Zach's sudden departure. But it gave her all the more opportunity for thinking of his strange behaviour and the more she thought the more angry she became.

No wonder he had not minded sleeping alone in his dressing room! Tonight, at the hotel, his every need would be catered for with fine professionalism. What was it Adelaide had said to him that very first time Regan had met her? 'When have you ever found cause for complaint regarding my hospitality?'. Perhaps there had been more hidden meaning in that than at first met the eye!

Well, he would not get away with it, Regan decided. She would not allow him to leave her trapped like a caged bird while he rode off wherever and whenever he pleased. If he chose not to teach her to ride, then she would find someone else who would – Tommy the stable lad, or Silas, the bent little groom who had once ridden the finest racehorses in the land. Or else she would teach herself – and why not? So long as the horse was a patient one and not likely to run away with her, she had all the time in the world to practise sitting on its back and controlling it as Zach did with a tug on the reins.

Breakfast done and her mind made up she left the house and went around to the stables. She was a not infrequent visitor and Tommy and Silas greeted her with the admiration she drew from them as a pretty woman and the respect due to her as Zach Casey's wife. But when she told the groom what she wanted, he shook his bullet-like head.

'I wouldn't like to go against the master,' he told her flatly. 'He said to me that he was going to teach you to ride himself, and what the master says, the master does.'

'But he's got so little time!' she pleaded. 'And I'm so isolated here not being able to ride at all. I can't go for walks into the bush, I might lose myself. And I can't go to town or anywhere else.'

Silas stopped what he was doing, leaning on the long-handled rake that was nearly as tall as he.

'I'll tell you what I will do,' he said at last. 'Mister Zach wants to teach you to ride himself, but he's said naught about you learning to drive the buggy. A lassie like you should be able to drive the buggy, and if it's all right with Mr Seamus, that's what we'll do.'

Regan waited for Seamus to return from the boundaries of the property in a fever of impatience and when he did he raised no objection to her learning to drive the buggy.

'Sure, it's a grand idea,' he told her absently, his mind still preoccupied with the problems of the farm. 'And a better man to teach you than Silas would be hard to find.'

Regan nodded her agreement. Silas was a wonder with horses, though it was his misfortune that he would never look as good as Zach in the saddle.

That afternoon she had her first lesson and when it finished, Silas praised her aptitutde.

'We'll make a decent driver of you before the summer's out,' he told her in his slow drawl and although she was pleased he thought she had done well, she was anxious to make faster progress than he had predicted. The end of the summer seemed a lifetime away – she hoped to be proficient long before then.

When Zach returned next day and learned what she was doing he seemed less than pleased, and the dark expression on his face gave her a small thrill of triumph.

If he had thought he could ride off to see his mistress and she would remain at home doing exactly what he wanted her to, he was much mistaken! And perhaps next time he lay in bed in the Commercial Hotel he would stir uncomfortably each time he heard a buggy pass in the street outside!

She continued with her lessons in the days that followed and they became something of an obsession with her. Out in the bush, bowling along between the tree ferns and the brush, with the dwarfing eucalyptus stretching their branches to the sky above her and the dust rising in puffs beneath the wheels, it was easy to forget that she was a prisoner here on Ballymena. When the flies settled on her bare arms, neck, and even her face it was not pleasant, but at least it relegated Zach's infuriating behaviour to the back of her mind for a while, and when the thrill of controlling the sturdy little pony was intoxicating her, she could almost believe that one day she would find a way to get the better of Zach, too.

Since returning from Robertson he still slept every night in his dressing room and for some reason it set her nerves on edge. She did not want him sharing her bed –

heaven forbid! – but somehow his careless rejection of her wounded her more deeply than any love-making he could have forced upon her. To know he could sleep on the other side of the door with no desire whatever to take advantage of his marital rights was a slap in the face that hurt her more than she would have believed possible. Why, he never even tried to kiss her, and as the days passed she felt more and more used.

It must be as she had thought – there could be no other explanation for his behaviour. He was taking his pleasure with Adelaide – that painted, jumped-up whore, and using her, Regan, for a front and nothing more!

Not that it was much of a front! It would hardly deceive a fool! thought Regan, and she cringed at the thought that the household might, by now, be beginning to suspect that she and Zach were not the blissful newly-weds the district was supposed to believe them.

Every morning when she rose she dutifully rumpled the pillow and sheets, but she fancied Maggie was looking at both her and the bed with a puzzled and critical eye. And Seamus, too, sometimes appeared to be on the point of saying something when she found herself alone with him.

But he did not, and she wondered if perhaps her doubts were a result of her over-sensitive imagination. Zach, after all, acted with perfect chivalry towards her when there was anyone to observe them, and only she could be truly aware of the irony as he placed a protective hand on her shoulder or her waist or opened a door to usher her upstairs to bed.

Once or twice Regan almost confronted him with her suspicions as to his motives. Once or twice in the strained times they spent together, she began to turn the conversation towards Adelaide and his relationship with her. But at the last moment she always drew back without really knowing why. Coward, she upbraided herself! But what could she say? To make him admit he wanted her only as a convenience was to make her humiliation complete.

Christmas was fast approaching, though Regan found it hard to believe it could be so in the middle of a scorching

summer. But Zach assured her that Seamus always insisted on an old-fashioned English Christmas whatever
the weather, and one morning at breakfast the talk turned
to the invitations and entertaining that marked the festive
season.

'Sure I wanted to talk to Jud Trenoweth about the
property,' Seamus remarked. 'And it's time we invited
him and his brother to dinner. They're our neighbours
when all's said and done and except for the wedding I've
never set eyes on the lad who voyaged out with your two
selves.'

Regan said nothing. Any mention of Dickon Trenoweth made her remember too clearly the terrible night
when his gun had caused her father's death. But so far as
she knew, Zach had never recounted the circumstances to
Seamus and she had no wish to go into them now.

'Jud's in town at present I believe,' Seamus went on.
'He told me he had accounts to go into at his office and if I
know that clerk of his, it'll take him a week and more to
put them straight. He's the one weak link in Jud's empire
and if his mining interests go on turning up gold he should
get rid of him and put in a man who knows his business
better.'

'*Gold*?' Regan repeated, startled, 'Jud Trenoweth has
found gold?'

Seamus nodded, gulping at his hot, sweet tea.

'He's struck lucky, from what I hear of it. Two of our
oldest hands disappeared yesterday – gone to work for
him, or so Mitchell tells me. A smell of gold is enough for
most men and Jud's struck a good seam, if there's truth in
what I hear. But he's welcome to it. I'll stick to the sheep I
know. They've looked after me so far and I reckon they
always will. I'm big enough now to survive what the
elements can throw at me, and I wouldn't want to sink my
capital in a search for El Dorado.'

There was a moment's silence at the table. Then Zach
said easily:

'If Jud's in Robertson, I'd better ride over and take the
invitation to him there.'

At once Regan's hackles were up. There he went again,
snatching the first opportunity to get to Robertson – and

Adelaide! Well, this time she would spike his guns!

'I could go if you like,' she said demurely.

They both looked at her, and she went on, 'I can drive the buggy now, remember, and I could be there and back before nightfall.'

'I don't care for that idea!' Zach snarled and Regan felt a stab of triumph.

I'll wager you don't! she thought, but aloud she said sweetly:

'I can be spared much better than you and besides I'd like to put my new skill to good use.'

'You've not enough experience!' Zach began, but Seamus interrupted him.

'Now don't spoil it for her, Zach. I like to see a girl with some spirit about her. I'll write a note to Jud whilst you're preparing yourself, and you can show us what a good horsewoman you've become.'

Zach's face darkened and he pushed back his chair and marched from the room. When he had gone Seamus leaned across and patted her arm.

'Take no notice, Regan. 'Tis only your good he's thinking of. But he does not realize if he tries to cage you, he'll lose you. And I wouldn't want to see that happen.'

There was a tone of regret in his voice and Regan knew it was not of her that he was thinking at that moment. Had he tried to cage Zach's mother, she wondered? Was that why she had run? And did Seamus still regret the fact and wish her back again? A sudden warmth for the old man rushed through her veins and she caught at the hand that lay on her arm, squeezing it gently. Feeling as she did about Zach, there was nothing she could say that would answer Seamus's unspoken question. But at that moment, for the first time, she found herself wishing it were not so.

Leaving the breakfast room she went upstairs to get ready for her drive, and to her surprise she found Mary Mitchell in her room, her arms full of fresh linen.

'Sorry, Miss Regan, I didn't expect you back from breakfast yet,' she said, But Regan knew it was a propriety only. Mary Mitchell was not the least bit sorry to be there and her tone said so only too clearly.

'It doesn't matter, Mary. Carry on with what you're doing,' Regan said and the housekeeper bent over the bed, turning back the carefully rumpled sheets while Regan set about changing into a light, summery dress suitable for her drive.

'I'm going to Robertson,' she explained and Mary Mitchell gave her a sly, sidelong look.

'On your own?' she asked.

'Yes. Why not?' Regan returned defensively and the housekeeper shrugged.

'It's just that I thought Mr Zach would have taken you. It would be an ideal opportunity for the two of you to spend some time alone together.'

Regan turned sharply, her cheeks flaming. She knows! she thought wildly – it was there in her tone – an implication too blatant to be missed. And for some reason she was delighted . . .

'Mr Zach and I have all the time alone together we want!' she snapped, but as she left the room, going back down to the hall, she was not only full of dislike for Mary, but also disgust with herself. Why had she been so defensive? Why had she not told the housekeeper to mind her own business? She did not know.

Tucking Seamus's invitation to the Trenoweths into her reticule she went out in search of the buggy. She had thought it might be ready and waiting for her at the door but it was not, and she started towards the stables to look for it.

Halfway across the yard, however, Zach's voice arrested her.

'Regan – just a moment!'

She stopped, turned towards him. His face was still thunderous, and she stiffened. 'Yes?'

He reached her in a few quick strides. 'Regan – I don't want you driving to Robertson. I don't think you know enough of the country yet – nor have you had enough practice in driving a buggy.'

Her chin came up. So he was still trying to stop her – he still thought he could snatch the opportunity to go to Robertson himself.

'I shall be perfectly all right,' she told him coldly. 'I'm a good driver, though you may find that hard to believe, and your father has faith in me even if you have not.'

'That's got nothing to do with it,' he argued and a new thought struck her.'

'You need not worry I'm going to run away again,' she told him.

Between his hands his riding whip twitched.

'I forbid you, Regan. As your husband . . .'

'Ha!' The snort of derision was torn from her lips. 'And what sort of husband do you think you are, Zach? Why you don't even sleep with me, and I declare the whole house knows it!'

A muscle moved in his cheek. 'People's opinions matter little to me, Regan,' he began, and still smarting from her encounter with Mary Mitchell she cut in angrily:

'I wouldn't expect them to, Zach Casey. After all, you're half native!'

His face changed suddenly from controlled anger to sheer fury and before she could move or even cry out his hands shot out, pinioning her arms in a grip of steel.

'Zach!' she whimpered, eyes like saucers. 'You're hurting me . . .'

He pulled her closer, his fingers still biting painfully into her arms.

'Don't ever say that again!' he grated at her.

'Zach . . .'

For a moment longer he held her, like a rag doll, limp and frightened, then he released her so roughly she almost fell.

'Go to Robertson, Regan, if that's what you want,' he growled. 'And if you're bushwhacked or raped on the way, it's no more than you've asked for.'

Then, without another word, he turned on his heel and left her, shaking and close to tears.

So unnerved was she by Zach's attack that if it had not been for her fierce pride Regan might have changed her mind about the trip to Robertson. But if she did that it would mean Zach would have his way – and it was not in her nature to capitulate so readily. Taking a grip on herself she went into the stables and found the buggy Silas had ready for her. Then, with his advice ringing in her ears, she set off.

It was a hot day and she did not press the horse but for all that she reached Robertson by midday. The town seemed unusually noisy, with gangs of men who looked like diggers roaming the streets and Regan realized they were probably chasing the chance to be involved with Jud's find.

Without more ado, she drove up the narrow street, reining in the horse outside the rough wooden building that she knew to be Jud's estate office, and climbing down onto the path. As she tethered the horse, however, the sound of angry voices wafted out to her through the open windows and she hesitated, uncertain whether to go or stay.

The one voice belonged without doubt to Dickon, the other, though she knew it less well, was Jud's harsh drawl. What they were saying she could not be sure – nor did she want to eavesdrop, but there was no mistaking the venom of the quarrel, and within the torrent she thought she caught the word 'gold'.

So that was it. They were quarrelling over the mine. Gold truly was the root of all evil.

As she stood awkwardly in the road, not wanting to intrude into the quarrel between the brothers, the door suddenly flew open and from within she heard Jud's angry voice.

'Don't try to tell me how to run my business, Dickon!'

Then Dickon himself appeared, storming out of the office so tempestuously he did not even seem to notice Regan. For once the smile was missing from his face and he was white with fury.

As he stamped away down the street she turned to watch him go. A group of miners was emerging from the Commercial Hotel and he was swallowed up by them. For a moment more she looked after him, wondering just what had precipitated such a fierce quarrel between the brothers.

Then suddenly her breath caught unevenly and all thought of the pair was driven from her mind as she stared wide-eyed towards the group of miners, and in particular one slightly-built, fair figure that she would have known anywhere.

'Richard!' she breathed.

CHAPTER THIRTEEN

For a moment, as she stood staring, in disbelief, it seemed the world stood still. Then Regan picked up her skirts and began to run along the pavement.

In the space of those few seconds a thousand thoughts cascaded through her mind. Could it really be him? Could it? Or was it just a mirage in a desert? Oh, dear God, she had waited, she had prayed, and now . . .

'Richard!' she called, her voice rising with trembling hysteria. 'Richard . . . wait!'

The one figure detached himself from the group and turned towards her voice.

It was him! But even in that first joyful moment she saw with a sense of shock how changed he was from the Richard she remembered. Gone were the boyish good looks that had made female hearts beat faster wherever their theatrical company had appeared. He was older, his face grown haggard, and a beard straggled over his chin. As for his hair, it was unkempt and matted, while his clothes were ragged and caked with dirt. But it was him – it was Richard – and nothing else mattered.

Tears of joy stung her eyes and spilled over to run down her cheeks. But as she reached him her step faltered and she stopped, suddenly shy. She wanted nothing more than to throw herself into his arms but it had been so long, and so much had happened. Far too much . . .

Through the mist of tears she saw his blank disbelief, saw him shake his head from side to side as a man shakes off sleep. But there was no smile of welcome on his face, only stunned amazement.

'Regan!' he gasped. 'Can it really be you?'

'Yes,' she whispered. 'It is me. Oh Richard, I thought

I'd never see you again.'

'But what are you doing here?' His voice was hoarse and there was a strange, wild look in his eyes, though Regan did not notice it. She laughed now through her tears at his surprise.

'Surely you haven't forgotten so soon – I came to Australia to join you! But I was beginning to think I'd never see you again!'

Still he stood staring, not answering her, and a first prickle of alarm ran through her.

'Richard!' she said sharply, catching at his hands. They were horny to the touch and when she looked down she almost gasped aloud at the state of them – calloused, grained with dirt, and the nails torn and broken to the quick. As an actor, Richard had had hands that were soft and white. Now, he possessed the hands of a miner.

'Oh my poor love!' she whispered. 'What has become of you?'

He shrugged. 'It's nothing. You can't dig for gold and not soil your hands. And it'll be worth a few blisters when I strike it rich.'

Again there was the strange, wild light in his eyes. This time she noticed it and the alarm began to spread, sending out fresh roots and suckers.

'Richard – we can't talk in the street after all this time,' she said desperately. 'There must be somewhere we can go and be alone. There's so much to say . . .'

She followed Richard's eyes to the group of gold miners now climbing the steps to the Commercial Hotel and shook her head quickly. They would find no privacy there – and she had no wish to conduct such an intimate conversation under Adelaide's powdered nose.

'My buggy's just down the street,' she suggested. 'We could drive out of town a little way.'

To her dismay Richard's face clouded and he shifted awkwardly. 'I can't leave just now,' he said apologetically. 'There's been a big strike somewhere around here and there'll be work for those who are first on the scene. I dare not miss out on it, Regan.'

'Oh!' she said, trying not to feel hurt. Gold mining was Richard's life, after all, and he looked as if he was desperately in need of work. 'Well, come and sit in the buggy anyway.'

She took his arm, not caring who saw them, and he went with her along the street. Every few steps he glanced over his shoulders as if afraid he would miss something, but when he saw Regan's buggy he stopped in his tracks, giving it his full attention.

'Is that yours, Regan? Where did you get a fine pony and buggy like that?'

She swallowed at the lump that rose in her throat. There was too much to say and she did not know where to begin.

'It's a long story,' she faltered. 'Didn't you ever receive my letter, Richard?'

'Letter?' he repeated vaguely.

'The one I wrote telling you Father had had a win on the gaming tables and we were using his spoils to come and join you,' she explained, and when he did not reply she stopped, turning to look at him with her eyes narrowed against the glare of the sun. Something was wrong, she knew it instinctively, though just what it was she could not be sure.

'You weren't in Melbourne when the ship berthed,' she went on desperately. 'I didn't know where to find you. It was terrible Richard. I didn't know what to do!'

'But you managed all right,' Richard said absently. 'In fact you look as if you've done very well. I'm glad about that, Regan.'

'Richard . . .' She broke off. She was beginning to realize what it was that was wrong, although until now she had not wanted to admit it. Richard had not greeted her as the girl he loved and wanted to marry. That was impossible now, of course, but he was not to know that. Yet he was talking to her as if she were an old friend, nothing more – an old friend he was quite pleased to see though not overjoyed; in whose affairs he was interested, but not really concerned.

'*Did* you receive my letter?' she asked, cold suddenly in spite of the heat of the sun.

His eyes fell away from hers. 'I was in the diggings – it took a long while to reach me,' he muttered evasively.

'But you did get it before we berthed?' she pressed him. All her first excitement at seeing him had died now and she was taut with dread. But she had to know, and even before he spoke his face, hang-dog with guilt, had given the answer.

'I couldn't have reached Melbourne in time,' he faltered miserably. 'And in any case we thought we'd found a rich seam. If I'd left it, someone else would have had the gold I'd sweated for. You do understand, Regan?'

Understand! She couldn't have answered him to save her life. He *had* received her letter. But he had not come. While she had searched the streets of Melbourne, half-crazy with despair, he had been digging in the goldfields, caring more for the elusive dust than he did for her . . .

'And did you find your gold?' she asked at last, her voice harsh with tears.

His face fell, whether with shame or with the memory of his disappointment she did not know.

'It wasn't as good as we expected it to be,' he admitted. 'But it's going to be different from now on, Regan. This time . . .' He broke off, eyes beginning to shine once more, and suddenly, too clearly, she found herself remembering what Zach had told her about the way the lust for gold could affect a man, getting into his blood like a fever until he could think of nothing but his quest for the shining nuggets.

It would be different with Richard, she had told him. But now, facing the poor ghost of the man she had once loved, she knew it was not different at all.

Could Richard not see what it was doing to him? Had he no idea of the way it had destroyed his body, his mind, his soul? She raised a trembling hand to her lips and as she did so Richard's eyes widened. He reached across, catching at her fingers and she realized that for the first time he had noticed the gold ring on the third finger of her left hand.

'What's this?' he asked roughly.

A nerve jumped in her throat. Did he still care after all?

'I'm married,' she said awkwardly. 'So much happened to us, I can't begin to tell you, and I had no choice . . .'

'And this buggy is your husband's?' he asked.

She nodded. 'Yes. His father is a sheepmaster. Oh, Richard, please let me explain. Please try to understand...'

'Of course,' he said distantly. 'I'm glad you're settled, Regan. It's better that you should be. The goldfields offer no life for a woman. I've seen pretty lasses age from a Queen of the Diggings to an old hag in the time I've been here. Of course, it's different for a man.'

Not for you, Richard, Regan thought wretchedly. Not for you. But before she could find the words to express the depth of misery that was in her, he turned, looking back down the street to see the group of miners emerging again from the Commercial Hotel.

'Regan – I must go or I may miss my chance,' he muttered urgently. 'I'm glad you're settled, truly I am.'

She swallowed at the lump in her throat and pointed to Jud's log-built office. 'This is where you'll find the owner of the gold mine,' she said thickly. 'If you go in now, you'll be first in line.'

The eager light came back into his eyes. It tore at her heart, reminding her strangely of something – or someone.

'Thanks, Regan!' He squeezed her hand and was gone, making for the door to Jud's office, and she stood watching him go, unable to believe that the man for whom she had crossed the world could dispense with her so readily. Why, he had not even asked after her father, who had treated him for so long as his own son...

The thought brought her up sharp and her heart began to pound as she realized suddenly just who it was that Richard reminded her of when his eyes had lit up with hungry delight at the prospect of gold. Just so had Thomas's eyes shone when he had heard the rattle of dice or seen the fall of cards! The cause might be different – the fever was the same. It lured a man until he was obsessed by his craving. It had destroyed Thomas and now it would destroy Richard.

With a sob she turned away and suddenly she found herself thinking of Zach. Brute he might be, monster he might be, but no sick greed would ever make him forget all else. He was his own master, proud and strong – if he had a weakness he would stamp on it, she knew that instinctively. He liked to gamble, it was true, but he gambled only what he could afford. And although he had never known what it was to be poor, she could not imagine he would ever waste the best years of his life grubbing in the barren earth for gold. Whatever he was, he was also dependable in a way Richard had never been. And in spite of all that had gone before, he had taken better care of her . . .

The gaggle of miners came up the street, brushing roughly past her as they went into Jud's office and Regan remembered abruptly her reason for being here. The invitation! In seeing Richard again she had forgotten all about it. Now she pulled it out of her reticule and stood uncertainly on the path. She had no wish to go into his office while it was full of miners and she didn't think she could bear to face Richard again. But she could hardly take the invitation back to Ballymena after having driven to Robertson especially to deliver it . . .

As her mind raced, she remembered Dickon. He must still be in town somewhere and if she could find him that would be good enough. Whatever he and Jud had quarrelled about would no doubt be forgotten by sundown and the invitation was addressed to them both. Leaving the buggy hitched up outside the office she walked the length of the street, hesitating only when she reached the Commercial Hotel. Facing Adelaide was not a prospect to be relished, either. But there was nothing for it. If Dickon was there, she would have to go in.

She climbed the steps and went into the hotel. After the brightness of the day outside it was so dim in the lobby it took her eyes a moment or so to become accustomed to the darker light, and as she stood uncertainly, a voice addressed her.

'If it isn't Mrs Casey! What brings you to Robertson, Regan?'

It was Dickon. She swung round to face him, noticing as she did so that he had regained all his usual composure.

I was looking for you,' she said with relief. 'I've an invitation to deliver to you, but Jud's office is full of miners.'

'And the genteel Mrs Casey would not wish to soil her hands with dirty miners!' The voice was Adelaide's. She had appeared as if from nowhere and clearly had over-heard their conversation. 'Though I thought I saw her arm in arm with one earlier in the street.'

Regan coloured. Did she miss nothing? But Dickon was smiling, clearly treating the statement as a joke, and as he took the invitation from her his hand remained on hers a trifle longer than was necessary.

'I'm sure Jud and I will be only too pleased to accept. Now, do you mean to tell me that you have come all the way to Robertson on our behalf, my dear? The least I can do then is to offer you luncheon! What can you provide, Adelaide?'

'Oh no, I couldn't . . .' Regan said hastily, and Adelaide fixed her with a shrewd look.

'I declare Zach must be quite crazy to allow you out alone!' she said nastily. 'Every man in town, it seems, is seeking your company! But Zach is a fair-minded man. I suspect he adheres to the old adage: "What's sauce for the goose is also sauce for the gander" – or, in this case, "What's sauce for the gander is also sauce for the goose".'

Regan gasped, momentarily stunned by the blatantly pointed remark. Adelaide possessed a venomous tongue – she had learned that the very first time she met her – but this went beyond venom. At Regan's elbow, Dickon chuckled unpleasantly and the sound brought her to her senses.

'How you do run on, Miss Jackson!' she returned brightly, determined not to allow Adelaide the pleasure of knowing how much she had discomfited her. 'You have the quaintest turn of phrase! I assure you, Zach was not at all anxious to allow me to drive here today, but I insisted. He has more than enough to do at the homestead.'

Adelaide's eyes glinted coldly.'

'I dare say he has,' she remarked archly. 'Even before you came, Zach always found plenty to do there.'

'What do you mean?' Regan asked before she could stop herself, and Adelaide's mouth twisted with triumph as she realized she had pierced the younger girl's armour.

'Why look around the place, my dear,' she murmured.

'But when your eyes come to rest on the evidence of his ardour, do not judge him too harshly. A bush farm can be a lonely place for a man, and Zach has always ensured that the child is well cared for.'

Regan's heart seemed almost to stop beating. What was Adelaide saying? Surely she could not be suggesting that Zach had found solace with Mary Mitchell? And that Queenie was in reality his daughter? But there was no other child at Ballymena . . .

As if reading her mind, Adelaide smiled with grim satisfaction.

'The mother is a poor, pale specimen. I don't blame Zach for preferring you – though I dare say Mrs Mitchell does not see it that way. But have you not noticed how fond he is of the child? He fairly dotes on her, wouldn't you say?'

For a brief, heart-rending second Regan had a vision of the reunion between man and child when they had first arrived back at Ballymena, and the small moments of closeness she had witnessed since then. Zach *was* fond of Queenie and she had been surprised that such a hard man could be so gentle and understanding with a child. But she had thought nothing of it, and even now . . .

'You go too far, Miss Jackson!' she said coldly. 'How dare you make such statements? If this were England, you would find yourself in a court of law, charged with scandal. As it is not, I dare say Zach will deal with you in his own way.'

Adelaide's eyes narrowed, then she threw back her head and laughed.

'I dare say he will!' she sneered and Regan could have bitten off her tongue for giving her the opportunity for the further barb. With a small, determined movement she lifted her chin.

'Perhaps you will excuse me, Miss Jackson,' she said haughtily. 'I have a long drive ahead of me. Good day to you – and to you, Mr Trenoweth.'

Then, without another word, she swept past the start-led Dickon, down the steps and into the street. She was trembling violently from the encounter but she was determined not to show it, and it was only when she had turned the buggy onto the homeward track and left the town behind that she dared give vent to her feelings, squealing so loudly with rage that the pony leapt forward in the shafts and she had to employ all her new-found skill to steady him down again.

'How dare she say such things?' she fumed. 'A beastly whore like her – who does she think she is?'

But as the first flush of anger began to cool, Adelaide's words still rankled, sending shoots of doubt through Regan. Zach and Mary Mitchell – was it possible? As Adelaide had said, the homestead was isolated and women were few and far between. It would also explain why Mary Mitchell had so resented her arrival. She had guessed it was because the housekeeper had thought her position in the household might be usurped. Could it be that was not her only reason?

'No!' Regan cried aloud. 'No, I won't believe it!'

It was ridiculous, crazy. She had never seen any intimate exchange between them – no look, no touch, not even the tense awareness she had noticed between Zach and Adelaide. And as for Queenie, no child could be less like Zach. She was fair to gingery like her mother, but if Zach's blood ran in her veins, somewhere it would show itself. That darkness of his would dominate, always. No, his fondness for her had nothing to do with her parenthood, Regan was sure of it. The charge had been Adelaide's way of discomfiting her, that was all. And yet . . .

Regan pulled herself up mentally, aware suddenly of the gnawing hurt deep within her. The anger had gone now, but the pain had not. It remained, sharper than she would have believed possible and connected, in some strange way, with the idea of Zach and Mary Mitchell.

There never was anything between them! she told herself firmly, and the very necessity of the thought took her by surprise.

Why should it matter to her what Zach did, had done, or intended to do? Why should it be of the least importance to her if he made love to every woman in the land? But it did. It mattered very much. Surely . . . surely it was not *jealousy* that was tearing her apart? Jealousy over Zach, whom she hated?

Or did she hate him? At the thought of him, a spiral of excitement twisted within Regan and her hands tightened on the reins. She had experienced that stab of sharp delight once or twice before – and always when he had been close to her. Why should she feel it now, out here alone on the dusty track? What was happening to her? What was it?

She raised her hand to her face, brushing away the dust that was clinging to her damp skin and at that very moment a sharp crack like a pistol shot rung out, loud in the still afternoon, and the dead branch of a eucalyptus under which they were passing came crashing down, missing both Regan and the pony by a mere hair's breadth. Regan screamed and the startled pony, taking advantage of the loose reins, plunged forward.

'Whoa, Lucky!' Regan cried, but her voice seemed only to excite the pony more. Faster he went, his drumming hooves raising a thick, choking dust from the path so that she could hardly see, and no matter how she tugged on the reins, it was to no avail.

Dear God, he's running away with me! she thought in a panic.

The track was rough now, full of potholes and ruts, but they did nothing to deter the frightened animal. If anything, the violent lurching of the buggy only served to madden him even more. Over a hillock they went, bouncing right into the air as the wheels hit the ground and the jolt sent Regan tumbling off balance so that she lost the reins. With a squeal of fear she landed in the well of the buggy and the pony chose that very moment to veer off the track and into the scrub. For seemingly endless seconds they careered on, and Regan thought her last moment had come. Then the undergrowth became thicker, acting as a brake on the buggy wheels and gradually the pony's headlong gallop slowed first to a canter and then a trot before he stopped beside a tree fern, blowing and sweating.

Shaking from head to foot, Regan pulled herself up and tumbled out of the buggy. Her legs almost gave way beneath her and she gripped the side for support, working her way round until she reached the pony. Then she stood for a moment holding his lathered head. Thank God he'd stopped and she was all in one piece! The buggy could have been jerked to flinderjigs and she could have been thrown out and killed. Or she could have lain unconscious here in the brush for hours, even days, and no one to find her! The thought brought on a fresh spasm of trembling and it was only when it subsided that it occurred to her to wonder how she was ever to get the pony back onto the track. The buggy wheels were firmly anchored in undergrowth, and ahead the bush was thick and virgin. Regan caught at the bridle, trying to turn the animal, but he stood his ground, unwilling, now that he had stopped, to move again.

'Come on, you beast! Come on!' she urged him in shaking tones, but to no avail, and the effects of shock washed over her again in a chill tide.

If she couldn't get him back on the road, what on earth would she do? And even if she managed that she didn't relish the prospect of driving all the way home again. Lucky could bolt again – anything could happen –

Weak tears filled her eyes and she lay her head down on the pony's neck.

'Oh Zach, Zach, why aren't you here?' she sobbed, and it was a moment or two before she realized what she had said – not only that, but she meant it with all her heart.

If Zach were here, it would be all right. He would know what to do. If Zach were here he would have the buggy back on the road in no time and drive it home himself. If Zach were here he would take care of everything. But Zach was not here. Regan spread her shaking arms across the pony's sweating rump, tears making pale streaks on her dust-caked face, and the ache of longing swelled within her until she felt she would burst with it.

Zach. Zach. Zach.

Suddenly a multitude of memories were passing before her eyes like slides in a magic lantern show – the way he had covered her with his blanket aboard the *Maid of Morne* and slept himself with only his cloak to keep out the cold; the hours he had spent searching the streets of Melbourne for her when he could so easily have let her go to her fate;

the strength of his arms when he had carried her, swooning, to the couch on their wedding day. Since he had taken responsibility for her, whenever danger or circumstances had threatened her he had been there, strong yet gentle, a tower to rely upon. Yet she had chosen not to notice it. How could she have been so blind? Why, he had even tried to prevent her driving alone to Robertson today and she had been foolish enough to dismiss his warnings as pique because he wanted to make the journey himself. Surely after the weeks she had spent with him she should have known him well enough to know he would never demean himself so? But she had defied him, ignored his sound common sense as she had ignored his warnings about the dangers for a girl in the streets of Melbourne and now she was in a pretty pickle. Would he come to look for her when she did not arrive home? Probably – though it would be no more than she deserved if he did not. And in any case . . .

Regan lifted her head from the pony's rump, narrowing her eyes against the sun. She would not want him to find her here like this. Her pride would not stand for it, especially now – now that she had realized how much she cared for him.

In the beginning, he had wanted her, but now it seemed it no longer made any difference to him whether she was there or not. He thought her a fool most likely, a stupid, conceited nit-wit – hadn't he said as much on more than one occasion? But once he had thought her attractive, even if all he felt for her now was pity, scorn and a sense of responsibility. And if she tried very hard, maybe she could make him revise his opinion of her, and earn the regard she longed for.

But to be found weeping in the middle of the bush was not the way to make him respect her again.

The thought gave Regan courage, and strength, and hitching up her skirts she returned with determination to the task of trying to guide horse and buggy back to the path.

CHAPTER FOURTEEN

It was almost an hour later when Regan finally persuaded the unwilling Lucky back through the bush to the road and by the time she had managed it her dress was torn to ribbons and her hair hung limply on her cheeks. Her face was itching too from the bushflies that kept settling upon it and she had only just avoided swallowing one. No one, not even a native, could swallow a bushfly without being sick, she had heard, and she was grateful for her quick reflexes and lucky escape. But her mouth was sore and swollen all the same and she looked a sorry sight as she once more clambered into the buggy and set the pony's head for home.

He was in no hurry now – his escapade had tired him, even more than it had tired her and the sun was low in the sky when at last she saw the golden yellow hulk of Bally-mena on the horizon.

At once she was tense and trembling again and strangely shy at the thought of seeing Zach. She looked a fright, she knew, but it was more than that. He'd seen her in worse states before this. No, it was facing him with her new-found emotions that she found so formidable a prospect. Before, she hated him and her hatred had buttressed her against anything he could do or say. Now, suddenly, she felt as naked as the day he had caught her in the bath tub, afraid that he would know, just by looking at her, that things were different with her, and make capital from her discomfort.

Mustering all the composure she could, she turned into the drive, but before she could reach the safety of the stables she heard the clatter of hooves loud in the still evening air and Zach rounded the corner on his huge black horse, Tarquin.

When he saw her he reined in immediately and dismounted, landing so close to her pony that he was able to take the bridle all in one movement. Then he stood between the two horses, looking up at her with a face like thunder.

'Where have you been until this hour, Madam?' he demanded.

She raised a dirt-encrusted hand to brush aside a lock of red-gold hair.

'I – I had a little mishap,' she said weakly.

'I can see that. What happened?' His tone was rough and it brought the tears prickling behind her eyes again. But she was determined he should not see them.

'Lucky took it into his head to run off into the bush,' she said brightly. 'A falling branch startled him and he just went as if the devil was after him.'

'In rough country? He hasn't injured himself, has he?' Zach turned swiftly to the pony, running a practised hand over the fetlocks and pasterns, and the knot of tears grew in her throat.

Just a short time ago she had been longing for Zach, convinced that if he were there he would look after her and make sure she was safe. Now she was home, dirty, dishevelled, with a tear-stained face, and all he could think about was the pony. He wasn't concerned about her at all! He hadn't even asked her if she was harmed!

'Well thank you very much, Zach!' she flared. 'It's nice to know where your priorities lie. This high-spirited beast runs away with me, and all you can think of is whether he has any cuts or bruises. I could be lying dead in the bush for all you care!'

Zach glanced up at her, his dark face hard.

'If you were, you'd have no one to blame but yourself. You're not experienced enough to drive a pony all the way to Robertson and it would have been your own fault if you'd come to grief. What's more, I should have held you responsible if the pony had been injured. So don't expect me to have any sympathy with you over your fright, my sweet. If you'd listened to me in the first place, it would never have happened.'

'Oh!' she squealed in outrage. After all she had been through, that was all he could say! And the love she had felt for him a few minutes earlier was fuel for her anger, too. How could she have been so stupid as to want him – and want him to want her? He was a beast – the very devil in disguise. 'Oh, how I hate you, Zach Casey!' she cried.

Then, with a little less aplomb than she would have liked, because her joints were already stiffening up from the jolting they had received, she climbed down from the buggy and walked away from him towards the house, the unshed tears sparkling like diamonds in her eyes.

As he watched her go, Zach swore softly to himself. Little fool, she'd risked her own neck, and the pony's, and caused him more anxiety in the last hours than he cared to admit. Yet even now he wanted her, with a longing that ached in his loins like a festering sword-thrust. With her hair awry and her face dirty and tear-stained she had looked so vulnerable it had torn at his heart and he had wanted nothing but to take her in his arms, crushing her lips beneath his and kissing away the tears from her cheeks. His body had remembered too clearly for comfort the roundness of her body's curves, the soft sweetness of breast and belly and thigh, and the torn and dusty dress that now concealed them had somehow only made them more desirable. Not even the fact that she hated him could stop him from wanting her, fool that he was. And she surely hated him . . .

He turned abruptly, calling to Tommy the stable lad to come and relieve him of Lucky and the buggy to which he was harnessed. Then, with an athletic thrust, he swung himself up onto Tarquin's broad back. There was only one way to relieve the tension that ached within him – a good, fast gallop through the cool of the evening. With a cry, he drove his heels into Tarquin's flanks and horse and rider disappeared down the drive in a cloud of dust.

Zach did not return for dinner and Seamus's usual good humour slipped as the meal progressed with no sign of him.

'First you're missing, then Zach,' he said to Regan when they eventually decided to begin without him. 'Sure wouldn't you think he'd know better than to ride away just when it's time for a meal to be served.'

Regan felt her cheeks turning hot with guilty embarrassment. Now that her first outrage had cooled a little she had the uncomfortable feeling that Zach had been right to accuse her of risking both herself and the pony – she was not experienced enough to drive so far alone and what had happened only went to prove it.

'I think he was angry with me,' she said awkwardly.

'Yes, I suppose he was. And when he's angry, Zach likes to get out under the stars,' Seamus said absently and Regan realized that he was thinking not only of his son, but also the woman who had borne him – the native girl he had loved and lost.

'Is he very like his mother?' she asked softly.

A look of surprise crossed Seamus's face, then his blue eyes misted and he nodded slowly.

'In some ways,' he agreed. 'For the most part, he's my son. His mother left while he was still a young child. She was restless for her own people, you know, and nothing I could give her could ever replace for her the life she was born to. If I bought her the richest jewel in the crown of the King of England she would not think it one quarter as bright as the stars in the velvet sky above the bush. So she went – nothing could hold her – and Zach was raised as a civilized Irish squatter. What I call civilized, at any rate,' he added with a twinkle.

Regan nodded, not wanting to interrupt. It was the first time Seamus had ever talked to her of Zach's mother and she waited, enraptured, for him to continue.

At last he did, drawing on the Bengal twist he always smoked when dinner was over.

'In most ways, Zach's the perfect sheep farmer,' he said thoughtfully. 'He knows the land and he knows the business – with the head he has on his shoulders he'll never need to employ a manager. That's the best way, for if you can do the job yourself you know you're not being cheated out of what's rightfully yours. Zach's hard, but he's fair, and if he's a temper – well, you can guess, he got that from me. But there are some things he didn't get from me. Some things where blood will tell. His need for open spaces, for one thing. His fear of being caged another. I thought all these years it would keep him from marrying and settling down. I've watched him shy away from women who wanted him. Then you came along, m'voreen, and changed all that.'

A lump rose in Regan's throat.

'I think I've let you down on that count,' she said softly. 'I don't think I've changed him one little bit.'

Seamus patted her hand.

'Marriage must mellow him,' he told her gently. 'And you must have patience. I'll say no more for fear of embarrassing you, but when two people are close . . .'

She did not reply. There was nothing she could say. So Seamus, at least, had not realized there was anything wrong. Perhaps if he thought Zach treated her strangely at times he put it down to his 'native blood'. Well, that at least was a mercy. And in some inexplicable way there was something satisfying about the mistaken assumption – as if she had briefly seen through Seamus's eyes the way things could be and liked what she saw.

I'll tell him I'm sorry, she thought. When he comes home, I'll tell him he had a right to be angry with me.

She went to the window looking out into the night that had fallen swiftly, but there was no sound of galloping hooves and fear began little tormenting twists within her.

Where could he be? Supposing there had been an accident? After her own fright of this afternoon it was all too easy for her to imagine. If Tarquin, galloping through the bush, stumbled, Zach would be thrown. He was an expert rider, yes, but even an expert could come to grief. Supposing at this very moment he was lying hurt somewhere in the bush, feeling as abandoned as she had done this afternoon? Supposing he was dead and she could never tell him she loved him . . .

The thought caught her with almost as much surprise as it had done earlier and she pressed her hand over her mouth as if she might somehow give away what she was feeling to Seamus, now sitting quietly over his books. She loved him, yes, and sometimes she hated him. The two seemed inseparable. Love – hate – how close they were in reality. How often one masked the other!

Fleetingly her mind returned to Richard. Never, in all her life, had she felt so about him. She had believed she loved him because she had known nothing different, but it had been a pale ghost of the emotion that racked her now. And somehow it seemed as though she had always, instinctively, known that. Sometimes, she thought, casting her mind back to the days before Thomas had been shot and Zach had claimed her, sometimes she had been aware of a restlessness within her, a strange certainty that there should somehow be more than the gentle affection she had felt for Richard and he for her. It was only when the world had turned topsy-turvy that she had longed so desperately for the old order as a safe haven from the storms that enveloped her. Now, with a calm assurance, she knew it would never have been enough for her. She had known heights now, and depths, and she could never go back to being satisfied with less.

It was like the song she so often sang, she thought – 'The Flowers In The Valley'. Richard had been of the ilk of the red and green knights, whose passion was not strong enough to carry off the maiden. But Zach was the Knight in Yellow. 'My bride, my queen, thou must with me'. He had given her no choice, and she loved him for it. And now . . .

She stared into the silent dark, tears aching in her head. Suppose it was too late. Suppose she could never tell him now how willingly she would come . . .

Abruptly she turned to Seamus, unable to keep her fears to herself a moment longer.

'You don't think he's had a fall, do you?' she burst out, her voice trembling.

Seamus looked up, his eyes very blue in his weathered face, and smiled at her gently.

'Don't worry, m'voreen, Zach's too able a horseman for that. No, he's most likely ridden far enough for his anger to burn itself out – and that could be a long way. I've known him ride to Robertson when the mood took him. A tot of rum and a game of cards and his temper will burn itself out.'

'Yes, I see,' Regan said meekly, but inwardly her anxiety had been overtaken once more by an explosion of searing jealousy.

So Zach had ridden to Robertson! That was it! Denied the chance of seeing Adelaide today he was using her mishap with Lucky as an excuse to absent himself from dinner and seek his pleasure at the Commercial Hotel! What would Seamus say, she wondered, if he knew that in addition to a tot of rum and a game of cards, Zach also counted Miss Adelaide Jackson as one of the attractions of the town? In all likelihood he would never believe it – he was so clearly proud of his hateful son – and she would not be the one to disillusion him.

'Perhaps I'll go to bed then,' she murmured. 'After my adventures today I declare I'm quite exhausted.'

Seamus rose, smiling at her gently.

'You're a wise girl as well as a pretty one,' he told her, and even when the bedroom door had closed after her, she was still wondering what he meant.

It was very late when Zach came home. Regan had lain awake for what seemed like hours, fuming and torturing herself by imagining where he was and what he was doing. Eventually she had drifted into a fitful slumber, but the sound of his horse's hooves on the path outside must have wakened her, for she heard him come into the house and a few minutes later his steps coming up the stairs.

Her first reaction was overwhelming relief. He was safe – not lying somewhere injured or dying – and the welcome knowledge made her limbs and even her stomach go weak. Then, as she came fully awake, the anger began again.

So, he had decided to come back. He had had his pleasure with Miss Adelaide Jackson and then come arrogantly home, not caring that she knew it. She was his wife, yet he ignored her and sought an evening's entertainment with his lady friend. Why, it was more than flesh and blood could stand!

She heard him go into his room and close the door behind him. Then suddenly she froze. That small, creaking sound – surely it was the handle of the connecting door? Her eyes flew open and it came into view – yes – the ornate carved handle was turning!

If she had not been wide awake before she was now, every nerve tingling while the blood sang loudly in her ears. He was coming into her room! Since their wedding night he had never done that. Always the connecting door had remained firmly closed but now – now, it was opening, slowly, stealthily. What did he want with her? Had Adelaide not provided for his needs? Was he now going to take her, Regan, against her will? She was his wife, yes, and he had every right. And a few hours ago she would, had he but known it, given herself willingly. But if he thought he could creep into her room at dead of night and force himself upon her, he was much mistaken!

Regan closed her eyes again and lay quite still, feigning sleep. He was in the room with her now – though she could not see him she could sense his presence. For a moment there was silence, broken only by the sound of his breathing, then into the stillness his voice murmured:

'Regan?'

She did not move a muscle.

'Regan?' he said softly again. 'Are you awake?'

Still she lay motionless, though her heart hammered so loudly against her ribs she felt sure he would hear it. For what seemed a timeless eternity he stood there and she felt his eyes upon her. Then the door whispered over the carpeted floor again, the handle creaked, and she knew he had gone. Half-afraid, she opened her eyes. Yes, the room was empty. Her breath came out on a sigh and she knew she should be relieved to be left alone. But she was not. Her body ached, more with longing than with the effort of remaining motionless. And her heart felt as abandoned and empty as the empty room.

On the other side of the door Zach loosened his shirt buttons and stood for a moment staring through the window at the velvet blackness of the summer's night.

Damn her, he thought. Damn this woman who had come into his life and taken it over. Until he had met her he had been his own master – master of his emotions, his actions, his future. No more. From the moment he had set eyes on her on the *Maid of Morne* he had wanted her – made up his mind to have her – and set out to achieve that objective with the confidence that had come from past experience. He had not expected her to love him at once. If she had done there would have been no challenge, no chase. But it had never occurred to him that he would not, in the end, win her.

Now, however, he found himself forced to face the truth.

She did not love him. She hated him, feared him and resented everything he tried to do for her. And nothing, it seemed, would change that.

Perhaps, Zach thought, he should try to find the fiancé she was clearly pining for, and reunite them. Perhaps if he gave her to another man he could find peace himself at last. But the thought sent a frenzy of jealousy coursing through him. To think of another man holding her as he had held her, kissing her, caressing her, bringing her to the height of passion he knew instinctively she was capable of and finally possessing her was more than he could stand.

With an angry movement he took off his jacket, throwing it carelessly on the floor. Tonight he had sought release for his tortured pride and emotions riding Tarquin as hard as the black beast would go. Then, at the Commercial Hotel, he had attempted to lose himself in a game of dice and the contents of a bottle of rum. And Adelaide had been there, flirting and flaunting and making it clear that his marriage had changed nothing. They had been lovers before, they could be lovers again, he knew. Had he wanted it, he could have found release with her without a doubt. And for a little while, sore at Regan's repeated rejections of him, he had been tempted to take advantage of her ready loving.

But something had held him back – the vision of untidy, red-gold curls and a dirty, tear-stained face; of flashing green eyes and a determined chin held high, and delicate rounded curves beneath a tattered dress. And he had known that to make love to Adelaide would prove a momentary respite only. It might, for a little while, ease the pressing ache within his loins. It could do nothing for the ache in his heart.

So he had ridden home again, kicking on the tired Tarquin. He had thought, foolishly, that she might be lying awake, as disturbed as he by the state of their relationship and he had come to her room in the vain hope that even now they could find some common ground, some basis for a new beginning.

But it was not to be. She was sleeping soundly, like a baby who has not a care in the world and he knew he must face the truth. It was no longer practical to go on hoping that the marriage might yet succeed. No longer possible to continue the fight to win her.

'Damn her,' he said aloud again, but it did no more to ease the weight of misery inside him than the ride, the rum or the dice had done.

Jud and Dickon took up their invitation a week later and though their presence made a change at the dinner table, Regan was soon bored by the business talk the four men engaged in. Jud was well pleased with his mining interest, he told them, for there was more gold coming to the surface than he had dared hope, and men had come from all over to work for him. But although it was better to do things on a large scale, it was not easy to keep an eye on all his employees and be sure they were not cheating him and pocketing the profits for themselves, and in this respect it was good to have the help of his brother – another member of the family could be trusted where itinerant fortune hunters could not.

As he said this, Regan found herself remembering the quarrel she had overheard and wondering whether there were any disadvantages, too, to family involvement, but before she could think about it too deeply, Dickon was begging her to entertain them as she had done aboard the clipper ship.

'She's a beautiful singer,' Seamus agreed. 'And sure now she has her piano, she doesn't lack for musical accompaniment.'

It was true. The piano Zach had promised her had arrived and she had spent many happy hours tinkling on it. As a child Thomas had taught her to play and now her pleasure in the beautiful instrument, finer than she had ever thought to own, was marred only by the sharp sadness that Thomas himself could not be here to play upon it. How he would have delighted in it! she thought. How lovingly his fingers would have touched the keys!

To hide the spasm of grief that threatened her, she sat herself down at the keyboard, and because it was almost Christmas she picked out the tunes of some of her favourite carols, though it seemed strange singing of snow and holly berries while the windows were all thrown open to the balmy summer's evening!

That night, when they had left, she was in a strange mood. Since her visit to Robertson the previous week Zach seemed hardly to have spoken to her and the pointed avoidance hurt her deeply in spite of herself.

Why should I care what he does? she asked herself. But the fact was she did care – very much. Even knowing he had gone that night to Adelaide could not stop her wanting him and she did not know which was worse – the days when he worked on the drought-beleaguered land and she did not see him at all, or the ones when she had to endure his arrogant attitude towards her. It hurt, knowing he did not want her, while the thought of him with Adelaide was a knife-thrust in her heart.

She missed his company, too, more than she could tell. Though since their wedding night he had never suggested they should share a room, at least they had begun to talk and communicate. Now all that had gone again.

He even goes to see Adelaide for his conversation now, I suppose, she thought wretchedly.

But the piano was a boon. It helped keep her mind occupied and even lulled her to drowsy peace when sleep refused to come. And that night, when the guests had gone and Seamus and Zach retired to bed, she crept back downstairs, sitting in the half-light fingering the notes of a new carol.

How long she sat there, she did not know, perhaps she had even dozed off at the stool. But suddenly she was aware of not being alone and spinning round she saw Zach.

At once her heart leapt. What did he want with her? Could he have come to urge her to come to bed? With the pulse-rate of a sleeper roused to awareness she bridled defensively in anticipation of his attack.

'I'm not disturbing you, am I?'

In the lamplight his face was a mask, though for a second she thought she saw beyond it and glimpsed . . . what? Her breath came harder as she looked at him. He was half ready for bed, his shirt unbuttoned to reveal the matted hair of his chest, though he still wore the light grey trousers that accented his narrow hips and long, muscled thighs. How masculine he was, she thought. And his eyes, dark and burning, were starting fires inside her so that she found herself wishing, ridiculously, that he would take her again with the mastery that denied her choice, the mastery that left her helpless.

He took a step towards her and breath seemed trapped in her lungs. Suddenly she was alive and aching with wanting him and she knew that it was this that made her restless day after day. To know she loved him and have to accept he no longer wanted her, to be so near and yet so far, it was torture of the most exquisite kind. And now . . .

Her fingers tightened on the handles of the piano stool and she waited. He was closer now, so close she could feel the warmth of his body, warmer even than the summer night.

'It isn't your playing that keeps me awake,' he said. His voice was harsh and her mind raced. Did he mean . . . could he mean . . . that it was something else about her that caused him sleeplessness?

At the thought a small involuntary gasp escaped her lips and he stopped abruptly. She felt his mood change and harden as clearly as she saw the tightening of his lips.

'I came to look for my pocket watch,' he said swiftly. 'I seem to have mislaid it and I wondered if I had left it here.'

'Oh.' Feeling vulnerable and foolish in case she had misjudged his motives, Regan busied herself in helping him to look for the missing watch. But when the search proved fruitless he stopped beside her, touching her arm so that his fingers seemed to be burning through the thin fabric of her wrap.

'Don't you think you should come to bed now?' he said.

Her heart leapt again. Could there be an invitation behind his words? Had she been wrong – did he want her? Then fear of rejection flooded her again. She had been hurt too often. If she made anything of this she would be hurt again, as surely as night must follow day.

'I'm all right. I think I'll practise a little longer if I'm not disturbing you,' she said carefully.

And it was only when he had gone and she was alone once more that she lay her head down on the keys and realized that for all her efforts she had not been able to avoid being hurt.

CHAPTER FIFTEEN

Christmas came and went and Regan was surprised to find the Caseys celebrated it in traditional style in spite of the hot summer weather.

To her, used as she was to the softer English climate, the dry heat was grinding and when she heard talk among the workers of bushfires, she trembled inwardly. When she had driven out into the bush she had seen the marks of other conflagrations – blackened stumps of ironbarks rising out of the new growth – and now she shrank from the thought of how fire would roar through the tinder-dry brush. Nothing would be safe from it, not man nor beast, and she sensed the waiting fear that was in all of them.

A week after Christmas, however, something happened that drove all thought of natural occurrences from their minds.

It was late evening and Zach, Seamus and Regan were lingering at the table after dinner. Zach had been out to the boundaries of the property and had been late returning; now he and Seamus talked, as they always did, of business, while Regan occupied herself with wondering if, when the weather became a little cooler, she dare ask Zach if he would keep to his promise and teach her to ride.

Suddenly through the windows that were still thrown open to catch the cooler evening air they heard the sound of galloping hooves and a moment later, raised voices.

Seamus and Zach exchanged looks and Regan's blood ran cold. Had the bush gone up? Was someone riding in to tell them a tide of flame was sweeping towards their land? She sat, paralyzed with fear, as the men pushed back their chairs, but before they could leave the room the door burst open and Jim Mitchell came in.

His clothes and face were thick with dust but it was not the pungent black dust that comes from smoke and fire. It was all Regan could do to keep from screaming at him to tell them what was wrong, but Zach and Seamus seemed as calm as ever, only the tautness of their muscles betraying their anxiety.

'Well, Jim?' Seamus enquired evenly, and the foreman took his cabbage-tree hat from his head, twisting it between his hands as he spoke.

'Terrible news, Mr Casey. I thought as how you ought to know right away.'

'What is it?' Zach asked impatiently.

Jim looked from one to the other of them, plainly determined to make the most of his moment of importance.

'It's Jud Trenoweth,' he said at last. 'He's been murdered.'

'*What*?' Afterwards Regan was never quite sure which of them it was who had spoken. Their breath seemed to come out on a concerted gasp, and they stared at Jim for a moment in utter amazement.

Zach broke the silence. 'When did this happen?' he asked sharply.

'Tonight – leastways, I suppose it must have been tonight,' Jim said levelly. ''Twas out on the Robertson road it took place. Jud was found not an hour ago, lying shot beside his buggy, and the gold he had with him gone – every last nugget of it.'

'You mean he was bushwhacked?' Seamus asked and the foreman shrugged.

'That's what it looks like, I grant you. Jud had been out to the mine and was on his way back to town with rich finds. But it's a mighty funny thing if you ask me. He weren't in the buggy when he were found, but beside it, as if he'd stopped and got down to talk to whoever it were killed him. Now I can't seem him doing that, can you, if a bushie came at him out of the trees? Jud's a hard man, and he knows this country like the back o' his hand. What's more, his horses could outrun any hereabouts. Why didn't he try to make a run for it, that's what I'd like to know? Why hand over the gold and get down, all convenient like, to be shot?'

Seamus shook his head. 'I'm sure I don't know, Jim. It'll all come out in time, I suppose. But it's a shock all the same, even if the man was asking for trouble by driving about alone and unprotected with a buggy full of gold.'

Zach nodded his agreement. 'There are plenty of men who would murder for it,' he said briefly. 'Gold – or the greed for it – is a sickness. I've said that often enough but it's no more than the truth.'

Regan stirred uncomfortably, thinking of Richard. It was a sickness with him, right enough. Though it would take a harder and more violent man than he to take it to extremes and kill for the love of it.

'Who found poor Jud?' Seamus asked.

The foreman gave his hat an extra twist and directed his gaze straight at Zach.

''Twas Miss Adelaide,' he said.

Regan saw Zach start involuntarily.

'Adelaide Jackson?' he asked sharply.

The faintest smile touched the corners of Jim's mouth before his face once more resumed the solemn expression of a bearer of ill tidings.

'That's right,' he confirmed. 'She'd been out visiting, or so I heard, and she came upon the murder on her way home.'

Regan shivered. Dear God, it could very well have been *her* who had found Jud. The thought of coming upon a dead body in a clearing was a terrifying one and she wondered if she would ever be able to drive out again without thinking about it.

'Have you heard how she's taken it?' Zach asked, and at the concern in his tone Regan felt a twist of jealousy.

Seamus, however, chuckled. 'Knowing Adelaide, it's likely she never turned a hair,' he said with a twinkle. 'A pioneer of the old school, that's Adelaide. Why, I wouldn't put it past her to have been the one to kill him herself, if she had a reason!'

Regan's eyes widened. 'Surely you don't think . . .' she began.

'No, of course not,' Seamus reassured her, and Jim broke in:

'Not Adelaide, Miss Regan, but somebody he knew – leastways, that's what they're saying in Robertson. Jud wouldn't have stopped that buggy of his for a bush-whacker, they say, and if you ask me, that's not far out. Though whether the truth will ever come out, that's another matter.'

After he had left the room, Seamus and Zach went on discussing the killing, much to Regan's discomfiture. Remembering how she had driven alone through the bush, she would have preferred to try and put the atrocity from her mind, and besides, thinking of a man being shot reminded her all too sharply of her own father's death.

She was still rankling, too, at the memory of Zach's concern for Adelaide, and when in the course of the conversation he pondered aloud whether he should ride to Robertson and offer his services to help find the men who had committed the murder the all-too-familiar jealousy stabbed at her, try as she might not to let it.

Go to help find the culprit, indeed! All he wanted was a chance to make sure Adelaide was none the worse for her ordeal!

Forcing a small smile, she stood up.

'I think I'll retire,' she murmured.

Seamus fixed her with his shrewd gaze.

'You're looking quite pale, m'voreen. This news has upset you, hasn't it? You mustn't let it. This is a wild country, yes, but these things don't happen every day, so you must put it from your mind.'

She nodded. 'I'll try,' she promised meekly, and Seamus turned to Zach.

'Sure, see her to her room, boy. Never mind talking with me. It's an old man I am. I've been alone with troubles before and I dare say I will be again. But your wife needs you.'

Regan tried to protest, but Zach rose with exaggerated courtesy, putting a hand behind her waist to shepherd her to the door.

The nearness of him set her pulses racing; his touch was like a firebrand on her back. Why could he do this to her, she wondered? How could she still want him this much, knowing that all his thoughts were with the painted saloon girl turned hotel owner? Her emotions churned within her and she was terrified she would somehow expose them to his piercing gaze.

As soon as they were out of Seamus's hearing, she hissed at him over her shoulder:

'You've no need to be concerned about me, Zach. I'm quite capable of putting myself to bed, you know.'

His mouth touched her ear, his hot breath whispering into it.

'I know that, my sweet. But if you don't want my father to know it too, you'd better play your part a little better than you have been doing. I'm not surprised you never were successful as an actress. Your talent for deception seems to fall short of your musical abilities.'

'Oh!' she squealed indignantly, and it was only when she was alone in her room and Zach had returned downstairs for a last tot of rum with Seamus that the irony of the remark came home to her.

If only he knew she was play-acting every waking moment! If only he knew the efforts she was constantly making to hide from him the fact that in spite of everything she wanted him just as he had sworn she would! Still I'd die before he would have the satisfaction of being proved right! thought Regan. I'd die before he should know I have so little pride and self-respect as to care for a man who cares nothing for me!

She undressed herself carelessly, throwing her clothes

down before packing them carefully enough not to arouse the suspicions of the maids. Though if they found her undergarments discarded in a hasty heap, they would probably leap to the wrong conclusion in any case and imagine that it was Zach who had tossed them there in the height of passion. But how wrong they would be!

She climbed into bed and lay wide-eyed and sleepless, staring at the ceiling while a million muddled thoughts chased themselves through her head.

How could she have guessed, she wondered, when she had sailed from England, the future that lay before her? If a fortune teller had even hinted at it she would have laughed and called her crazy. To lose her father so violently, to be claimed in payment of his gambling debts, to have Richard desert her in a strange land without a second thought, and to be tied to a rich squatter who cared not one jot for her – it was all so wildly improbable that if she did not pinch herself, she might believe she was only dreaming. And the life she lived was unreal too – with fine clothes and servants and a valuable piano of her own – luxuries to gild the harsh reality of life in the outback, where bushfires, flood and drought were everpresent threats and a man like Jud Trenoweth could be murdered by bushrangers or even, if what Jim had hinted at contained any grain of truth, by someone he knew and trusted.

In spite of the warmth of the night, Regan shivered. It was not a nice thought, that. Better that it should be a faceless bushranger than it should be someone she herself might have met on one of her visits to Robertson. Pushing the thought aside she turned her face into the pillow and willed herself to search for the elusive elixir of sleep.

Two or three days passed and they were no nearer finding Jud's killer.

The rumours persisted and everyone had their own favourite suspect or theory, but rumours could not make an arrest and there seemed to be no shred of evidence to connect anyone with the murder.

'I still think it was someone who worked for him,' Mary Mitchell said to Regan one hot morning at the beginning of January. 'Either that or it was the Trenton brothers. They're the most notorious bushies in these parts and they'll feel the rope around their necks before they finish, mark my words.

Regan nodded, trying to show interest. Privately she wished the atrocity could be forgotten, but she had no wish to upset Mary Mitchell. It was so unusual for her to make friendly small talk, and it eased the loneliness of the outback to have someone to gossip to.

'Gold – they can smell it a mile away!' she continued, but before Regan could reply, the door opened and Queenie came skipping in grasping a handful of envelopes.

'The mail's come!' she announced. 'And one of them is for you, Regan.'

'For *me*?' Regan could hardly conceal her surprise. Since coming to Ballymena, she had never once had a letter. Who was there to write to her?

Curiously she took it. The envelope was printed in a neat hand and told her nothing, so whilst Mary Mitchell sorted through her own mail she ripped it open and drew out the single sheet of paper. Then, as she began to read, her eyes widened and the blood drained from her cheeks.

An anonymous note! And what an anonymous note!

'*I have evidence to prove your husband was connected with the murder of Jud Trenoweth,*' she read. '*I would not like it to fall into the hands of the law, so if you wish to gain possession of it and thus save his neck from the hangman's noose, be at the Widow's Tree on the Robertson Road at noon on Friday. Bring with you 50 gold sovereigns. Exchange is no robbery.*'

For a moment Regan stared at the letter in stunned disbelief. It was a joke – it must be, and yet . . . Somehow, terrifyingly, she knew it was no joke. With trembling hands she thrust the paper back into the envelope and muttering some excuse to Mary ran upstairs to her room. Then, with the door firmly shut behind her, she scanned the contents once more.

Zach connected with Jud's murder and threatened with the hangman's noose! It was insane! She did not believe it.

That much she knew. But the note stated that the writer had *evidence* and threatened to hand it over to the law if his demands were not met.

Regan pressed her hands to her head, trying to make sense of the words that spun before her eyes. Who could have written the letter? And on what was the accusation based? What so-called 'proof' could they possibly have? It was a mistake, of course, it must be, and yet . . .

Supposing it was *not* a mistake but a deliberate attempt to frame Zach? There were those who would be jealous of the Caseys and be glad to see their downfall. Could the 'evidence', whatever it might be, be something that would stand up in a court of law, or at least throw enough suspicion on Zach to discredit him? It must be, surely, or why should anyone try to blackmail her for it? And if this was the case, did Zach have any way of proving his innocence?

Regan's racing mind flew back to the night of the murder. They had been at dinner when the news had arrived – and they had been late eating because Zach had been out to the boundaries. But the murder had occurred earlier in the evening – the very time for which he had no alibi! And besides . . .

With a shiver, she found herself remembering what people were saying in the town – that Jud must have known his killer. Was it possible they might believe the man for whom he had stopped his buggy was Zach? It was ridiculous – crazy. Zach was no thief and certainly no secret murderer. She knew that. He cared nothing for gold – or at least he did not care enough to kill for it. And he had no quarrel with Jud, no reason to waylay him in the bush and take his life. If Zach set out to kill someone, he would do it openly, with a hundred witnesses, the way he did everything else! But she had no way of proving it, and the only way she could discover the strength of the so-called 'evidence' against him was to keep the appointment as the letter bade her on Friday – tomorrow! – at the Widow's Tree! If she failed, and some damaging accusations fell into the hands of the law, heaven only knew where it would end. Maybe, as the letter suggested, with Zach on trial for murder, with his very life in danger.

If only he was here now so that she could talk it over with him! she thought, pressing her fingertips to her aching head. But he was not. He had ridden to Tacoomba, a day's journey north-east, to clinch a business deal and he was unlikely to be back before the time for the appointment had come and gone. Could it be that the blackmailer, whoever he may be, had known that and timed the arrival of the letter accordingly? It was possible. But if she wanted to help Zach she could not wait to find out. By hook or by crook she must keep the appointment herself.

But there was still the question of the fifty golden sovereigns. Regan had not a penny of her own – she had had no cause to want any. And she could not imagine where she could find a sum sufficient to meet the blackmailer's demand.

She could, she supposed, go to Seamus and show him the letter, but somehow she was unwilling to do that. It would doubtlessly raise his Irish temper and that could do more harm than good. If Seamus, fighting mad, kept the appointment, any evidence would most likely be handed over to the bobbies or the military and that would be an end of it. And someone would certainly add that Zach Casey had inherited his murderous temper from his father!

She stood for a moment thinking furiously. Supposing she was to tell Seamus she needed money to go shopping in Robertson for some new things for herself? It was a deception, yes, and she hated deceiving the old man who had treated her with such kindness. But she had to find out what evidence there was against Zach – and who it was who was trying to pin the murder on him. And deception was the only way she could hope to get the money in time.

Taking a grip on herself, she tucked the letter into her reticule and went in search of Seamus.

She found him in the study, sorting through his own correspondence. She hesitated in the doorway, wondering if he would be annoyed to be disturbed, but when he realized she was there he looked up and smiled.

'Good morning, Regan! What can I do for you this grand day?'

She swallowed hard, wishing she could cross her fingers behind her back as she had done as a child when she was about to tell an untruth.

'I'm afraid I've come to beg for money. There are some things I need from Robertson – I wanted to go and order them while Zach's away, so as to surprise him.'

Seamus's eyes became shrewd.

'You mean to drive to Robertson – alone?' he asked.

She coloured.

'Yes. I'll be all right. I'm more used to handling the pony now.'

The snowy-haired Irishman thought for a moment and she held her breath. Then he shook his head.

'I'm sorry, m'voreen. Whatever you want is yours, you know that. But Zach would never forgive me if I let you cavort about the country on your own again, and if something happened to you, I'd never forgive myself either.'

Regan began to tremble.

'But . . . what harm could come to me?' she protested.

'Sure the bush could go up, for one thing. It's tinder-dry as well you know, and there's not a horse on Ballymena that could outrun the flames with a buggy behind him. The fire leaps from tree to tree like a hungry beast – the speed it moves you wouldn't believe unless you'd seen it with your own eyes.'

'But it's not going to happen at the very time I'm driving the road, surely?' Regan said desperately.

'There's no telling when it will go up,' Seamus told her sternly, 'though we pray it won't happen at all. No, Regan, I'm sorry. I don't like refusing you, but I can't allow it. If there's something you need from Robertson, one of the men can go.'

Realizing it was useless Regan left the study, then stood for a moment in the hall wondering what she could do next. She must keep the appointment, that much she was determined on, be it with Seamus's permission or without. But what good was a meeting with a blackmailer if she had nothing with which to pay his demands?

Briefly Regan considered again whether it might be best to tell Seamus the truth. But at once she decided against it. If the Irishman went in with all guns blazing, it could only do more harm than good. Why, there might even be another killing if he took it into his head to try and take the evidence from whoever it was who claimed to have it.

No, there had to be another way. But what – what? How could she raise the money demanded? She had not a penny of her own; nothing . . .

She caught herself up abruptly as she suddenly remembered Zach's Christmas present to her. It was a brooch, as beautiful as any she had ever seen – tiny, star-stud diamonds offsetting an emerald that Zach had said reminded him of her eyes. She had fallen in love with it and it meant far more to her than the value of the stones, priceless though they were. Zach had bought it for her, and although she knew he had given it to her merely to preserve appearances, she still treasured it as his gift. But she would give it and willingly if it meant saving him from being turned over to the law for something he had not done. Why, if the so-called evidence against him was strong enough, it might even put a noose around his neck. Men were hung here for less than murder. And if she could gain possession of the so-called 'evidence' and ensure Zach's safety, she would count her brooch well lost.

All day she was in a dream, going over and over the note and all its implications. And before long she found herself eyeing everyone at Ballymena with new-found suspicion.

Whoever had written the note and planted it in the mail had known Zach was away. She was sure of it. And they had known, too, that she would know where to find the Widow's Tree – though she supposed everyone hereabouts must know of it – the eucalyptus from whose towering heights a branch had come crashing down, ten years and more ago, impaling the best-known shearer for miles around and making a widow of the wife who had borne him eight children. What was more, to set a time and date for the meeting, the sender must have been reasonably sure she would receive the note in time. And that meant only one thing. It was someone she knew – and knew well, maybe. Of that she was fairly certain. But it was not a pleasant feeling to think that someone Zach trusted might be plotting against him, and she wondered with apprehension who it was she would find waiting for her beneath the Widow Tree.

That night Regan slept little and when she rose she went straight to the window, scanning the sky for any clouds that might be the first welcome sign of rain. Seamus's warning of the speed with which a bushfire could strike had gone home, though at the time her mind had been full of more urgent considerations, and now she felt a sick dread at the thought of driving through the tinder-dry brush. If only she had kept Zach to his promise to teach her to ride! A fast horse, with only her scant weight to handicap him, might outrun flames where a pony and buggy could not. But it was too late now to think about that. She had not learned to ride, but she could drive the buggy. If she was to help Zach she must do the best she could with that and hope she did not have to take the consequences.

At breakfast she was nervous and subdued and Seamus plainly thought it was his refusal to lend her the money that had upset her.

'Zach will be home by tonight and I'm sure he'll arrange for you to have whatever it is you want,' he comforted her.

'If *he's* not caught in a bushfire,' Regan retorted rebelliously.

Seamus shrugged. 'It's a danger we live with and have grown used to. And now, my dear, I must ask you to excuse me. I have to ride out with Jim Mitchell and the work will take all day as it is.'

Regan's heart leapt. So Seamus would be away at noon! That would give her a chance to take the buggy out unobserved.

When breakfast was done she went to her room, slipping the precious brooch into her reticule and hoping it would be enough to satisfy the greed of the blackmailer. Then she prepared herself for the drive. It would take the best part of an hour to reach the Widow Tree, she knew, and she could not risk being late in case the blackmailer should think she was not coming and leave, taking his 'evidence' with him. So, in good time, she went to the stables and asked for the buggy to be made ready.

Tommy, the stable lad, seemed surprised, but he was used to obeying the Casey's instructions and he did as she asked. As she drove away from Ballymena her heart was beating a tattoo and beads of perspiration that owed more to nervousness than to the heat, stood out on her face.

As she drove, she looked around fearfully, watching for any sign of fire – and the other thing she feared – meeting Seamus face to face on this side of the property. He could have come this way for all she knew, and she had no idea how she would explain herself should she run across him. But with fierce determination she swallowed her fears. She had to do this, for Zach's sake. He had saved her from difficult situations many times – now it was her turn to do something for him. And even if she had owed him nothing she would still have wanted to help him, no matter what the dangers to herself. To see him implicated in a murder would be more than she could bear, loving him as she did now. To think of him hanging for a killing of which he was innocent was insupportable.

How strange, she thought. Once I should have rejoiced to think of him suffering. Not now!

The sun was high in the sky when the Widow Tree came into view and at once her pulses began to race once more. Now, soon, she would discover the identity of the black-mailer and the strength of the 'evidence' he had against Zach. Was he already there waiting for her?

As she reined in the pony in the clearing beneath the tree, a black shadow fell across the grass, and turning, her heart pounding within her breast, she saw a man coming towards her.

CHAPTER SIXTEEN

As the man crossed the clearing towards her, a small gasp escaped Regan.

The dark, stocky figure was familiar, just as she had

feared it would be, but the identity of the blackmailer still took her by surprise. It was Matt, the jack-of-all-trades servant who worked for Adelaide at the Commercial Hotel!

'*You!*' she murmured.

The man looked around quickly, as if to make certain Regan was alone, and when he was satisfied an unpleasant smile twisted the corners of his mouth.

'I'm glad you decided to keep our appointment, Mrs Casey. But then, I thought I could rely on you.'

Regan drew herself up tight, ignoring his leering implication.

'What do you want with me?' she asked, her voice harsh with nervousness.

For a moment the man did not answer. His amused eyes roamed over her and she fumed helplessly as she realized how much he was enjoying his power over her.

'I thought I explained that in my letter, Mrs Casey,' he drawled at last. 'In fact I was under the impression I had made myself admirably clear, and we were meeting here today to do our best to save the neck of your dear husband from the hangman's noose.'

Ever since she had received the letter yesterday she had been unable to forget the awful threat that hung over Zach if he was implicated in Jud's murder. Now, hearing the words spoken aloud, she could not suppress a shiver.

'Zach is innocent!' she said vehemently. 'I know he is! What evidence could you possibly have to prove otherwise?'

A grin spread across the man's face and she wished she dared strike out at him.

'Don't distress yourself so!' he chided. 'It's good to know you have such faith in your husband and I sincerely hope it is well-placed. But I fear he may have difficulty in explaining even to you how his property came to be found at the scene of the murder.'

'Property?' Regan repeated sharply. 'What property?'

The man reached into his pocket and when he withdrew his hand Regan saw that he was holding a small pouch. His eyes never leaving her face, he opened it, and extracted a pocket watch which he held out towards her.

'Zach's watch!' she gasped as her eye took in the distinctive markings. 'How did you come by that?'

As she spoke she reached out instinctively to take it, but Matt withdrew sharply.

'Not so fast, my dear Mrs Casey! Not so fast!'

'Where did you get Zach's watch?' Regan asked again. Matt's small, mean eyes held hers.

'It was found by Jud Trenoweth's body. If necessary I could swear to that in a court of law, though I hope most sincerely that it will not come to that.'

'Found by Jud's body? You mean to tell me that Adelaide . . .'

'*I* found it,' Matt said smoothly. 'When we came upon the scene of the murder I naturally got down to investigate and I found it lying in the brush almost under the buggy wheels. I said nothing to Miss Adelaide or to anyone. As I mentioned in my letter, I was anxious it should not fall into the wrong hands.'

'Oh!' Regan's mind was racing as she took in this new turn of events. So Matt had been with Adelaide when they had come upon the murdered man – she had only assumed her to have been alone. But how had Zach's watch come to be there on the very spot where Jud had been killed?

'It would look bad for him, don't you agree?' Matt's gnarled hand clenched and unclenched over the watch, giving Regan tantalizing glimpses of it. 'I'm sure even you find it difficult to believe in his innocence in the face of such evidence.'

Regan drew a sharp breath, her mind flying back to the night Zach had returned to the drawing room when she had been playing the piano. He had been looking for his watch then and he had never found it. She had heard him comment on it several times and curse the loss. And that had been some time before Jud's murder. No, for Zach's watch to have been found by the body was no proof at all – in fact to her it would have been proof, had she needed it, that Zach had no connection with the attack. But who would believe that?

'Well, Mrs Casey?' the man pressed her. 'Do you agree I did the right thing in making this damning piece of proof available to you, rather than turning it over to the authorities? As a good citizen I suppose that is what I should have done. But I did not care for the idea of putting a noose around your good husband's neck.'

'You mean you saw your chance of making some easy money!' Regan flared before she could stop herself, but the man did not appear put out by her insult.

'Don't let's talk about it in those terms,' he urged her. 'Let's say I'm helping Zach out and you're showing your appreciation. Now, do you have the money?'

Regan opened her reticule and slipped out the brooch. The emerald caught the sparkle of the sun, exploding to a small pool of green fire, and tears ached in her throat. She didn't want to part with it, oh, she didn't! But this horrid, gasping little man was quite right. Things could look very bad indeed for Zach if it came to light that his watch had been found at the scene of the murder. Useless to protest that it had no longer been in his possession then. That would be dismissed as the excuse of a guilty man – and everyone would expect his wife to back him up. Her own word that the watch had already been lost would be worth nothing. No, there was only one thing to be done – buy the so-called 'evidence' and take it safely home. That way and that way only could she be sure it would not put a noose round Zach's neck.

'I couldn't get the money,' she said swiftly. 'I don't have any of my own, and Zach is away. So I brought this instead. It's worth far more than you asked.'

She held it out and saw his small eyes widen with greed.

'The stones are real,' she went on. 'I'll give it to you if you'll give me Zach's watch.'

Seeing the wary look on her face he laughed suddenly. Zach Casey's bride might be an English girl instead of the native-born Australian Adelaide always maintained he would have taken for his wife; she might look too fragile to survive out here in the bush. But she was no fool and she had courage. He would tell his mistress that next time she treated him with the sort of disdain that made his hackles rise with helpless fury.

Slowly he held out the watch.

'As I said in my letter, exchange is no robbery,' he told

her. 'Put your brooch in my left hand and you can take
your husband's timepiece from my right.'

Regan did as she was bid, and as her fingers closed over
the watch relief surged through her. It was in her possession now, it could no longer be used to incriminate Zach,
unless someone discovered her here, carrying out the act
of barter . . .

Suddenly she was trembling again and desperately anxious to leave this clearing which had seen at least one
premature death, far behind her.

Pushing the watch into her reticule, she turned back to
the buggy, without another word to Matt. But she knew
his eyes were following her, and as she took up the reins,
his mocking voice reached her.

'Good day, Mrs Casey. It's been a pleasure doing business with you.'

As soon as she shook the reins, Lucky began to walk
back to the path and it was all she could do not to urge him
to an immediate canter. The afternoon felt heavy now, and
oppressive, and every nerve in her body was stretched to
breaking point. It was as if there was some sort of threat
hanging in the still air, she thought, and the whole of the
bush was waiting for it. Why, even the pony was jumpy.
She could see it in the small, impatient movements he
made as he trotted along the track – a flick of his tail here,
a twitch of his ear there, a dozen different muscles quivering independently in his back and rump.

Afraid he might be able to sense something she could
not, she looked around her fearfully. Though she could
see no clouds above the eucalyptus, the sky seemed to
have darkened and she thought she heard thunder roll in
the distance. At the sound her spine seemed to turn to
water. A dry storm! That could be the very thing to start a
bushfire. One arrow of lightning striking a dessicated tree
would be all that was needed and the tinder-dry bush
would go up.

All the stories she had heard on Ballymena of bushfires
came rushing back to her and she glanced from side to side
imagining the way the fire would leap and bound, with
gums exploding to send showers of sparks into the hot,
acrid air and all the birds and animals fleeing from the

inferno. Dear God, if that happened she would not stand a chance! Seamus had been quite right. To drive out today as she had done had been the height of foolishness.

Yet even now, her whole body was tingling with fear, Regan knew that given the same circumstances, she would do the same thing again. Whatever happened, she had the evidence against Zach safe in her keeping. No one could now claim to have damning proof of murder to lay at his door. No matter what the dangers she would encounter, they were small compared with the danger to Zach if someone tried to pin Jud's killing on him. And if that had happened and she had not done everything in her power to prevent it she would never, ever, have forgiven herself.

As Lucky bowled along the dusty track she thought of the man who had blackmailed her so successfully and she felt an echo of the surprise that had run through her when he had come across the clearing into her view and she had recognized him.

Adelaide's servant, Matt! Who would have thought it? Yet now that she came to consider it who else could it have been – unless it was Adelaide herself? If the whole thing were not a complete hoax it had to be someone who had been on the scene and fairly promptly, too.

But how had Matt – or anyone else for that matter – come to find Zach's watch beside the body? Surely Zach could not have dropped it there himself? It would be too great a coincidence to suppose he could have lost it at the very spot some bushwhacker had chosen to hold up Jud. And that left only one alternative. The murderer had dropped the watch. That, of course, was the conclusion Matt had reached. Only he had not known that Zach had already lost the watch, some time before the murder . . .

Perhaps it was stolen by one of the sundowners when we were shearing, thought Regan. But if that were the case she was surprised Zach had not missed it before. And there was still the nagging thought that local people believed Jud had known his killer. If that were so, and the same person had somehow been in possession of Zach's watch, then it must be someone they both knew and who had been with Zach in the recent past.

Another roll of thunder rumbled in the heavy air, making Regan sharply aware once more of her danger. She straightened up, urging Lucky to a canter, and he surged forward between the dusty tree ferns and ironbarks.

Don't let there be a fire! she prayed silently, but it was not only of her own safety she was thinking. It was as if she could see beyond that now, to the awful destruction of the bush. She didn't want its dense green to be shrivelled and blackened; she didn't want the birds and animals to die in the agony of a holocaust. Without realizing it she had come to love the outback just as she had come to love Zach. To the timid, it might be a cruel and unrelenting place, but to those prepared to take it on its own terms it was exciting, challenging and full of unexpected beauty. Like Zach himself, she thought, and a strange, sharp pain drove through her loins so that she urged Lucky on faster still.

Before she had gone much farther she felt the first spots of rain heavy in her hair and as big as farthings on her face. In the open buggy she had no protection from it and in the space of a few minutes her thin dress was soaked through and clinging to her. But she felt nothing but relief and wild exhilaration. It was not going to be a dry storm after all! The rain was pattering on the leaves and making puddles on the ground that was baked too hard to absorb it, and it was the most wonderful feeling in the world! She lifted up her face so that the raindrops ran over it, sticking out her tongue to catch them and delighting in the sweet taste. Rain! Shivering and wet in England, she had hated it. Now, it was like the nectar of the gods.

And it seemed like an omen, too, of a fresh beginning. Perhaps even now it wasn't too late to begin again. Perhaps even now she could make Zach love her . . .

By the time she was within sight of Ballymena, Regan was drenched, her clothes sticking to her body and her hair hanging limply on her cheeks, but the storm was already passing over.

Regan trotted Lucky up the drive and around to the stables. For once there was no sign of Silas or Tommy, so she set about unharnessing the pony herself and wiping down his steaming flanks.

It was quiet in the stable yard except for the stamping and twitching of the horses, and when she heard a voice coming from one of the boxes, Regan jumped in surprise, twisting round sharply.

It was Queenie. First her head appeared over the top of the door, then her small, straggly body, as she hoisted herself over and stood looking at Regan with wide, amused eyes.

'You're wet!' she said unnecessarily.

Regan nodded. 'Yes, I am. But it was good to see the rain, so I don't mind.'

'We didn't think you'd like getting wet and dirty.' Queenie was still regarding her with solemn concentration. 'We thought an English girl would be hopeless. But you're not so bad, really.'

'Well, thank you!' Regan returned, amused. 'To tell you the truth, Queenie, I didn't think you liked me very much.'

'Well . . .' Queenie rubbed her finger along Lucky's nose and wiped the grime from it onto her skirt. 'It wasn't that I didn't like you, Regan. It was just that I didn't want you to marry Zach. I used to think he might marry me when I grew up, you see. But I know now that was a bit foolish of me. He'd have had to wait far too long, wouldn't he?'

Regan suppressed a smile.

'I think he would, Queenie. And I'm sure there's some very nice boy for you somewhere. You'll have your pick when you grow older. I think you're very lucky, really.'

Queenie nodded slowly.

'Yes, I suppose I am. But so are you. Just now I can't think of anybody I like better than Zach.'

And neither can I, thought Regan, though she just smiled at Queenie. She was glad the child had accepted her a little – it seemed like yet another good omen for the future.

She went on unharnessing Lucky, though she was glad when Tommy came into the yard and relieved her of the last of the jobs. Not that she didn't want to do them – there was something very relaxing about being out here surrounded by the animals – but she was terrified of doing something wrong or omitting some important precaution, and bringing Zach's wrath down on her head.

'You'd better go and get into some dry clothes, Mrs Casey,' he advised her and she nodded resignedly.

'Yes, I suppose I'd better.'

Queenie remained in the stables and when Regan entered the house it felt as empty as when she had left it. Seamus was obviously still out with Jim Mitchell and she was glad of that. To have met him face to face and have had to explain her soaking had been one of the things she was afraid of. And Zach could not have returned yet, either.

Leaving a trail of damp behind her she climbed the sweeping staircase. Then, in the privacy of her room, she opened her reticule and drew out the watch.

In a moment she would send for a tub of hot water and fresh clothes. Just now the most important thing was to satisfy herself with the knowledge that the so-called evidence was safely in her possession and could no longer be used to incriminate Zach.

As she looked down at the watch, however, a small perplexed frown wrinkled Regan's forehead. The timepiece was Zach's right enough. She was in no doubt as to that – the markings on the face were so distinctive she would have known them anywhere. But the pouch that held it was strangely unfamiliar.

Zach's pouch, she was sure, had been of the smoothest leather, soft and dark from much use. This one was too new, too shiny and too stiff. And by comparison it appeared cheap and roughly made.

As the thoughts ran through her mind Regan's heart seemed to miss a beat. If she was right – if this pouch was *not* Zach's – then surely that could mean only one thing. It belonged to whoever had been using the watch and had been at the scene of Jud's killing – the person who had perhaps actually murdered the property owner!

For a moment Regan stood, almost overwhelmed by the enormity of the realization. Then she crossed the floor to Zach's dressing room. She could be mistaken about the pouch – memory played such odd tricks sometimes it was a possibility she could not entirely discount. But if she found Zach's pouch still in his possession she would know that so far, at least, her assumptions were correct.

Zach's dressing room was in a fairly ordered state; she guessed the maids had been in to tidy up after he had left. She looked around her, not sure where the pouch would be and unwilling to pry more deeply than necessary. Regan was too fond of her own privacy to enjoy desecrating someone else's.

Her eye skimmed over his coat, hanging behind the door – he always rode out attired in breeches and shirt – to the dressing table and wooden chest. There was a box atop it, a small, polished wood box inlaid with mother of pearl, and it seemed to her the likeliest place for him to keep his odds and ends as well as his treasures. Swiftly she crossed to it, flipping up the lid and looking inside.

At once she could see that the pouch was not there, and she was just about to close the lid again when something caught her eye – something that glowed in the dim interior with the richness of a ruby . . .

Her eyes widened and her stiff fingers probed the contents of the box. She must be mistaken, surely! But that ruby! It looked for all the world like her own – the one that had been stolen from her father's pouch on the *Maid of Morne* while he lay dying . . .

Trembling suddenly and icy cold from head to foot she drew the ring from the depths of the box, and as the fresh sunlight-after-rain slanted through the window catching the facets of the beautiful stone and turning them to liquid gold she knew she had not been mistaken.

It was indeed the ring that had belonged to her dear, dead mother.

But what was it doing here – hidden amongst Zach's possessions?

CHAPTER SEVENTEEN

As Regan stood looking down at the ruby ring a million chaotic thoughts chased themselves round her spinning brain.

The last time she had seen it had been when her father had placed it, for safety, in his pouch aboard the *Maid of Morne*. Yet after his death, when she had wanted to use his sovereigns to pay off his gambling debts to Zach, she had found both them and the ring missing and a handful of pebbles in their place. Now, it was here – in Zach's dressing room, hidden away in the box where he kept his personal possessions.

But how – why?

Regan shook her head, unwilling to even allow birth to the terrible thought that was trying to force its way through the turmoil of her mind. Holy Mary, she must not for one second allow herself to wonder if it had been *Zach* who had rifled through her father's pouch as he lay dying! It was insupportable! Yet what else could she think? What other explanation could there be?

Against her will, Regan's mind was drawn back to the last hours of her father's life in Zach's cabin. She had hardly left his side long enough for an intruder to have substituted the pebbles for the sovereigns – that was what had puzzled her at the time. But could Zach have gained access to the pouch, perhaps while she slept? It was, after all, his cabin and no one would question him being there.

She had supposed, when she had got around to supposing anything, that someone had entered the cabin while she and most of the rest of the passengers and crew were on deck for the burial. It had been a vile thought and it had left the field so wide open that speculation had been pointless. Now, however, she found herself remembering that Zach had been nowhere to be seen that grey afternoon. She had thought his conscience had kept him away – and when, afterwards, she had returned to his cabin to collect her things and her father's, she had found him there alone. Could it be that he had been taking the opportunity of going through her father's belongings for anything of value? Why, it would not even have been a question of 'going through' them. He would know exactly where to find the sovereigns and the ring. Hadn't he seen both when he had beaten Thomas so thoroughly at dice?

She shuddered violently and the whole of her world seemed to shudder with her. If Zach had done such a thing, then it undermined the whole of her life here, the respect that had begun grudgingly and grown day by day and the love she now bore him. For it would mean that Zach was not at all that he seemed to be, but a thief and a cheat. And if those things – then why not a murderer too? If she could be so wrong about him that far then anything was possible.

But why? Why should a man of his means stoop to stealing a few sovereigns and a brooch, if indeed he had? She had seen now the empire to which he was sole heir, and benefitted many times from the generous way he spent his money. To take a handful of sovereigns from her and then repay her a hundredfold with fine clothes, a piano of her very own, jewellery worth as much, and probably far more than the ruby ring – it made no sense at all. Unless . . .

A chill ran through Regan's veins as she remembered the scene in the cabin when she had returned from the burial. Zach had insisted she should pay her father's debt in the way he had designated – by remaining with him. Even now, months later, she could still hear the cold determination in his voice – 'I won you, my dear, fairly and squarely in a game of dice'. But she had been equally determined not to succumb to such a fate. She had been willing to give him every last penny – and the ring as well – it would secure her freedom. And it would have done, if it had not been stolen. So was it possible Zach had anticipated her intention and substituted the pebbles so that she had nothing with which to barter? Had he deliberately rendered her penniless to place her at his mercy?

Dear God in Heaven, that could be it!

She looked down at the ring in her hand, glinting red fire at her, and she had the sudden fanciful notion that it was a reflection of her heart's blood. She had thought she would give anything for its return, so precious had it been to her as the last thing she had to remind her of her dear mother. But she had not realized how high the price would be. If only she could turn back the clock an hour and not know what she knew now! But that could not be. Zach had tricked her most cruelly, and she would have to live her life with the knowledge.

'Regan! What are you doing?'

The voice, like a whiplash, cut through her thoughts and she spun round, clutching the ring defensively to her. Zach! She had been so engrossed she had not heard his step on the stairs; now he stood framed in the doorway, his face dark with accusation.

For a moment she returned his stare while her heart pounded so loudly in her ears it sounded like the roar of the sea.

'What are you doing?' he asked again, and somewhere within her the storm broke.

'*You* ask me that?' she cried. 'You dare talk to me as if I had no rights here? After what you've done?'

His eyes narrowed. 'What are you talking about?' he asked harshly.

'This!' She stretched her arm out towards him and opened her fingers to reveal the ring lying in the palm of her hand. 'This, Zach Casey – my ring, stolen from me aboard the clipper. How did *you* come by it, I would like to know?'

'*Your* ring?' he repeated blankly. Then his brows came darkly together. 'What are you saying, Regan? You're not suggesting, surely, that I . . .?'

'Yes!' she cried. 'Yes, why not? You were determined to have me! And you knew that if I paid off my father's debt you would have no claim on me. You took it to keep me prisoner! Why else should it be here, hidden amongst your things? Why else? You see, you have no answer!'

He moved towards her, anger naked in his face, and she thought he was going to strike her. Fear coursed through

her, but hot on its heels came defiance. She had seen him
now in his true colours; let him do his worst.

His hands closed over her shoulders, holding them in a
grip of iron, but her eyes still blazed into his.

'Don't think you frighten me now, Zach!' she grated at
him. 'And don't think you can pretend you didn't know
my ring was here, either, because I won't believe you.'

'Of course I knew it was there!' Zach snarled. 'I bought
it for you from a trader I met in Robertson because I
thought it was similar to the one you had lost. I was
keeping it for your birthday.'

His voice carried conviction and she hesitated. *Was* it
possible he had bought the ring from a trader? But no, it
was surely too great a coincidence. Only a fool would
expect her to believe that the mysterious thief should have
turned up in Robertson of all places!

'A likely story!' she rasped.

'Regan, I swear to you as God is my judge . . .' Zach's
face had been close to hers, blotting out the room; now
suddenly as he realized there was no lessening of the cold
disbelief in her eyes he thrust her aside with an angry
movement. 'What am I to say to you? Your mind's made
up, isn't it? And if you really believe I would stoop to such
a trick, then there's no more to be said.'

Unexpectedly tears ached in her throat. Oh, why did it
have to be this way? Why?

'What am I supposed to think?' she cried. 'You'd made
up your mind to have me and that was the only way, I
suppose. You were so desperate for a woman – any
woman – you'd stop at nothing!'

'Not *any* woman.' His voice was low and harsh.

'Yes, any woman. You'd been at sea too long and you
were crazy for – for, oh, you know what! It blinded you to
everything else. You couldn't wait until you got back to
Australia for your paramour. You had to have me there
and then. But your conscience wouldn't allow you to rape
me without some excuse, would it? You had to believe
you had the right!'

Zach spun round; his eyes were like blazing coals.

'Yes, Regan, I wanted you! From the first moment I
saw you, I wanted you! You were like a fever in my blood,

damn you, making me forget my senses just as the poor fools in the diggings forget theirs at the scent of gold. I took you, yes. I thought to make you mine. But I did not trick you or rob you. If you believe I did, I will give you gold and to spare and you may leave this house without delay.'

A chill ran through her. Once, she would have given the world to hear those words. A moment ago, hating him, she had wished never to see him again. Now, suddenly, with the door of the cage flung wide she did not way to fly. But neither did she want her captor to know of the treacherous longing that even now gnawed at her heart.

'Well, what am I supposed to think?' she cried again. 'This is my ring – I'd know it anywhere.'

Zach stood unbending.

'The time has come for an end to this farce, Regan. We can go on with it no longer. I thought I could make you love me, but it seems I was wrong. Now either you believe me when I tell you I bought the ring in good faith from a dealer, and you live with me as my wife, or you go, with my blessing and half of everything I own. I will not be miserly with you. That much I owe you. But you must make your choice!'

She stared at him as the meaning behind his words ran arrow-straight through the turmoil of her thoughts.

'As your wife!' she repeated. 'I have never refused to live as your wife, Zach. Since we took our vows my bed has been open to you. It is *you* who refused to take advantage of it.'

'Because you would so plainly take me on sufferance only,' he told her harshly. 'There is precious little pleasure, Regan, in making love to a block of wood!'

'You didn't let that stop you when you raped me with my father scarcely cold!' she threw at him. 'You used me not once but three times, and you had no fine sensibilities about my response then!'

He did not answer and she knew she had scored.

'Of course, it was different at sea,' she persisted. 'You didn't have Adelaide to run to then as you do now.'

'What are you talking about?' he demanded.

She laughed aloud.

'Oh Zach, don't pretend! I'm not the fool you think me. I know you go to that whore Adelaide for your fun! The only thing I can't understand is why you married me and not her. Did your business interests conflict, or was she not a suitable wife for you? I pray you, do enlighten me!'

With a quick stride he was before her again, his fingers once more biting into her arms through the wet fabric of her dress.

'Stop it, Regan! I warn you!'

Breath caught in her throat but her eyes held his.

'Oh, you're threatening me now, are you? Don't you like to hear the truth about your mistress?'

'For the last time, Regan, she is not my mistress!' Zach grated. 'She was once, I grant you. But no more. Since I met you there has been no one else. You have been the only one, I swear it, though if I could but have forgotten you with another, I would willingly have done it. But we can't go on tearing one another apart. You hate me and I suppose I can hardly blame you. It's my misfortune that I still love you.'

Within her something sweet and sharp twisted painfully. He was close to her, so close that their breath seemed to be one and she could feel his heartbeat as if it were her own. Yet the only reality was the echo of his words, clamouring round and about her ringing ears.

'You *love* me?' she whispered.

'Yes, damn you.'

'You *love* me?' she repeated again, like one in a dream. 'I don't believe it!'

He moved impatiently.

'I don't know what else I can do to make you believe it. Or why I should try. It's over. There's nothing more I can do. I'll try to find your fiancé for you, Regan, and set you up with enough money to finance his digging until he grows tired of it.'

'No!' she whispered.

'I owe it to you,' he went on, as if he had not heard, and she caught at his shirt.

'Zach, no, I don't want it! Listen to me! I didn't know you loved me. I thought – oh, I didn't know what to think! I've been so confused – so terribly confused. I did hate you, it's true. I blamed you for my father's death and I swore to him that I'd make you pay. And I hated you for what you did to me. But not any more. Not any more!'

'You mean . . .? His fingers bit deeply into her shoulders and it seemed to her she was suspended in time and space.

'I mean I love you too, Zach. Oh dear love, you'll never know how much I love you!'

For a long moment they stood motionless looking at one another and their eyes said everything their lips could not. Disbelief gave way to wonder, misery to soaring joy, and the world shrank to the circle of their arms.

Then Zach's hands slid from her shoulders to her back and it seemed to her they burnt like branding irons through the wet fabric of her dress.

'Regan!' he murmured raggedly. 'Oh, Regan!'

Mesmerized by each other's eyes they drew together and Regan felt as if her whole body was alive with the quivering sweetness. Deep within her sharp tongues of delight were flicking and every tiny nerve ending from head to toe was yearning for his touch. As his mouth covered hers her lips parted as a flower unfolds in sunlight and his probing tongue started a fresh fever within her. Hungrily she clung to him, her hands exploring the rippling muscles of his shoulders, glorying in the hard strength and the pressure of his hips against hers made her wish she dared run her hands the length of his back to feel the tautness of his buttocks and thighs. But she could not; her love was still too new. It made her shy.

As if reading her mind he held her away for a moment, smiling down into her eyes before pulling her close and covering her lips once more with his own. The kiss grew deeper and she felt the sudden urgency in his body while his hands moved restlessly across her back, fumbling for the fastenings of her dress. But this time she made no move to stop him. She wanted to be free of its cloying folds, wanted to feel him against her with nothing between.

With a low moan she pressed herself against him and as her yielding body thrust against his manhood he could restrain his need for her no longer. Leaving the bodice that clung wetly to her skin he lifted her bodily, carrying her across the dressing room to the makeshift bed and lying down upon it. With a swift movement he divested himself of his trousers and hoisted her skirts about her waist. Then he lay down beside her, running his hand over her belly to the hillock beneath. Her flesh burned beneath his touch and her muscles tensed, but as his fingers probed the softness of her thighs, searching for the hidden hollow, her breath came out on a sigh and she parted her legs slightly to him.

The movement stirred his senses and awoke all the suppressed desire that was in him. It was all he could do now not to mount her instantly and possess her. But he had sworn a vow not to take her until she wanted him as he wanted her and even now, while his body throbbed with desire, the severity of that vow implanted in his mind held him back.

He threw back his head and the muscles in his throat stood out in hard knots.

'Oh, Regan!' It was a cry of longing and despair and her own need reached out to it. Instinctively, not knowing what she did, she rolled onto her side and as their bodies touched and the burning hardness of him drove between her legs, a sword-edge of desire, urgent and bitter-sweet, twisted within her loins. Beneath the taut wet fabric of her dress her nipples swelled and hardened and she wished she could tear it away. But to do so would mean moving her hips from his, leaving the probing hardness that was bringing her most secret places to singing awareness, and she could not bare to relinquish that, even for a moment.

With a sob she pressed herself closer to him and together they rolled over on the narrow bed. Yet still he held back, afraid of hurting her again, and suddenly her shyness had gone as if it had never been.

She slid her hand between them, feeling the damp hardness of his belly, and when he realized what she was about he took her hand in his, guiding it downwards until it enclosed his manhood. For a moment she almost recoiled with shock at the feel of it, but her need was burning within her, making everything seem different than it had before.

His weight on her eased and she arched her back, holding him poised at the orifice. The desire was screaming within her and it seemed to her that nothing in the world mattered but that she should feel his body within hers; know the release of his juices in her innermost sanctum.

'Take me!' she moaned.

It was all he needed. With a single thrust he entered her and as the softness closed in around him he could wait no longer for release. He moved within her with swift, searing strokes that seemed to tear her apart. She felt them like sword-thrusts, but this time she gloried in her pain.

For a few brief seconds his body worked and she raised her own to meet it while her loins cried out at the exquisite sweetness. But soon – too soon – it was over. His fingers bit into her arms until the pain made her gasp and his ragged breath hastened with each stroke to a crescendo. At the last he cried out with such vigour that it heightened her own passion, and for a few moments more he worked within her. But it was not enough and as she felt him soften a sense of loss permeated her.

She clung to him, almost sobbing with unfulfilled passion, as his manhood slipped from her to wetly between her soft thighs.

'Don't go – don't leave me!' she whimpered, squeezing him to her still.

Tenderness suffused him. He had been right. There was fire beneath the ice and a passion to match his own. What pleasure she had brought him! – pleasure deeper and more rewarding than any he had ever known. Now it was his turn to take her to the brink of paradise and beyond. Without moving away from her he slid his hand between them, easing his fingers into the hollow he had lately vacated. He heard her soft moan of delight, felt the sticky wetness that was evidence of his release. Gently he caressed her while he covered her face with kisses and her body writhed against him, arching and twisting as she climbed the heights. Then, at the last, he heard her breath catch and come out on a shuddering sigh, her hips moved convulsively just once, and she lay still.

Gently he rolled away from her, looking with love at

the way her eyelashes fringed her cheek beneath her closed eyes and the full, satisfied curve of her mouth, and as he did so he noticed with a shock the lank ringlets, still-wet and straggling along the line of her jaw.

He had seen she was wet, of course, when he had first entered the dressing room, but with all that had occurred since it had been driven from his mind. Even the fact that her clothes were soaked through had hardly registered through his all-consuming desire for her. Now, he looked at her crumpled wet dress and the tangled corkscrews of her hair and found himself wondering where she had been when the storm broke.

'You'd better get out of those wet clothes, my love,' he said softly to her. 'I don't want you dying of pneumonia now that I've found you.'

She opened her eyes and smiled at him drowsily, the smile of a contented cat just fed on cream.

'I suppose that's just a ruse to get me to undress for you.'

He laughed.

'It's a bonus, yes, but that wasn't what I was thinking of. If you fall ill out here we're miles from a doctor and you're not as hardy yet as we native-born Australians. How did you come to get so wet?'

The veil of rosy sweetness shifted slightly and she found herself remembering with a shock her drive through the tinder-dry bush and her rendezvous with the abominable Matt. It seemed like a bad dream now, and she did not want to make it real by telling him about it. Sometime she would have to. But not now. Not yet. Better to make the magic of this moment last a little longer.

She swung her legs over the side of the narrow bed, standing up and looking down at the crumpled dress, hanging like a wet rag about her legs.

'You're right – I'd better take it off!' she said with a laugh.

She turned and sat on the edge of the bed, presenting him with her back so that he could finish undoing the fastenings. He did so, pressing kisses on her soft flesh as it was revealed. Then he lay back, hands behind his head, watching her with love and pleasure as she stepped out of her dress. There was nothing now to hide her nudity, nothing to impede her firm, rosy body with its thrusting breasts, curved hips and soft thighs – she had bowed to the necessity of the summer weather and left off her corset when she had realized the heat made it insupportable, though no one, looking at the tiny circle of her waist, would have guessed it. Now she stood before him, nude, but she felt no sense of shyness or shame. His loving had carried her to the summit of passion and she glowed with pride and delight in knowing that she had done the same for him. How could there be shyness between them now? She was his wife, his lover, his queen. She stretched luxuriantly, throwing back her head so that her damp ringlets reached halfway down her back and catching her lip between her small, pearly teeth.

Never, not for one moment, had she guessed it would be like this. She had known restlessness, yes, but not even in her wildest dreams had she imagined the exhilaration, the wonderful, glowing completeness that suffused her now.

As he looked at her, Zach felt his own desire stirring once more. She was all he had known she would be, and more. The last months, when he had been tortured by the nearness, yet inaccessibility of her, had been hell. But he would go through it all again if it meant coming at last to this end. He had had women before. But never like this. Always, when it had been over and his passion burnt out, he had been ready to leave, afraid that the woman who had satisfied his needs would want more from him than he was prepared to give.

But with Regan it was different, just as he had known it would be. Whatever it cost him, he could never have enough of her. And as long as he had her, he would want no other.

Smiling, he levered himself up and lifted her in his arms. She was like a feather and he stood for a moment luxuriating in the feel of her breasts through the tangle of his hair on his chest, her ringlets, wet against his cheek, and the gentle pressure of her arms twined round his neck.

Then he whispered in her ear:

'It's time I took you in the comfort of my own bed, my love. We have a lot of catching up to do and I think we should begin it right away!'

Then he carried her through the connecting door, turned back the covers and laid her down upon the bed where she had slept alone since her marriage.

'You may do what you please with me, Zach,' she murmured.

Then his lips were on hers and once again there was no more time for talking.

CHAPTER EIGHTEEN

This time their love-making was slower and gentler without the urgency of that first, crazed encounter. Their lips and hands lingered, exploring each other's bodies and finding fresh delights with every passing moment.

When Regan held back, hesitant and shy, he gently taught her, and his questing tongue, teasing every part of her body, brought her to fresh and hitherto unimagined peaks of desire and pleasure.

When at last he took her once more it was with tenderness and she shivered with the sharp wonder that he could arouse in her. There was no frenzy now. He withdrew once or twice to kiss and caress her yearning body and when he re-entered her it was as if the heavens were rent by forked lightning. Only at the last did their eagerness rise once more to fever pitch. His teeth gripped her nipple until she cried out, but she did not try to draw away. Rather she thrust it deeper into his mouth and their bodies moved in unison as they came together to the glorious apex of their passion.

When it was over they lay in each other's arms, their sticky flesh clinging together as if not a single inch of them would willingly give up the other, and drowsed in the rosy glow of contentment.

Then, as her body returned to a more normal state, Regan's woman's curiosity reasserted itself.

'Has it ever been that way for you before?' she whispered, her lips moving tantalizingly against the base of his throat.

He pulled her up into the crook of his arm so that her forearm lay across his chest and one slender leg was bent up to rest on his hard muscular stomach.

'You ask too many questions, Regan.'

'*Has* it?' she persisted.

'If you're asking me if you're the first woman I've made love to, the answer is no,' he told her. 'But then I think you know that already. But with you, it's special.'

'Better than with Adelaide?' she pressed him, half afraid, for how could she, who had been a virgin until he had taken her, ever hope to compete with an experienced professional like the hotel owner?

He turned to look at her, his black eyes amused.

'Why do you always harp on about Adelaide?'

'Because – well, it's obvious you and she . . .'

'Oh, Regan, my love!' He twisted a still-damp corkscrew ringlet between finger and thumb and she thought he might be laughing at her. 'You have nothing to fear from Adelaide. We have been lovers, yes. I can't deny it. But that was all over a long while ago.'

'You mean – before you met me?' she whispered.

'Long before. Adelaide and I have known one another since we were children,' he told her gently. 'I suppose you could say we learned the art of love together. I taught her about men, she taught me about women. I liked her, admired her, as a friend, nothing more.'

'But you said you were lovers,' Regan pressed him.

'Yes, but not in the way you and I are,' he explained. 'Our bodies did the mechanical thing, out of curiosity at first and then from habit. There was physical satisfaction, yes, but nothing more. I could never have married Adelaide.'

'Did Adelaide feel the same way?' Regan asked.

Zach shifted a fraction uncomfortably.

'Adelaide wanted me to marry her,' he said truthfully. 'She felt that as native-born Australians we should stick together. I tried to tell her it would never work but she found it hard to accept that. Until I brought you home with me I believe she still thought that I would weaken in the end.'

'Yes, I see,' Regan murmured, feeling for the first time a glimmer of pity for Adelaide. Of course she must have wanted Zach – what woman would not! – and to have to settle for the role of friend after sharing the intimacies Zach had described must have been a bitter blow both to her pride and her happiness. But if Zach did not love her, then that was all there was to it. A weaker man might have allowed himself to be coerced. Zach had known there could be no lasting happiness where love did not exist – though when the boot had been on the other foot he had been ready enough to take the chance!

'I suppose that's the reason she disliked me so,' Regan said softly. 'She would have turned me off you if she could. She must have been very angry to find I wasn't deterred so easily.'

Beneath her knee she felt Zach's stomach muscles tense.

'Why? What did she say to you?' he demanded.

'Oh, she told me that you . . .' Regan broke off, aware suddenly that to relate Adelaide's charges to Zach would be to set the cat among the pigeons and no mistake. She held no brief for Adelaide. From the day she had arrived, the hotel owner had gone out of her way to treat her unpleasantly, and it would serve her aright for Zach to know just what she had been prepared to stoop to in an effort to get rid of Regan. But not only Adelaide would suffer if Regan passed on the claims the former saloon girl had made concerning Zach's relationship with Mary Mitchell.

Zach himself would say nothing, of course. What she told him would not go beyond the four walls of their bedroom. But if he thought it was being said that he was the father of little Queenie, he would be terribly hurt. The easy affection they shared would be gone forever, for he would be afraid others might place the same construction on his bond with the child, and the loss to both of them would be great. Better that he should go on as he always had, ignorant of the evil smear that Adelaide had tried to lay at his door.

'Well?' Zach demanded again and Regan smiled, nestling her face into his chest.

She had no need to fear Adelaide now. She could afford to be generous.

'Oh, nothing really. Just the sort of thing you'd expect from a jealous woman,' she murmured. 'I can't even remember the details now.'

Zach did not press her further. He lay quietly for a few moments, stroking the satiny smooth skin that covered one of her shoulders, and his touch sent ripples of pleasure coursing over her bare skin.

Then at last he said: 'The ring, Regan – you do believe me when I tell you I had no idea it was yours when I came by it?'

She nodded. She had no doubt of it. The Zach she loved and who she now knew loved her could never be a cheat and a thief. Ruthless, yes. Hard, yes – perhaps sometimes if it suited him cruel, even. But never mean or underhanded. Never that.

'I believe you,' she whispered. 'But whoever stole it must have been here – in Robertson. You do see that, Zach?'

'Yes, but it's not so strange as it sounds.' Zach's voice was distant, as if he was deep in thought now, and she wished there had been no need for harsh reality to intrude into their idyll. 'Everyone on the ship came ashore in Melbourne, after all, and Robertson is not so far away, as distances go. This is not England, remember, but Australia. Besides, dealers travel too. It's possible the man I bought the ring from got it in Melbourne himself.'

'I suppose so,' she murmured, but she was still searching her memory for a face from the *Maid of Morne* that she might have seen again in Robertson. Was the thief now a miner in the goldfields, perhaps even working for Jud? For some reason it was a frightening thought, and she shuddered in spite of the steamy heat of the day.

Zach's fingers moved reassuringly among her ringlets.

'I'll tell you what I'll do, Regan. I'll try to find the dealer again and discover how he came by it. I'd like to know who was rat enough to rob you with your father newly dead – although as you have pointed out to me, I likely owe him a debt of gratitude. Had you been able to pay off your father's debts, I believe you would have done so, and you would have been lost to me forever.'

Her lips curved; they felt fuller now, just as her body felt languorous.

'I surely would. So perhaps I, too, owe the thief some thanks. You were right, Zach, when you said I did not know my own heart! I hated you so I declare I would have killed you, had I but had the opportunity. But to quote from one of William Shakespeare's plays: *All's Well That Ends Well*, and now I have my mother's ring once more, I count the sovereigns well lost.'

Zach shifted slightly beneath her.

'How did you come to find the ring, Regan?' His voice was still low but there was an edge to it as he framed the question and Regan felt the blood rush to her cheeks. He was wondering why she had been in his room, prying amongst his things. She knew just how he felt – she valued privacy herself and always had. But to explain why she had been looking through his chest she would have to tell him of the blackmail threat – a story she hardly knew where to begin, and one she was not anxious to start on now. Zach would have to know, of course, and he would be pleased with the return of his watch. But to tell him now would be to break the spell completely and throw them back to harsh reality. And besides . . .

Supposing he reacted as she had feared Seamus would react? She could all too easily imagine the fury that would possess him when he learned what had happened and it would be very like him to saddle Tarquin and ride full tilt to Robertson to have it out with Matt. And the fact that the man had taken her brooch would only make it worse. Blows would likely be exchanged and who knew where it would end? Perhaps there might yet be a murder charge to be laid at Zach's door – and this time one that was based on fact!

'I – I was thinking about your lost watch,' she said truthfully. 'I wondered if when you mislaid it you also mislaid its pouch.'

'The watch only,' Zach told her. 'The pouch was coming unstitched and I had given it to Mary for mending. But why should you wonder such a thing?'

'Because . . .' Her mind raced furiously and when she could think of no explanation except for the truth, she resorted to her new-found power over him, running her fingers along his bare chest and planting kisses at the base of his throat until he pulled her to him, holding her body steady on his with one strong hand while the other caressed the curve of buttock and thigh.

'Witch!' he whispered against her hair and she smiled to herself, wondering if she would always be able to evade awkward questions so easily.

'I believe you made a spell to bring the ring back,' he teased her. 'And now since it's yours, you may as well wear it. It wouldn't be right for me to keep it for your birthday now. Have you put it on your finger yet?'

She stiffened, a tiny cold shiver run through her as she stretched out her two bare hands. She had been holding the ring when she had accused Zach – she had shown it to him – but where was it now? In all that had happened since she couldn't recall putting it down or even having it.

'Zach – I don't know what I've done with it!' she cried. 'I had it – but now . . .'

He laughed loud enough to rock the bedchamber.

'I gave you other things to think about. Is that it?'

'Yes. Oh, Zach, suppose I've lost it!'

All else forgotten she was off the bed in a moment and scurrying through to the dressing room. He followed at a more leisurely pace, still laughing at her anxiety.

'It's here somewhere, don't fret.'

'I know, but if it's lost again – my mother's ring . . .'

'It's not lost.'

Together they searched and at last she saw something gleaming in a dark corner beneath the makeshift bed. Sure enough it was the ring. But by the time it was safely on her finger the subject of Zach's watch had been forgotten again.

'I have work that must be attended to before dinner,' Zach told her. 'If I am absent for much longer, Jim will doubtless come searching for me, and that, my love, may well prove embarrassing for you.'

'It certainly would!' she squealed. 'But Zach, I can't go downstairs as I am! Would Maggie think it very odd if I asked for a tub of water so that I can bathe?'

Zach threw back his head and laughed at her.

'You must learn to stop worrying about what other people think – and particularly the maids,' he scolded her. 'They are paid to do as you tell them, not to wonder about the reason behind your request. You are a Casey, now, Regan, and you must begin to act like one.'

'High-handed and arrogant, you mean,' she teased him, enjoying the new-found confidence that allowed her to say such things, and he wagged an admonitory finger at her.

'Had I not already neglected my work too long, I should certainly put you over my knee and spank you for that remark, Madam,' he told her with mock severity. 'As it is, I shall pretend I did not hear it and you may think yourself lucky not to have your bare backside warmed!'

She smiled, pulled on the emerald green robe that he had bought her in Melbourne and perched herself back against the pillows to watch him dress himself. How beautiful he was with his strong brown limbs and his hard muscles! And a few minutes ago all that strength had possessed her more utterly than she could ever have believed possible – and in so doing had somehow become hers. Excitement and desire stirred deep within her once more and she drew her knees up to her chin, willing herself not to let him know that at this moment, more than any other, she wanted nothing but to be his, again and again until there was nothing left of her but a pale shadow. And even that shadow would worship and adore him . . .

When Zach had been gone a little while the tub arrived, along with grinning Maggie with a jug of hot water. She set it down and would have stayed to wash her mistress if Regan had not forbidden it. She wanted to be alone now, to sink back into the warm water and remember every touch, every kiss, every word of love. The scent of the soap was like powerful incense in her nostrils, evoking the most poignant of memories, and the warm, gently lapping water was sensual on her skin.

She lay back with her neck resting against the rim of the bath, half-drowsing, and after the most pleasant of her thoughts had run their course she found herself thinking again of Zach's watch, discovered by Matt at the scene of the murder.

It was a strange thing, she thought, and the more she considered it the stranger it seemed. That Zach's watch should have been found beside Jud's buggy was odd enough in itself. That it should have been picked up by someone who recognized it was more odd still . . .

She drew up tight suddenly, raising her head from the rim of the bath and drawing her brows together in perplexity.

How had *Matt* known it was Zach's watch? There was nothing on it to state the name of the owner. It was of a distinctive design, it was true, and easily recognizable, but only by someone sufficiently intimate with Zach to have seen him use it. Surely Matt had never had occasion to be in Zach's company that long? He could only have glimpsed it on odd occasions when Zach had been at the Commercial Hotel.

But there was another who had come upon the scene of the murder and she would know Zach's watch very well! Could it be that *Adelaide* was behind the blackmail that had been extracted from her today?

Regan stood up, towelling herself dry while the new ideas chased themselves round inside her head. Matt would do as Adelaide told him, not a doubt of it. He had worked for her for so long it would come as second nature. And he had not shrunk from what many would think an unpleasant task, but rather enjoyed the superiority that had come not only from being in command, perhaps, but also from knowing something she did not. Yes, the more she thought about it the more she sensed Adelaide's hand in the plot. Why, it was even possible that the watch had not been found at the scene at all, but planted there. Zach was often at the Commercial Hotel and he could have lost it there not at home at all, and it could have been found by Adelaide and kept for her own purpose.

But why should she do such a thing? She did not need

the money she had demanded. She was a wealthy woman in her own right and fifty gold sovereigns would mean little to her. It made no sense at all. Could it be that she was seeking revenge for Zach's dismissal of her as mistress and would-be wife? Had her alley-cat mind devised some way of making him – and Regan – sorry?

As she prepared for dinner, Regan's mind was churning. Should she tell Zach of her suspicions? She did not know. All she was sure of was that they sounded too fantastic to be true – the figment of a wild imagination. If she presented them to him with no vestige of proof he would likely think she had dreamed the whole thing – and tell her so in no uncertain terms. But she could not simply dismiss it from her mind. Something strange was going on and it somehow threatened Zach. She was determined to find out what it was. How she could do that she did not know. But on one thing her mind was made up. She would find a way.

Dinner that night was a strange meal, as Regan floated midway between ecstatic happiness and the restless anxiety that her reasonings had started in her. But she managed to hide them from Zach, chattering and laughing so that even Seamus noticed and asked what sort of a day she had had to put her in such an excellent temper.

For a second she caught at her lip, wondering if he had heard that she had taken the buggy out against his instructions, but when she saw the twinkle in his eye she knew her fears were unfounded.

'What is it, then?' he pressed her.

'Oh, it was such a relief to see the rain!' she murmured truthfully, and then blushed furiously as Zach's amused eyes met hers across the table.

She blushed again when at bedtime Zach excused himself from his usual last drink with Seamus and accompanied her up the stairs. Did he not even care that his father should know what he was about? she wondered. But when she whispered as much to him, he only laughed.

'Oh, Regan, Regan, first you do not want anyone to know we are not living as man and wife, and now you do not want them to know that we are! You must make up your mind, my love, which it is to be!'

'I just don't care for everyone to know such private things!' she answered hotly and he took her in his arms, kissing her eyes, her cheeks and the tip of her nose.

'This is the first time I have been able to share my bed with you since that night in the hotel in Melbourne,' he told her. 'And I assure you I do not intend to waste a minute of it. Now, take off your dress as a good wife should – or do you want me to take it off for you?'

'Well, why not?' she laughed, and her whole body began to tingle as his fingers stroked the soft flesh above the low neckline of her green gown and explored gently, teasingly, downward.

Oh, it was so good – so good! Better than she could ever have imagined!

She threw back her head so that the length of her body pressed against his and his lips took hers, crushing them in a hard kiss that left her breathless. Then his fingers moved to the fastenings of her dress and as she felt them give, one by one, the sharp expectation within her made her almost cry out.

'If I am to undress you, it's only fair that you should undress me!' Zach whispered in her ear, and when she hesitated he guided her hands to the buttons of his shirt. Shyly she fumbled with the first while he returned to the fastenings of her dress, stopping every whitswhile to kiss her so deeply that the room spun around her, and when his chest was laid bare she pressed her face into it, feeling the coarse curling hair tickle her cheek and tasting the salt of his flesh beneath her questing tongue.

'Oh, Zach!' she whispered. 'What have I done to deserve you?'

He held her away and she saw the passion flame once more in his eyes.

'Whatever it was, forget it, love, and begin to pay your dues to me now!' he joked gently.

Then his arms were around her and as their marriage bed enveloped them, all else was forgotten in the explosion of mutual love.

Nothing could have kept Regan from sound sleep that night. Her mind and body were so satiated with love that she sank into a sweet, dreamless repose almost before he had rolled away from her and when she next opened her eyes morning light was streaming through the window and she had not moved an inch. Even her hands were still folded on her stomach where they had held Zach's hand.

But he had moved. It was his kiss on her forehead that had wakened her and she looked up to see him standing, fully dressed, beside the bed.

'Zach!' she whispered, fighting her way through the mists of sleep, but he placed a finger to her lips.

'There's no need to disturb yourself, love. But I have business that takes me out early and I did not wish to leave without telling you I had gone.'

She nodded, still half asleep.

'I understand, Zach.'

'I'll see you at dinner if not before.' He kissed her lightly, 'Go back to sleep now. It's early yet.'

Then he was gone but although she closed her eyes once more, sleep did not return. Instead she lay thinking of all that had happened, reliving their loving with relish, and returning once more to the problem of the watch.

She would have to decide what to do about it – and soon. But Zach would not be here today . . .

Zach would not be here today! The thought brought her wide awake and she sat up, feeling the already-warm sun on her face. This would be an ideal opportunity for her to go to Robertson to see Adelaide to try and elicit an explanation from her. By tonight she would then have the full facts to put before Zach.

She got up bathed and dressed, anxious to put her plan into immediate action.

Seamus was in the breakfast room and he greet her with a smile.

'You'd have no objection to me driving to Robertson now we've had some rain, would you?' she enquired primly.

Seamus laughed, shaking his head.

'There are times when I pity that son of mine. When you get an idea in your pretty head you don't let it go too easily do you, Regan? No, I've no objection to you driving to Robertson today. But take care of yourself whatever you do. Zach seems more in love with you than ever and 'twould break his heart if he lost you.'

She touched his arm glad that this time at least she could reassure him.

'He'll have trouble losing me, I assure you,' she smiled.

By the time she was ready Lucky was harnessed to the buggy and Regan drove out onto the Robertson road. The sun was already high and in spite of her nervousness about the coming interview there was a song on her lips as she bowled along the track.

It was only when the outskirts of Robertson came into view that the nervousness returned, making a knot in her throat and tingling in her veins.

The street seemed busier than usual, with miners and the like milling about, and there was a crowd on the path outside the Commercial Hotel which took Regan by surprise.

But as she drew close enough to be able to see the hotel itself a gasp of horror escaped her lips. There was an air of dereliction about the square stone building. The windows were black, gaping chasms, the walls darkened and streaked, and the awning that had proudly proclaimed 'Commercial Hotel' hung at a crazy angle.

Shocked, Regan reined in Lucky and called to a passer-by:

'What's happened here?'

'Fire,' came back the reply. 'The place was gutted in the night.'

'But how?' Her mind was racing. The bush had not gone up. So why should the Commercial Hotel have caught fire? And what a fire it must have been! She shivered at the thought of the flames roaring through the sleeping hotel, and another thought occurred to her.

'Did everyone get out safely?' she asked.

'Most everyone.' The man spat into the gutter.

'You mean someone didn't?' Regan pressed him.

He looked up at her, rheumy eyes narrowed against the sun.

'They were too late to save Miss Adelaide,' he told her flatly. 'She was found in her room upstairs. When they got her out, she was dead.'

CHAPTER NINETEEN

'Dead – Adelaide?' Regan's lips moved automatically but every drop of blood seemed to have drained from her body. 'You can't mean it!'

'Oh, it's true right enough.' The man, who had been hanging about to see what there was to be seen, was clearly enjoying passing on his knowledge. 'It's a sad day for Robertson, to lose a lady like that. And the hotel too – the best drinking bar for miles around. It'll be back to the grog shanties again, I dare say.'

'Oh, never mind the bar!' Regan exclaimed, climbing down from the buggy and tethering Lucky to a handy post. 'Buildings can always be put up again. But to die in a fire – that's terrible! How did it start? Do they know?'

The man shook his head, grinding out his Bengal twist on the path.

'I haven't heard, Miss, but from the number of bobbies and military buzzing around, there's something peculiar about it if you ask me.'

'What do you mean?' Regan asked.

The man had begun to move away, but he looked at her over his shoulder and pulled a knowing face.

'Make what you like of it, but I reckon it was no accident,' he supplied furtively.

Stunned, Regan stood staring at the blackened shell that had once been a prosperous hotel. She could still hardly believe her eyes – it was such a shock to see it in this condition. And it was impossible, too, to believe that Adeliade was dead – beautiful, vital, hard-boiled Adelaide, with her ambition and her viper's tongue and her obvious love of life.

Regan held no affection for her. From the moment she had set eyes on her she had disliked her and their brief acquaintance had only given her cause to like her less. But she would not have wished this upon her. To die in a fire must be to die horribly. Regan could think of nothing more terrifying than to be trapped in a burning building – unless it was to be caught in the holocuast of a bushfire. But even that seemed to offer some chance of escape, while the blackened stone walls and a tower of flame shooting up a staircase offered none.

But why had she not managed to escape if there were others who had? wondered Regan. Had she been sleeping so heavily that she did not hear when the alarm was raised – or had she stayed behind too long trying to collect together any belongings she was desperate to save? Either way, it was a terrible thing, and not one she cared to dwell upon.

With a shudder she tore her eyes away from the wrecked hotel. What now? If Adelaide was dead there was nothing for it but to drive home again with all her questions unanswered.

She was about to unhook Lucky's reins from the tethering post when a voice from behind her took her quite by surprise and she spun round to see Adelaide's servant, Matt, approaching her.

His ugly face was even more haggard than usual, soot-streaked and tired, and beneath his bloodshot eyes were dark circles as large as saucers. And his clothes were grimy, too, evidence that he had been at the hotel when the fire had broken out.

'I thought that was you, Mrs Casey,' he greeted her, and the menace in his voice made her take a backward step away from him. 'You've been to feast your eyes on the results of your husband's actions, I have no doubt. Well, you can report back to him that he can be well pleased with his night's work.'

'What are you talking about?' Regan asked, frightened. There was something almost mad about the man – as if he had taken leave of his senses – and she felt a threat in the air between them.

'You think I don't know who did this?' he threw at her. 'There was only one man who could have wanted Miss Adelaide dead – wanted it enough to go to these lengths. And that man is Zach Casey!'

'You're insane!' Regan cried, trying to unhitch Lucky. 'Why should Zach want Adelaide dead?'

Matt caught at the reins, holding them securely around the post and so preventing her escape.

'Because she could prove he had killed Jud Trenoweth!' he stated. 'Yesterday I sold you the evidence of that. But it wasn't I who found it. It was Adelaide. She gave it to me and asked me to meet you for her.'

'I thought as much!' Regan said softly. 'I thought she must be behind it – you would never have recognized Zach's watch. But she would.'

'That's right.' Matt's voice was low and dangerous. 'And when you and Zach realized that, he decided he would be safer with her dead. That's the way it was, isn't it? Admit it, Mrs Casey!'

'No!' Regan cried. 'No, that's ridiculous. The fire's unhinged you! Zach knows nothing of this – nothing at all. And he would never harm Adelaide. In any case, it would be a pretty stupid way to do it, wouldn't it? To set a hotel on fire to try and kill one person? Why, she could have escaped like everyone else. Now, release me at once! I wish to leave.'

But Matt made no move to do as she bid. Still holding the harness securely he moved closer to her and his eyes, burning like twin coals in his haggard face, struck fresh terror to her heart.

'Not so fast, Mrs Casey! I have not finished with you yet. You think Miss Adelaide died in the fire, do you?'

'Well, didn't she?' Regan demanded.

Slowly, menacingly, the man shook his head.

'I see your husband has spared you the grisly details. No, Mrs Casey. Miss Adelaide did not die in the fire. She was already dead when it started.'

'*What*?' Regan cried. 'What are you saying?'

The fingers of his free hand closed around her wrist in a vice-like grip.

'Miss Adelaide was stabbed to death,' he told her. 'That was why she did not escape. No doubt your precious husband believed that if he burned the hotel around her, he could destroy the evidence of what he had done. Perhaps he hoped her body would be charred so that the marks of the knife would be disguised and no one would stop to ask how she died. But he reckoned without me. As soon as the alarm was raised I looked for her. If he thought I would leave her to burn he misjudged me. And I found her dead – stabbed – and her nightgown soaked through with her own blood.'

His voice faltered and Regan shuddered. Would this nightmare never end?

'Well, Zach had nothing to do with it, I swear it!' she cried. 'He's innocent of this, just as he's innocent of Jud Trenoweth's murder. But now I suppose you'll try to blackmail me about this, too!'

'You stupid woman!' Matt grated at her. 'Don't you understand what I've been saying? I never meant to blackmail you at all. It was Adelaide.'

Regan was incensed by his tone even more than by his restraining hand on her wrist. She had decided for herself that Adelaide had been behind the 'blackmailing' and she had come to Robertson to learn the answers to the questions that unsavoury episode had raised. Well, Adelaide may be dead now, but here was someone who could give her the answers. Perhaps Matt had obeyed his mistress blindly – certainly she could tell from his distress now how attached to her he had been – but surely he must have known something of what lay behind his mission?

She lifted her chin, her eyes meeting Matt's squarely.

'Why should Adelaide want to blackmail me?' she demanded. 'Fifty gold sovereigns would be nothing to her, and as for my brooch – she must have dozens just as fine.'

'Aye, so she has – and since you ask me, I will tell you what I believe to be the truth of the matter,' Matt snapped at her. 'It's my belief that Miss Adelaide was trying to protect your worthless husband. She had a regard for him, though he treated her cruelly, and she did not want to see him hang. But had she returned the watch to him herself he would have known she knew of his guilt and she was afraid for her life. By disguising its return as blackmail she hoped to keep from him that it was she who knew the truth. For she must have known better than most how violent he could be. And she was right to fear him, was she not? She was right when she thought he would stop at nothing to save his neck. Well, now 'tis time for him to pay for what he has done, for I intend to turn him over to the law!'

Wildly Regan looked around. She could see the uniformed figures amongst the crowds that still milled curiously about outside the Commercial Hotel and she turned cold at the thought of Matt going to them with the story he had just told her. It was nonsense, every word of it. She knew that. But would they?

'Why should they believe you?' she asked desperately. 'I have Zach's watch now, remember. You returned it to me.'

An unpleasant smile crossed the man's face.

'And I have your brooch Miss Casey,' he murmured.

Regan's eyes widened with fear as the implications of his statement came home to her. He had her brooch – proof that an exchange had taken place! Holy Mother, how could she have been so stupid as not to realize it! She had played into his hands, and no mistake!

'The authorities are bound to wonder why you were willing to part with it if you truly believe your husband innocent,' Matt went on. 'And do not even bother to tell me Zach was at home with you last night. I would not expect you to say anything else. As for your being here in Robertson this morning, why, even that adds to the case against you. It's plain you came to discover the results of your husband's handiwork. There can be no other explanation.'

Horrified, Regan stared at him. She knew there was not a word of truth in his wild accusations, but even to her they hung together far too well for comfort. How much more convincing would they sound to those who wished to believe them? Desperately she caught at Matt's arm.

'Please – please stop this!' she begged. 'Zach is innocent! I swear it!'

But the man only looked at her with such hatred in his eyes that she knew it was hopeless.

'He'll pay for what he's done,' he grated out vengefully, and with a sob Regan jerked the bridle from his hands and climbed into the buggy.

Nothing she could do or say here could help Zach now.

But she must get back to Ballymena quickly and warn him of what had happened. Only that way, perhaps, could she save him from the hangman's noose.

As she left Robertson behind, hysteria was rising in her in a warm tide and she urged Lucky forward at a reckless pace. She had to find Zach – she had to! Oh, why hadn't she told him before what had happened instead of trying to take care of it all herself? At the time she had believed she was doing it for the best, but now she realized that by meeting Matt and acceding to his demand for blackmail she had only made the case against Zach look blacker than it would otherwise have done.

But it didn't make sense, any of it. First Jud murdered, now Adelaide, if Matt was to be believed – and strangely, Regan did believe him, for she felt sure he was genuinely upset by her death, and suspected he might even have been a little in love with her.

But there was so many questions as yet unanswered. Why had Adelaide set up the blackmail plot? Matt thought it was because she wanted to save Zach's neck without him knowing that she knew the truth. But Regan knew it could not be that. Adelaide had had nothing to fear from Zach, and she would have known it. If she had really been concerned with saving his neck she would have returned it to him quietly – or buried it somewhere in the bush and forgotten all about it.

But she had kept the watch to use for some private purpose of her own – and now she was dead. Someone had gone to the Commercial Hotel when everyone was asleep and stabbed her to death before setting fire to the place. But who? And why? Could it be the same person who had also killed Jud? Was there a link between the two deaths?

Regan's eyes widened suddenly as the explanation struck her and she wondered wildly why she had not realized it before.

She had known all along it had not been Zach who had dropped his watch beside Jud's buggy during the struggle that had ended in the landowner's death. Therefore it followed that whoever had committed the murder had dropped it. The watch, of course, would not have concerned them – if found it could easily be identified as Zach's. But the pouch it had been contained in had not been Zach's. The pouch belonged to the real murderer and might give a clue as to his identity. Perhaps the man responsible had heard that Adelaide had been first on the scene. Perhaps either she or Matt had talked to someone about finding evidence. And the murderer, whoever he was, wanted that evidence before it could implicate him – wanted it badly enough to kill for it.

But who – who – who? Who would Jud have stopped his buggy for? Who had had the opportunity to gain possession of Zach's watch? And who now could have gone to Robertson and knifed Adelaide? Find the person who could be the answer to all three questions and that person would the murderer!

Fiercely Regan drove the buggy on, heedless of the bumps and potholes. Zach might know the answer. Between them they might be able to arrive at it before the military or the bobbies came to pick him up.

Regan had hoped that she would find Zach in one of the paddocks on the Robertson side of Ballymena, but there was no sign of him, and as she turned into the drive she thought the homestead looked deserted too, slumbering in the warm afternoon sunshine. Even the stables were deserted. She unharnessed Lucky herself and hurried into the house.

Perhaps if she was to have another look at the strange pouch it would yield up a clue to the identity of the murderer, she thought. There must be something about it that she had not noticed before, something sufficiently damaging to make the culprit want it back – and want it back badly enough to kill poor Adelaide in an effort to get it. She had noticed nothing before, but that did not mean there was nothing there.

As she went in through the front door she saw that she had been wrong about the house being deserted. Queenie was there, sitting halfway up the sweeping staircase with her dolls arranged around her.

'Regan – hello!' the child greeted her. 'I'm glad you're back. I'm here all alone and I'm running out of things to do.'

Regan bit her lip. Fond as she was of Queenie she could not entertain stopping to play with her now.

'Where is everyone, then?' she asked.

'Oh, Mr Davey came riding over to say his baby was coming, and Mama and Kathy have gone to help,' Queenie explained, matter-of-factly. 'I wanted to go along too, but they wouldn't let me. It's not fair, really. I've never seen a baby born.'

'Your turn will come,' Regan assured her, sparing a sympathetic thought for Mrs Davey, labouring in the heat of the afternoon with only neighbours to help with the delivery. 'Why don't you make believe your dolls are babies and put them all to bed?'

'I can't do that – they're at sea at the moment,' Queenie informed her with great disdain. 'This is my ship – didn't you know? And you're standing right in the water.'

Regan suppressed a smile, climbing from the hallway onto the stairs.

'Oh dear, I'm all right now, am I?'

'Yes,' Queenie said doubtfully, adding as an afterthought, 'unless we get shipwrecked, of course. And we might be.'

'I'll disembark quickly, then,' Regan smiled, glad of the excuse to escape.

She ran up the stairs and into her room. Zach's watch and the mysterious pouch were still in her reticule. She delved into it and pulled them out.

The pouch was stiff and shiny beneath her fingers and again she had the impression that compared to Zach's it was cheap and poorly made. But she could see nothing about it to identify its owner or make it a danger to him.

Though if it was something obvious, Adelaide would have seen it in any case, Regan thought. Carefully she opened it, drawing out Zach's watch and looking inside. It was empty and she was about to close it again when something caught her eye – something marked into the leather on the inside.

A tremor ran through her and she hurried towards the window and the better light. Yes, there was something inked on the uncut side of the leather – letters, words!

Anxiously she strained her eyes, then, as she made them out, breath caught in her throat.

It was a London address – presumably the name of the maker! No wonder whoever had lost it had been anxious for its return! If pursued, no doubt the craftsman would be able to point a finger at whoever it was he had made the pouch for. But London! The owner must either have come from, or been in, England – and fairly recently! The newness of the pouch bore witness to that.

But who? Who fulfilled all the conditions she had already thought of and had a connection with England? Most people hereabouts had been in Australia a long while. Zach had been to England, it was true, and only yesterday Regan might have been forced to wonder, if only for a second, whether he might after all be involved with the crimes in some way. Not now. Zach was innocent she knew. But who else. . . ?

Dickon Trenoweth! It came to her in a flash and she stood holding the pouch with fingers suddenly turned nerveless. Dickon Trenoweth had come from England. Dickon Trenoweth had been here at Ballymena the night Zach had lost his watch – she had been playing the piano after their departure when Zach had come downstairs looking for it. He could easily have taken it – she had never liked him and it could be that he was a thief. Why, Jud had been transported years before, perhaps for something similar, and it could be that the weakness ran in the family. But was it possible he had murdered his own brother?

Regan stood staring into space, her mind racing. It could be that Dickon had killed Jud and then stolen the gold nuggets to make it look like a bushwhacking. It would explain why Jud had stopped – as he never would have done for a stranger. It would explain why such a tough, suspicious Australian should be caught so much off his guard. But what could have triggered such a killing?

Unless there was a quarrel. Suddenly Regan's mind was winging back to the day she had driven to Robertson to deliver Seamus's invitation to Dickon and Jud. She had almost walked in on a terrible quarrel between them; she had stood in the street outside and heard their raised voices. Then she had seen Richard and the whole incident had been forgotten. But now as she cast her mind back, snatches of what she had overheard came back to her and it was enough to convince her.

There had been some kind of a power struggle going on between the brothers – Dickon, perhaps, had wanted to cut himself in on Jud's empire, and the tough old former convict had resisted. Hot words had been exchanged and in the end Jud had paid with his life.

As for Adelaide – Dickon could as easily have been responsible for her killing as anyone else. But if she was right, and suddenly Regan was quite sure that she was, then Dickon was the most dangerous of criminals – a thief and a murderer without a vestige of conscience. He had killed twice, and if he believed himself threatened, he would likely not hesitate to kill again.

Tingling with sudden fear, Regan thrust both watch and pouch back into her reticule and hurried from the room. She had to find Zach and tell him what she knew, and she had to find him now.

Queenie was still on the stairs, looking more bored than ever.

'You're not going out again, are you, Regan?' she groaned. 'Oh, let me come with you, please!'

Regan bit her lip. She did not particularly want Queenie with her when she found Zach and told him of her suspicions, but it did not seem right to leave the child here alone either – especially now she knew there was a double murderer in the vicinity.

'All right, come along,' she said. 'No, leave your dolls where they are – they can captain the ship while you're away.

Her voice was too hard and bright, but Queenie did not appear to notice. Leaving her dolls, she trotted along behind Regan to the stables and stood watching while she harnessed Lucky once more to the buggy. Because of the trembling of her hands it took Regan longer than it usually did, but at last she was finished. She climbed into the buggy and was just about to drive off when Queenie touched her arm.

'Regan – there's a big, black cloud over there.

Shouldn't we take our wraps in case it rains again?'

Regan sighed with impatience. For herself she would have taken a chance – she was too anxious to find Zach to worry about a little thing like a storm of rain. But if she got Queenie soaked to the skin, Mary Mitchell was sure to be furious.

'Wait here, I'll fetch them,' Regan commanded and leaving the child sitting in the buggy she ran back to the house.

The quiet inside was still unbroken, but as she climbed the stairs, something odd caught Regan's eye. Queenie's dolls – surely she had left them sitting upright on the stairs? Now they lay in untidy disarray in the hall, as if someone had kicked carelessly into them . . .

It was a passing thought. Regan lifted her skirts and ran up the stairs and along the passageway. The door to her room stood ajar; she pushed it open and hurried in. Then she stopped dead in her tracks, the blood leaving her cheeks, her legs suddenly turning to quivering jelly.

'Holy Mother!' she whispered.

For the room was no longer as she had left it. Drawers had been pulled out, spilling their contents across the floor, the door of her robe hung open, even the sheets had been ripped from the bed.

And in the midst of the chaos was the figure of a man – a man who turned to her with desperation and murder in his eyes.

It was Dickon Trenoweth.

CHAPTER TWENTY

'Regan – my dear!' Dickon straightened up from the tumbled contents of the chest and even now the perpetual smile was still there on his lips. 'I'm so glad you're here. I'm sure you'll be able to help me.'

She tried to speak, but no sound came, and when she

tried to back away from him her trembling legs refused to obey her.

'What are you doing here?' she managed at last.

'I think you know that, Regan,' Dickon's voice was silky. 'You have something that belongs to me. Suppose you give it to me – that would save us both a good deal of trouble, would it not?'

Desperately, Regan tried to inch towards the door, but Dickon was too quick for her.

'Don't try to run away so soon!' he urged her, grasping her arm roughly, and she wondered why she had never before seen the menace that lay behind the smooth, smiling countenance. 'Tell me first where I can find what I am seeking. Then, if you insist, you may leave . . .'

Regan's mind, numbed at first by shock, was beginning to function once more. Dickon would have her believe that if she did as he asked and handed over the pouch, he would leave her in peace, but she knew that would not be. He must know that she would tell Zach everything the moment the opportunity arose and *that* he could not allow. Dickon had killed already to protect himself – he would do so again, without hesitation, and to give him the pouch would be to sign her own death warrant. But so long as he did not know where it was there was a chance for her, for she was the one person who could tell him . . .

'I don't know what you're talking about,' she said wildly, trying to gain time. 'How should I know what you're seeking – or why you think you will find it in my bedchamber?'

Dickon's fingers tightened around her wrist.

'Very well, Regan, if you insist on playing games, I shall have to do my best to discourage you. Adelaide Jackson played games, too. She played very dangerous games and now she's dead. I wouldn't like to think the same fate was going to befall you.'

Regan paled, and he went on: 'Perhaps I should refresh your memory. At a secret meeting you were given a certain leather pouch. It belongs to me, and I'd like it back. So hand it over, my dear, if you want to save your pretty neck.'

Regan's breath came ragged, but she thanked her stars

she had left her reticule in the buggy when she came back for the wraps. It gave her a breathing space at least – and might mean the difference between life and death.

'I tell you I don't know what you're talking about!' she said again. 'What makes you think I've got your pouch? I declare you've taken leave of your senses, Dickon.'

His eyes hardened, though his lips still smiled their damnable smile.

'Adelaide told me so before she died. She didn't know the pouch was mine, of course. Why should she? And, unfortunately for her, I did not believe her. It seemed such a very unlikely story!' He smiled reflectively at the memory of Adelaide's wild denials and his own persuasive knife at her throat in the night-time quiet of the Commercial Hotel.

'So why do you believe her now?' Regan asked.

'I have since heard it from another – Matt – the ugly little runt who ran her errands for her,' Dickon told her. 'He has been telling the whole of Robertson that Zach is a double murderer and that you bought the evidence of his treachery. It will not be long, I suspect, before he is arrested and I shall be safe. But I must have my pouch. It could spoil everything if it was discovered to be mine. Though I suppose I could claim he stole it from me. Why should that be any more difficult to believe than that I was using my pouch to house his watch? After all, it would be my word against the word of a suspected double murderer!'

'You rat!' Regan cried. '*I* know you stole Zach's watch, when you were a guest in this house!'

Dickon's eyes narrowed to glinting slits in his smooth face.

'Indeed! You know too much, I fear! I suppose you also know that it was I who killed my brother?'

Regan felt a rush of revulsion. How could he stand there, calmly boasting of the evil things he had done?

'I guessed as much,' she returned, throwing caution to the winds. She could not, after all, be in greater danger than she already was, while if she could keep him talking, there was always the chance help would arrive. 'Why did you do it?'

'He treated me like the child I was when he left England,' Dickon said petulantly. 'I could have been a great asset to him in his business but he resented me, and the fact that I had an easier start in life than he. He refused to count me in on his deals.

'But that was no reason to kill him, surely!' Regan protested.

'Oh, I didn't mean to kill him!' Dickon returned pleasantly. 'I waylaid him that day to remonstrate with him; try once more to persuade him. In his office he was always too busy, and at home there was frequently someone around – one of his managers or overmen if not the servants. I thought that out in the bush we would be undisturbed. But nothing was different. He was still in a perpetual hurry with no time for someone he regarded as being as unimportant as me. He called me a fop, told me he thought I should return to England – he didn't want me here. His own brother! I ask you, what choice did I have but to kill him? It was the only way I could get my just deserts.'

'Your just deserts? But it was he who had built it all up!' Regan burst out before she could stop herself and as a dark spasm crossed Dickon's face her blood ran cold. Had she gone too far? Would he kill her now and have done with it?

'I was his brother!' Dickon reiterated. Then he gave Regan's arm a violent jerk. 'Enough of this chatter. Tell me where my pouch is – and tell me now. Or I shall have to burn this place around your ears as I did the Commercial Hotel. And perhaps this time I'll be successful in destroying it.'

'No!' Regan cried, horrified at the thought of beautiful Ballymena reduced to the same blackened ruin as the Commercial Hotel. 'You can't do that – and it wouldn't work anyway. It's not in the house.'

'Ah-ha!' Dickon crowed triumphantly. 'So you do know where it is! You shouldn't lie to me, Regan. I don't like it. Now tell me where it is, there's a good girl.'

She caught her lip between her teeth. She dared not tell him – she must not. If she did it would be the end for her. And besides, when Dickon had the evidence against him in his possession there would be nothing to disprove the charges against Zach. His life could yet be in danger of the hangman's noose if anything went against him.

Her eyes met his, frightened but defiant.

'How are you going to make me tell you?'

A flicker of anger crossed his face, then the smile returned, full of anticipation now. 'Oh, Regan my dear, have you no imagination? A pity. I shall not enjoy spoiling those good looks of yours. And your screams will haunt me at nights. But what must be, must be.'

He raised his coat and drew from his belt the revolver which had been the cause of Thomas's death. Regan stared at it, mesmerized by the horror as he rolled it lovingly round his palm.

'Where is the pouch?' he asked her softly.

She gritted her teeth to keep them from chattering.

'I won't tell you.'

Hardly were the words out than his hand struck her full in the face. She reeled backwards, her head buzzing from the blow, her cheek numbed and cold yet already beginning to sting fiercely. Dickon's hand shot out to steady her, holding her upright when she might have fallen, and his face was close to hers.

'You see – you're not made for violence. But that was just the beginning. Next time, Regan, it will not be my hand. It will be the butt of my revolver. And that will do far more damage. Now . . .'

Tears of fear and pain burned behind her eyes, and her lips felt too stiff to move, but somehow she managed to shake her head.

'If you hurt me, Zach will kill you!' she cried. 'And I won't tell you, Dickon, if you break every bone in my body!'

Sunlight glinted on the barrel of the revolver as he brought it back raised to come smashing into Regan's face. She winced away, eyes closed, waiting for the bone-shattering blow. But at that very second a sound from the landing brought her eyes flying open again and she saw Dickon hesitate.

A footstep! Someone was there! Thank God!

Then, as the door swung open, her relief was replaced

by new, sharp fear.

It was Queenie who stood there.

'Regan, I . . .' The child broke off in mid-sentence, her face puckering with bewilderment as she looked from one to the other of them.

'Queenie – run!' Regan cried, but too late. With a cat-like movement Dickon reached her, grabbing her scrawny shoulder and spinning her round. She squirmed and cried out, but he held her fast and as he pressed the nuzzle of the gun to the side of her throat, Regan cried to her again: 'Don't struggle, Queenie! Stay still!'

The child froze, her eyes huge with terror, and Dickon laughed.

'I'm glad you see the danger, Regan. It might help you to be sensible. In fact, I'm sure it will. You wouldn't like to see Queenie hurt, would you?'

'You monster – you wouldn't!' Regan grated, but he only laughed again.

'I would, my dear! I have too much to lose to turn soft-hearted now.' The gun bit into Queenie's neck and as she whimpered with fear Regan knew she had no choice. But at least the pouch was outside the house. Perhaps while Dickon was getting it, she and Queenie could escape.

'Well, Regan? Are you going to tell me?' Dickon asked impatiently.

'It's in the buggy,' she sobbed. 'In my reticule. I was going to drive out to Zach with it. We'd be on our way now if I hadn't come back for our wraps.'

Dickon's eyes held hers questioningly and she ran on: 'It's true! It's in the buggy outside, I tell you.'

'Oh, I believe you, Regan. But just as a small insurance for your honesty I'd like you to fetch it for me.' His tone was silky, but she knew the cold determination it covered and her heart sank.

'You mean . . .'

'I mean I'll wait here for you – with little Queenie to keep me company. I'm sure that with my gun at her throat you will be less anxious to trick me. Hurry now, Regan. I am beginning to grow impatient and I should like to be on my way.'

'You – you monster!' Regan gasped, but Dickon only smiled.

'The time for name-calling is past. Make haste, Regan, if you wish no harm to the child. And do not think to cheat me.'

Regan drew a shuddering breath. What chance was there that he would let either of them go when he had the pouch in his possession? Precious little, she was sure. It would be the end for them both. Yet she had no choice. To cross him now would mean certain death for the child. All she could do was obey his instructions and pray God an opportunity presented itself to her to gain the upper hand – or that someone else came on the scene. If one of the workers was in the stables, or if Mary Mitchell returned from Mrs Davey's confinement there was still a chance for them . . .

Oh Zach, Zach, where are you? Regan sobbed silently as her feet flew down the staircase and across the hall. Why today of all days do you have to be out working away from the homestead?

As she ran across the yard to the stables she looked wildly around in the hope that someone might be there but the place still slumbered in the afternoon sunshine and it seemed ludicrous that a life-and-death scene could be being played out against such a perfect backdrop. But the hammering of Regan's heart told her that ludicrous or not, it was true. She hurried across to the buggy, reaching into it for her reticule. When he saw her, Lucky pawed the ground restlessly as if eager to be gone, and into Regan's racing mind came the germ of an idea.

If she set Lucky loose with a good hard smack on his rump he might go for a gallop by himself. He was frisky enough. And if Zach or Seamus saw him running wild they might wonder if Regan had had another accident with the buggy and come home to investigate. It was a tall order, to expect that the pony would go in the very direction they were, and he might not go at all, but it was a better than nothing chance.

As swiftly as her trembling hands would allow she slipped Lucky's harness, then gave him the hardest slap on the rump that she could muster. He stood quietly, looking at her in pained indignation, but he did not move a muscle.

'Go, Lucky, go!' she urged. But still he would not move. The irony of it! Usually it was all she could do to hold him back. Now he would not get started. Squealing in despair she emptied her reticule into the buggy and picked up the pouch that might yet cost her her life. Then with one last kick at the pony, who still stood unyielding before the buggy, she turned and went back into the house.

What now? She did not know. But if she gave in, just like that, it would be the end for all of them.

In the bedroom Dickon still held Queenie captive. The child was whimpering with terror and outrage flooded Regan to think he could treat her so callously.

'Have you the pouch for me?' Dickon asked, and summoning all her courage she thrust her hand behind her back.

'Yes, I have, but I won't give it to you until you let Queenie go,' she told him boldly.

Dickon's mouth twisted.

'*I'm* the one making the conditions,' he sneered. 'Hand it over!'

'Let Queenie go first,' Regan insisted. 'She's only a child, and I don't suppose she even knows your name. Why, she's not quite right in the head – or hadn't you heard? Don't add to her tragedy!'

For a second it seemed Dickon hesitated and she wondered if her desperate ploy might work. Then he shook his head.

'You take me for a fool, Regan,' he said sadly. 'I can't let her go – nor you, either. You must know that.'

Regan swallowed at the lump of nerves in her throat. 'You won't get away with this, Dickon. Zach will see you hang!'

'Zach!' Dickon laughed. 'By the time I've finished it will be Zach who hangs. After this, there will be two more murders to lay at his door. Be sure I shall give evidence to point straight to him.'

'You devil!' Regan sobbed.

Dickon laughed unpleasantly but the sudden sound of

hooves on the path beneath the window made him start.

Regan know at once what it was – Lucky had decided to take advantage of his freedom. But Dickon did not know, and while his attention strayed momentarily to the chattering hooves she saw her opportunity.

With a swift movement she threw herself at Dickon, striking at the hand that held the gun to Queenie's neck, and shouting to the child as she did so: 'Run, Queenie, run! Quickly now!'

Caught off balance Dickon reeled and the child, crazed with fear, seized the chance. Like a small eel she wriggled away and was around the door before he could stop her. Desperately Regan tried to hold onto his arm but he was too strong for her. With an oath he threw her aside, running to the landing, and Regan blanched as she heard the sharp crack of his revolver. He was firing at Queenie! Holy Mother, would he stop at nothing? Sobbing she ran after him onto the landing in time to see Queenie's small figure disappearing across the hall. Praise God he had missed her! Again she caught at his arm, clinging on for dear life, and he whirled round on her, venting his anger.

Gone now was his smile. In its place was the most evil expression Regan had ever seen.

'You bitch!' he grated at her through clenched teeth. 'You think to make a fool of me? I'll show you, Madam, that you cannot. I'll make you rue the day you were born!'

With all the ease of his superior strength he twisted her arm behind her back and pushed her along the landing towards the bedroom.

'Stop it!' she sobbed. 'You brute! Leave me alone!'

But it was useless. The pouch lay on the floor where she had dropped it. He picked it up and thrust it into his pocket. Then he released her, taking a step backwards with the gun pointing directly at her.

'Take off your clothes,' he ordered her.

She stared at him, uncomprehending, and he waved the gun impatiently.

'Take off your clothes, Regan. I intend to have this killing laid at Zach's door, and it will look the more convincing if it appears 'twas committed in an intimate moment. An act of passion that went wrong, perhaps.'

'No!' she whispered, crossing her arms around her body protectively. 'I won't – I can't! I cannot unfasten my dress without help anyway!'

'Then I will help you.' He moved forward until the cold nuzzle of the gun lay against her bare neck and with a laugh he reached around to loosen the fastenings. His eyes glittered like a madman's and she shrank from the touch of his fingers. Then with a quick movement he tore at her dress so that it hung about her waist.

'Now take it off – or I'll kill you here and now,' he said in a low, throaty voice.

'No!' Regan cried suddenly. 'No, I won't! You'll kill me anyway – why should I make it easy for you? If you want me undressed for your slaughter you'll have to do it yourself!'

For a moment Dickon stood looking her up and down, and for the first time he found himself seeing her as a woman – a beautiful, desirable woman. Then, with a low grunt his hand shot out to close over her bare shoulder, his fingers biting painfully into the flesh as he pulled her towards him.

'Leave me! Leave me!' she cried, forgetting the revolver as she tried to struggle free, but it was useless. His smiling mouth closed over hers and she sobbed with disgust at his slobbering lips. What was he going to do with her? Holy Mother she would rather die than he should have her. Once before she had been taken by force but it had not been like this. She had not felt the sick revulsion that rose in her throat now like bile . . .

A shadow fell across the doorway. Over his shoulder she saw it and her eyes widened with shock. In the melee she had heard no footstep on the stairs and neither had Dickon. A scream came to her lips but it was drowned by a cry of anger that filled the room. Dickon released her abruptly, spinning round, and she saw Zach bearing down on them.

Relief and fear fused together within her. Zach was here! How or why she did not know, nor stop to wonder. But Dickon had a gun. He had killed before – what had he to lose if he killed again?

'Zach – Zach – look out!' she screamed, but heedless of her warning he came on.

Sobbing she grabbed at Dickon's gun arm and caught off balance Dickon fired wildly. The bullet caught Zach in the arm and blood spurted in a scarlet fountain.

Momentarily he drew up and Dickon pointed the gun once more – at Zach's heart.

'No!' Regan screamed, knowing that this time he could not miss. She grabbed again wildly at his arm and it was all the respite Zach needed. With a shout he was upon Dickon, punching him full in the face. The Englishman staggered backwards towards the open window and Zach followed, blood pouring from his arm, and as Dickon fought to regain his balance and aim the revolver he caught him again, a swinging blow beneath the ribs.

Again Dickon staggered back towards the open window. As the curtain caught around him he realized his danger too late. Wildly he raised his arms to save himself and Zach struck him the third time. Back through the window he went, the gun still in his hand, and Regan sobbed with fear and shock. Loud in the still afternoon she heard Dickon's cry, the thud as his body hit the roof of the verandah below, and a sudden sharp crack. Then there was silence.

Regan's breath came out on a gasp of horror and she ran to Zach. But he put her roughly aside, leaving the room and taking the stairs two at a time. Fearfully Regan crossed to the window and looked out. Below her, on the path, she could see the inert body of Dickon. The sloping verandah roof had broken his fall, but he had rolled from it to the ground and now lay there, unmoving. As she watched she saw Zach emerge from the house and a new fear flashed through her. Suppose Dickon was merely pretending? Suppose when Zach reached him he shot him at point-blank range?

She tried to call out a warning, but her throat was so parched no sound came and she could only watch helplessly as Zach turned him over. Then she gasped again, shock tingling through her like rivers of ice.

There was a scarlet stain on Dickon's shirt front – a stain that spread and darkened with every passing moment. It looked to her almost exactly like the stain that same gun had caused on her father's shirt, but higher, and in that second she knew. In falling Dickon had triggered off the cocked gun just as her father had done. But the bullet had gone through his heart. Dickon would not linger – there was no hope of saving him. The cold, calculating murderer was dead.

Holding her dress about her she ran down the stairs to Zach.

'Oh, my love, my love!' she wept. 'Are you much hurt?'

His fingers held the torn cloth tightly over the wound.

'It's a flesh wound only. Nothing to worry about.'

She sobbed with relief. 'And Dickon?' she whispered. 'Is he. . . ?

'Dead? Yes, more's the pity. I should have killed him with my bare hands if he hadn't been.'

'If he hadn't killed you first!' she cried. 'Oh, Zach, he's mad! He's the one who murdered Jud – and he's killed Adelaide too. If you hadn't come back I don't know what would have happened. Now, let me tend your arm before you bleed to death!'

She hauled up her skirt, tearing at her petticoat as she had done once before and binding it around his arm. But as her fingers worked deftly the enormity of all that had happened washed over her once more.

So many dead – so much killing – and now Zach's blood seeping through her petticoat as her father's had done. It was too much, too much! The hot afternoon air seemed to sing in Regan's ears and the world began to swim about her. Briefly she was aware of someone calling her name and strong arms holding her. Then her trembling knees gave way beneath her and she knew no more.

It was evening and dinner was done. Not that Regan had had much appetite for food, but Seamus and Zach had expected her to come in and she had had no desire to be alone.

The events of the day were too vivid to her still and she could hardly have felt less like the heroine Mary Mitchell had acclaimed her when she returned from the confinement and learned how Regan had saved Queenie from harm.

'I haven't given you the welcome I could have done, and I'm sorry,' Mary had wept in a rare display of emotion, and glad though she was to be accepted at last by the other woman, her praise had only served to upset Regan once more.

Now, she sat listening as Seamus and Zach went over what had happened for the hundredth time. They knew the whole story now, of course, from the blackmail on. Zach had had it out of her when he had carried her back into the house and she had regained her senses. She had been ashamed that she should have swooned when it was he who was injured, but he had given her little time to dwell on it, demanding every detail of what had occurred from the moment the blackmail note had arrived, and promising to do his best to retrieve her emerald brooch from Matt.

Now, as he twirled his brandy glass in his hand, he returned to the subject once more.

'Poor foolish Adelaide! She thought to make trouble between us, no doubt – plant seeds of suspicion against me in your mind. But she did not know that in her possession she held the real murderer's pouch – and for that she died. The world will not be the same without her.'

'It was almost without me, too,' Regan said in a small voice. 'It was the most fortunate chance that you came in early.'

'Yes, and Dickon has only himself to blame for that,' Zach told her grimly. 'I was riding back with news for you, Regan, about your father's possessions stolen aboard the *Maid of Morne*. While I was working today, the trader came by from whom I obtained your ring. I questioned him about it – without much hope, but since it was the finest he had ever handled he remembered it at once – and remembered from whom he had bought it. It was Dickon Trenoweth.'

'Dickon again!' Regan breathed. 'Of course!'

He was the one person from the ship she had not even considered as being the thief – yet now it fitted perfectly with his newly-revealed character. And he had had the opportunity, too. Clear in her mind's eye she saw him bringing her father's pouch to Zach's cabin on the night of the shooting. He had found it on the floor of the saloon, he had told them. What he had not said was that he had taken the sovereigns and the ring and substituted a pile of pebbles . . .

'What an evil man he must have been!' Regan said with a shudder.

'The same blood ran in his veins and Jud's,' Seamus said reflectively. 'Jud harnessed his acquisitiveness to do himself good, Dickon let it turn him bad through and through. But even Jud has brought his share of death to the country. Only today a man died at his mine, did he not, Zach? Some poor soul mad for gold and employed for a pittance, no doubt.'

For some reason Zach did not reply. Instead he pulled himself to his feet.

'We have talked enough for one day and Regan is tired. Shall we retire, my love?'

'I have no right to be tired,' she murmured as they went up the broad staircase. 'You're the one who is injured.'

Zach shrugged. 'It's nothing – a flesh wound only. It will heal soon enough.' The bedroom door closed after them and Regan was sickened suddenly as she thought of how violated it had been that day. She reached for Zach's hands, but he did not pull her to him as she expected. Instead he held her away, looking at her seriously.

'I know this has been a black day for you, Regan, but do you think you could take one more piece of bad news?'

She felt the blood chill in her veins and he went on: 'I believe you should hear it from me, now, rather than perhaps learn it as loose talk somewhere. You heard my father speak of a poor wretch killed today in Jud's mine? It was your old sweetheart, Richard Gammon.'

As his words reached her Regan swayed and Zach put out a hand to steady her. Shades of emotion flickered across her face and they tore at his heart. Then her eyes misted and she shook her head slowly.

'Poor Richard!' she breathed.

He looked at her closely; he had expected hysterics, tears at the very least, but not this calm acceptance.

'Regan – you do know what I'm saying?' he pressed her.

She nodded. 'Yes, Zach, of course I do. So Richard's search for gold brought him no happiness. I'm so sorry.'

'Nothing more?' he asked harshly.

She shook her head again.

'What more could there be? I'm sad for him, of course, but he's been dead to me for a long time, Zach. And perhaps it's better this way than that he should grow old and disillusioned.'

An unexpected lump rose in Zach's throat. Would she never cease to surprise him, this woman he loved? From the moment he had set eyes on her she had turned his world upside down. He had looked at her and cared more for her in a brief space of time than he had ever cared for anyone before. She had tempted him, rejected him, blamed him for her father's death, played havoc with his emotions. And she had lied for him, believed in him and placed her life in danger for him. To him she was more than lover and wife. She was the sun, the moon and the stars. Without her the world would cease to turn. And he wanted her more now than he had ever wanted her.

He put his arm about her shoulders and she lifted her face to his. There were tears on her cheeks, sparkling diamonds, but he knew instinctively they were tears for what had been and not for what could never be. Gently he kissed away the tears and at his touch he felt the responsive spark within both their bodies. Would it always be this way for them – explosive, primitive magic?

He drew her towards the bed, feeling the tremor run through her, then felt her pull away.

'Your arm . . .'

'I shall not even feel it, my love,' he whispered truthfully, and with a sigh of pure delight their bodies fused to one.

It was still dark when Regan awoke. She lay for a few moments beside the sleeping Zach, then turned back the covers and padded across the room.

It was velvet night outside, a million stars twinkling

above the mysterious bush, and a thrill of happiness tingled in her veins. She had come to this land not knowing what to expect and found far more than she had dared hope for. She had lost her father, it was true, and that would be a sadness always. But had he lived she might have left the *Maid of Morne* and never seen Zach again. Such was the way of life. She might never again tread the shores of England. But already she regarded the brave new country as home. It was here that her future lay, with Zach and with the children they would one day have, building together on Seamus's empire.

Her eyes misted and suddenly in the quiet she seemed to hear an echo of her own voice, singing as she had once sung for Zach.

There came a Knight in yellow was he,
Fair are the flowers in the valley.
'My bride, my queen, thou must with me!'
The Red, the Green and the Yellow.
The Harp, the Lute, the Pipe, the Flute, the Cymbal,
Sweet goes the treble Violin.
With blushes red 'I come,' she said;
'Farewell to the Flowers of the Valley'.